Hidden

Courtney Charisse

Black Rose writing

© 2015 by Courtney Charisse

All rights reserved. No part of this book may be reproduced, stored in a retrieval system or transmitted in any form or by any means without the prior written permission of the publishers, except by a reviewer who may quote brief passages in a review to be printed in a newspaper, magazine or journal.

The final approval for this literary material is granted by the author.

First printing

This is a work of fiction. Names, characters, businesses, places, events and incidents are either the products of the author's imagination or used in a fictitious manner. Any resemblance to actual persons, living or dead, or actual events is purely coincidental.

ISBN: 978-1-61296-419-5
PUBLISHED BY BLACK ROSE WRITING
www.blackrosewriting.com

Printed in the United States of America
Suggested retail price $16.95

Hidden is printed in Traditional Arabic

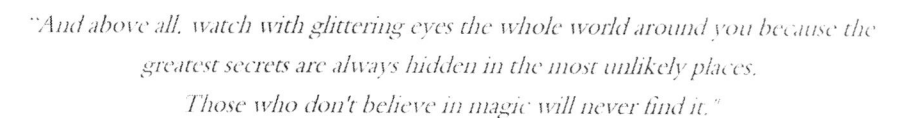

"And above all, watch with glittering eyes the whole world around you because the greatest secrets are always hidden in the most unlikely places. Those who don't believe in magic will never find it."
~Roald Dahl

Hidden

I

The War

I stood in the large library and cradled my two month old baby girl tightly in my arms. I looked into her huge bright brown eyes that combined well with her tanned skin. I adjusted her gold name plated bracelet before I looked out from my window at the chaos of a war that was happening right in front of my living quarters. Blazing fire was being thrown from both sides good and evil. Swords and other useful weapons were being drawn and used. My people good and bad were out there dying.

This war was everything that I don't represent. My kingdom was falling apart. I sighed thinking upon the fact that the bloodline of The Caylan sisters, the three most powerful beings in the dimension of Permia which included my two sisters and I was now broken, because this war was produced by my younger sister Kara.

Kara traded the purity in her soul for a power more evil, a wicked form of magic. Our older sister Marnie found her practicing witchcraft. Shortly after, it was brought to my knowledge that she had eloped with a warlock, and as the consequence for her actions, she was banished from our home and no longer part of the royal family. Being exiled meant that regardless of Kara's bloodline and the Caylan heritage, she is no longer eligible to be queen in Permia.

Being banished drove Kara mad and she threw a temper tantrum for not getting her way, which is to be queen and have complete control over both world's Permia and Earth.

For not getting her way, she created this monstrous war, and set out for the royal family which includes me, my husband Zion, our sister Marnie, Marnie's husband, their seven year old daughter Hannah and my little baby Eve, to be put to death.

Kara was good once. She practiced all things pure and was a sweet girl. At times she was a little rebellious, and liked drama and causing a scene or two but no one ever thought she was capable of the evil that she is and produces today.

Never did I ever think that I would one day have to go against one of my own sisters. It is sad to think of raising a weapon towards one of your own siblings, but in a situation as this one, it must happen.

I couldn't let Kara threaten me or my family anymore. I couldn't let her continue to take innocent people's lives. I couldn't sit back and let her destroy this world. Good has to be able to keep the bad in control to keep the grounds peaceful. I looked up to the dark purple sky and the moon before wiping away the single tear that was falling from my right eye. "How did it all come to this? I didn't think it would be like this." I asked myself. As I remembered the premonition that I had of this very war. Yes the premonition was horrible, the nightmare of a vision kept me awake for many nights. But I didn't think it would be this out of control, this huge or this much of a disaster.

I could hear footsteps in a short distance coming towards me, and I knew the alone time between my daughter and I would be interrupted in a few seconds.

"Emirah! My sister, we need you out there now, I can't go against Kara by myself. The darkness in her isn't like anything we've ever had to deal with before." My older sister Marnie said.

I turned away from the window to look at her. Her hair was braided in a long braid that rested comfortably at her side. She looked serious and ready for war in her silver and black armor top, skirt, knee pads and arm pads. I looked at her sharpened sword and shield and sighed.

"I don't want to leave her." I said gesturing to my innocent baby girl who was just staring up at me. "Emirah, if you don't get out there to help us, our entire kingdom, this dimension and even down there on earth will be in severe trouble. Baby Eve will be fine once the war is over, but she won't live to see tomorrow, none of us will if we don't end this." Marnie said. I looked down at my smiling baby girl. "She will be fine sister." Marnie assured me.

I didn't want to leave Eve but I knew I had a job to do, I knew that Marnie was right. I knew I had to go and help protect the world. That was my whole entire purpose of being. I looked down and kissed Eve's forehead. "My darling Eve, you are fragile and yet the most unique and strongest amongst all others on this land, having inherited ways of your father and mine. I love you with everything in me. And I promise that we will meet again." I whispered to the cooing baby.

"What are you doing?" Marnie asked me, watching closely at my every move. "Taking precautions." I replied. "If I am not to survive at the end of this, I want Eve to be safe." I continued.

I wrapped Eve up tightly in another blanket to keep her warm and caressed her cheek. "Elsa!" I called out. Shortly a beautiful woman with green eyes and waist length jet black hair approached me.

"Elsa, please, do me this huge favor. I need you to send Eve down there." I said to my best friend while pointing out the window to the large blue and green planet. Elsa's eyes widened. "Down... down to-to earth? Your highness...Emirah, you can't send Eve down there. You can't ask me to bring her down there, she doesn't belong there." Elsa tried to explain. "She has to be protected." I said with my voice raised a little. I was beginning to get frustrated even more than I already was. I lowered my voice and took a deep breath before continuing.

"Elsa... please do as I ask. Please see that she is taken to the first hospital seen. And if I don't come back, promise me you will take watch over her." I said with concerned eyes. Elsa sighed. "I promise." She replied. She gently took Eve out of my hands and ran off in a safe and war free passageway.

I walked back towards the window and looked out and peered up just in time to see a pair of wings flying off with my baby. This time I let the tear that was falling from my right eye, fall aimlessly down my cheek.

"Emirah..." Marnie called out. I nodded my head to signal that I heard her call before I walked off in the same direction as her, adjusting my armor material dress and picking up my sword.

Marnie and I walked out of the library and down the long white walled hallway. Soon we were joined by a handful of Permian warriors and together we walked out the side door entrance of our home, The Caylan Mansion. As soon as I set foot outside, the eeriness took me by surprise and I shuddered. I heard the clashing of swords, grunts, groans and cries, the rustling of the tree tops, along with a sudden new added effect of rumbling thunder.

I couldn't completely focus on the war. I wondered where Eve was, if she was safe and warm. I also thought about how no matter what happens to me, on Eve's eighteenth birthday her powers will quickly develop. Also more importantly no matter what happens, one day she will be crowned queen and rule Permia. I tried to block out thoughts and images of my daughter and focus on the warzone I was walking towards.

I stopped walking in the darkness as a dark purple color of light appeared in front of me, indicating that someone was orbing in. The warriors surrounded Marnie and myself as we waited for the face of the incoming orb-er to appear. Once I could recognize who had orbed in, I ran up to my husband, Zion.

"Zion!" I cried as I hugged him tightly. "It's great to see that you're okay." I said, still hugging him. "And you. I could sense you're very unhappy. I thought you were going to stay indoors with the baby, what's wrong?" he asked me. His big hands cupping my face. I stayed quiet, fought back burning tears and avoided looking into his purple glowing eyes.

"Where's Eve?" He asked. I stumbled on my words before replying. "I sent her to earth." Zion looked at me in disbelief and shook his head no. "She has to be some place safe just in case. Just in case..." I said trailing off. I couldn't finish my sentence. I also didn't want to believe that anything horrible could happen to Zion or me, but Kara's behavior made me realize that you never know what could happen. Zion looked at me with sad eyes before kissing my forehead and hugging me.

"This war is certainly a battle. But it's nothing we can't win. And once we win, we will get our daughter back and live in peace. I promise." Zion said. I nodded my head in agreement, and he wiped my tears away with his thumbs. "So let's do it. Let's quickly win this unnecessary war and get back to our life." Zion suggested. "Okay." I said choking back a little.

"We have warriors in all coasts of the forest. We will run straight into it, in the field. I want us surrounded on all sides except for frontward. Is that clear?" Zion asked our Permian warriors. The warriors answered in a chorus of clears and Okays.

I looked at Marnie who was standing on my left and then at Zion who was standing on my right before we all moved forward to the battlefield. Even though I was still concerned for my daughter, I had to shake the fragile state of mind I had off, and I did. I closed my eyes and quickly mentally prepared myself for what was just up ahead.

"Ready?" My husband asked. I looked at him and took a deep breath. "Then I'll ever be." I replied while drawing my sword. And that was it. Marnie, Zion, the warriors that were surrounding us and myself plunged into the warzone.

My sword collided with bodies, and I got through six opponents in the matter of minutes. Zion ran into the center of the violent fight and started attacking a large number of the enemy. Quickly the number of opponents surrounding him became too great for him and I ran over to help him, knocking anyone that got in my way to the ground. I stood side by side next to my husband and took a second to look at him. He nodded his head in approval and I nodded back before attacking the surrounding group.

Five bodies laid at my feet and eight bodies laid at Zion's. Forgetting the war around us Zion and I took a second to hug. "Thank you for helping me." He said. "Anything for you." I replied looking straight into my husband's purple fluorescent eyes. Zion quickly kissed me before I pulled away remembering that we were on a battlefield. I turned around, away from Zion and found myself staring into my baby sister Kara's Red Eyes.

"If you would have just let me stay in the mansion. If you would have let me take the throne, if you wouldn't have banished me, none of this would be happening big sister." Kara said with gritted teeth. "We can't let you do that Kara; you've gone mad, your wicked and pure evil now. A decision you made on your own. We will never let someone of those standards rule this kingdom." I replied. "Never is a *very* strong word." Kara spat as she quickly stepped closer to me and then jabbed me in the stomach with the one weapon that is lethal to any living creature, *The White Fire Dagger*. I looked from my stomach to my sister who had an evil smile on her face. "And because of that you and Marnie are responsible for everyone that dies including yourselves and your pathetic little families." She said angrily while forcefully pulling the dagger out of me and watching me fall to the ground.

    After only seconds but what felt like forever, I could feel my head being lifted onto someone's lap. I weakly looked up and found Zion's purple eyes. His eyes full of tears from sorrow and anger. I cried knowing that this was the last time I'll see him until we meet again in another realm. I cried even more in knowing that I would never see Eve again. I wouldn't watch her grow up and teach her *our* ways. I quickly prayed for her protection and that she remain shielded from any harm until the age of 18 which is the age of maturity in Permia. I prayed that she forgive me for leaving her, and that one day she will understand. I reminisced a recently taken picture of my family, all three of us happy and smiling. And then I did it. I finally closed my eyes.

II

Eighteen Years Later

I climbed up the basement stairs and entered the kitchen and saw my adoptive family eating breakfast. I grabbed water out of the refrigerator and began to walk towards the front door. "Oh my God Eve what are you wearing?!" My adoptive mom Mena asked.

This entire family annoyed me. They were seriously miserable people and wanted everyone around them to either be miserable like them or believe that they had the perfect family. They are the absolute definition of phony and miserable but if you were to tell them that, they most certainly will not believe it. "Blue skinny Jeans, and a black t-shirt." I replied while looking down at my casual outfit.

I looked at my "mother" and as always concealed my laughter. Mena is a short woman with quiet a large stomach and the rest of her is completely a flat square. Her dark hair was cut considerably short, making her look totally manly, but no one dared to question her sexuality. Even though I'm pretty sure everyone she comes across mentally questions it. She was wearing her thick 1960s eye glasses, and I swear with those magnifying glass looking glasses, she could probably see what a proton looks like, without a microscope. And she had the nerve to criticize me on how I look on a daily bases. "Ugh you look horrible! How come you couldn't dress up beautifully as my girls? Or put a comb to your hair!?" She asked smiling at her daughters.

I looked from her to my adoptive sisters. Allie looked just Mena in the face, boyish. She wore a long red sweater with black leggings and flats. Jen the prettier one out of their entire family wore a black turtle neck sweater, skinny jeans and boots that had a low heel on the bottom. "They are wearing normal clothes...they look pretty normal to me. They aren't wearing gowns or anything, maybe you should have your glasses checked." I suggested to Mena with a smile. Mena huffed and threw a piece of toast in my direction but surprisingly for her, I caught it and threw it in the trash. "Why would you do that you should have eaten it, wasting food!" Mena spat. "I didn't ask for it or want it, you threw it at me." I replied. "Selfish girl!" Mena practically yelled. This is what I put up with on a daily bases, welcome to my life people.

I shook my head at Mena's "stupidity" and walked away, and almost made it out the door before my adoptive dad Lance came down the stairs. He was the same height as Mena and almost has the same haircut as she does. But in my opinion, he was kind of goofy looking.

He has a pair of large googly eyes and a weird shape nose. He also happens to have a girlish voice. His vocal chords barley carrying any base. I believe that he and Mena switched roles when it comes to the whole husband and wife thing. Mena ran the house, fixed the cable boxes, and has a tool box, being manlier out of the pair. And I swear that's clear glitter nail polish shining on Lance's buffed fingernails.

"Why are you leaving so early?" He asked fixing a button on his shirt. "Because school is much less of an example of actual hell then it is here, and I'd rather be there then here." I said honestly and almost cutely. Lance rolled his large googly bug eyes and walked into the kitchen with his family, and I happily and quietly walked out the door.

I was the outcast in my house. The odd one, the adopted one. They were a real blood related family. I've been here since I was a baby; Mena says she brought me here because she felt bad for me. I was a two month old baby that nobody wanted. Someone left me. The only reason why I know my real name is because of a little bracelet I've had since I was a baby, it has *Eve Marie Caylan* engraved on it.

Whoever left me, wanted me to at least know my full name. And the expensive looking bracelet kind of proves that they didn't just abandon me in a dumpster or trade me for drugs or something of that sort. *But why leave me then?* I asked myself. I always asked myself that question but couldn't ever figure out an answer.

On a positive note, I always see the bright side in every situation. I'm not a miserable loser like my family, and I'm not totally horribly looking. On a negative note, my family despises me for it all. They always try to punish me or make harsh comments to try to get me upset. They even moved me from my tiny old bedroom upstairs and put me downstairs in their dingy, unfinished, bug infested basement, where I sleep on a dingy couch. Yes it's the epitome of dirty and horrible. But I will be eighteen soon, even though I am indecisive about *everything* regarding my life... the first of my plans after I'm legally an adult and finally graduate from high school, is to go to a faraway college and get the heck out of here. Without school, I would have nothing to live for. School is my salvation. Even though I am not particularly good at anything, have no special talents or a sense of direction when it comes to a career, being in school always saved me. The second of my plans is to change my name from *Eve Marie Keller*, back to *Eve Marie Caylan*.

I walked to my black mustang, which I paid for by myself, and got in the driver seat and set off to school. South Brunswick is filled with trees, roads and houses. Nothing special in this little suburban town. Probably the most boring town in New Jersey, but that's just my opinion. South Brunswick high school is very eclectic, kids from all walks of life go there. Compared to other schools surrounding the South Brunswick area, South Brunswick high school is definitely kind of posh. We have three cafeterias, three gyms, a spiral staircase, we can eat our lunch in an outside garden area and we watch our morning announcements on TVs located in every classroom. Yes, it sounds posh doesn't it?

"Hey Eve what's up girl?" A pretty Japanese and Hawaiian girl asked me, as I pulled up to my usual parking spot in the school parking lot. I smirked at her. "Hey Loren, how are you?" I asked. "Same shit, different day. Thank Bob Marley that we will be out of this shit hole soon." She smiled. I chuckled.

Loren has been a good friend of mine since last year. We get along really well but she does have her moments when she annoys the crap out of me, particularly when she gets around her *tree* loving friends. Loren's kind of a floater, just trying to figure out where she belongs in this world. For now she's just blending in with the crowd. "Just eight more months." I replied.

I'm not the most popular girl in school anymore. I used to be popular, specifically from seventh grade through tenth. However once I hit sixteen, something inside me changed. It was a mixture of feelings that I can't describe, perhaps anger, confusion, sorrow and getting no satisfaction from the world I live in. But I had no idea why I began to feel that way; I'm usually a happy girl. I used to be a people pleaser, hardly complained. I had lots of people love me, tons of people hate me; a lot that envied me and a lot that betrayed me.

I was the girl that portrayed an image for others. The "cool" and "popular" image. However Because of my sudden "depression" and sense of feeling "lost", I felt I could no longer pretend to be something I wasn't, unless my ultimate goal was to drive myself insane and end up having to go to therapy. Therefore I had to change before I completely crumbled.

I stopped cheerleading, I stopped going to parties, and I stopped wearing bright colors like pink and yellow. My social cred began ranking lower and lower. Most of the "friends" I talked to started to ignore me like I was invisible. Only a handful of my old friends still actually communicate with me now. It used to bother me but now that I'm a senior, I realized that once I graduate, I'm most likely never going to see these people ever again.

"High school is like a seatbelt, it's here to baby us until graduation and after that is when we have to take the belt off and slam on the damn gas pedal. Get as far away as possible." Loren said as we walked the hallway towards our lockers. "What are your plans after graduation?" I asked her. Loren sighed. "I don't know, maybe I'll go to the air force." She said. I gasped "really?" She nodded her head yes. "I've always wanted to go." I nodded in understanding.

"Hey baby girl." A guy's voice said from behind me. He put his arm around my shoulder and from the specific olive pigment color and smell of axe body spray; I automatically knew it was my friend David. David and I knew each other since the seventh grade; we were in all the same classes, and had all of the same friends. He was the popular boy in my group of past friends, and I was the popular girl. Needless to say that I am shocked that he still talks to me, when practically everyone else he hangs out with, could care less if I exist or not.

"What's up Dave?" I smiled and asked him. "Nothing new, what's up with you though?" He asked while putting in the combination to his locker lock pad. "Counting down the days until we leave here." I Replied. "So what are you doing this weekend?" he asked. I hesitated before responding. "Um I don't know probably sitting at home; listening to music, write some poetry, who knows." David turned to look at me. "You should come out, you know… hang out. I'm throwing a party and you should be there." he said. "Sounds good but I don't know David." I replied. "Come on! You never do anything fun anymore!" he whined. I rolled my eyes and shut my locker.

It's not that I didn't want to go to his party, or that I don't like doing anything fun; I just think it will be awkward going to a party where no one talks to you. "What happen to the crazy, always smiling, *tiny* girl I used to know?" He asked me. I frowned at him for calling me tiny, but it is true. I was blessed to only reach the height of five feet two inches. "I don't know where she went Dave, she just vanished." I replied. "Look Evie, you're coming to this party even if I have to drag you out of your house by your ass." David said. I smirked at the nickname he had been calling me since middle school.

"Hey Eve!" A voice called out to me. I looked up and waved hello to the angelic shaggy brown haired boy and smiled. "Hi Josh." I said giving him a hug. I've known him just as long as I've known David. Ever since we met, Josh has always been like an older brother to me. He was the football star and I was in cheer so our friendship was obvious and instant. "Hey what you get on your SAT's?" Josh asked me. I thought about it for a moment. "About a nineteen fifty, kind of slacking off." I confessed. I was pushing myself to do well to get in college so I could get away, and a nineteen fifty on my SAT's kind of bummed me out. Not because it was a bad score, but because I want to go to school far away like across the pond or something, and you have to have excellent grades to do that.

"What are you guys up to?" He asked. "David's trying to get Eve to go to his party this weekend." Loren said rejoining us from her locker. "Not gonna happen." I said as the first bell rang. "Ugh time to deal with annoying ass teachers," Loren said. "Useless classes," I added. "Yeah I'm definitely ditching." David smirked. Everyone looked at him curiously. "What? not my fault we live in the most boring rich town in New Jersey that nobody wants to live in." He said. I rolled my eyes. "See you guys in the gym." I said opening the locker room door for Loren and I. Loren and I quickly changed our clothes before walking out to the gym.

"My class! Let's go!" My gym teacher Mrs. Tom said. I watched her and chuckled. She was my favorite teacher, and she's the only teacher I could really get along with and talk to about anything. "Mrs. Tom do we have to run today?" I asked her. She turned to me and smiled. "Listen up first baby girl." she smiled while sitting on the floor with her legs crossed. Instead of sitting across from her, I sat beside her. It's not like I'm a teacher's pet or anything, Mrs. Tom and I just bonded well. "Listen up guys. We are having a fire drill. So we will be outside walking the trail all together. I want us all to stay together." she yelled over the class.

"Hey girl why you looking so dazed out?" Loren asked as she sat down next to me. I didn't even realize I was actually sort of day dreaming. "I don't know…You ever feel like you're tired all the time and you feel like every day is the same?" I asked her. Loren vigorously nodded her head. "Hell yeah, especially when I go home. Family sucks." She replied. "Why don't we do something crazy fun? We should drive up to six flags! It's Fright Fest tonight!" I suggested, getting excited about my idea. "I'm so down for that." Loren cheered. "I need a change of scenery. I want the guys to come to; you know the more the merrier." I said spotting David standing and talking with a group of girls.

"Hey Dave!" Loren called out. I turned my body to stretch, only for my hand to come in contact with Josh's head. "Sorry!! Didn't see you there." I said to him. "Don't worry I'm not made of glass." he smirked.

"You rang?" David said when finally reaching us. "Yeah, we are heading down to Six Flags later tonight for Fright Fest." Loren said. "You guys wanna come?" I asked looking at both guys. "What is this like a date?" David asked. I snorted and Loren burst out laughing. "With you two? Is that a serious question?" She asked sarcastically. David frowned. "We'll come and bring a few other people too." Josh said. "Cool beans." I replied with a chuckle.

My last class for the day was math, the worst subject ever! I walked to my class and spotted a pretty brunette girl with glasses with her head in her math binder. I smiled at her before sitting next to her. "Hi Tiffany, did you do the homework?" I asked with a smile. "Yes, you need it?" She asked in a friendly tone. "Uh huh, I just want to check it." I sighed. Tiffany took the paper out of her binder and handed it to me.

I took Tiffany's paper and checked both her and my answers. I felt a little bad for taking her paper, even if it is to only check my work. I "take" her papers almost every math class. I wondered if she ever gets annoyed at me for it.

No matter how hard I apply myself, math just doesn't add up to me. "Hey everybody. How is everyone?" My teacher Ms. Burns asked. "Good." Everyone but me replied. I seriously dreaded math, so much that each day I had the class, I would feel hot, dizzy and my stomach always ended up feeling like a washing machine. I self-proclaim myself to having a math phobia. "Hello Eve." Ms. Burns greeted. "Hi," I greeted back.

From my point of view, it seemed that Ms. Burns had taken a like to me. She always pushed me and wished me to do well in class. She always paid special attention to me in and out of the classroom. I figure the reason is either because she likes me, or she figures that I need a lot more attention since I am a special math challenged student. I'd like to believe it's the first option but it's most likely the ladder.

"Now class, today we are going to learn about slopes. There is an X axis and a Y axis that you have to mark and add to the graft by adding a point on the grid." Ms. Burns said. She then wrote X equals eight and Y equals two over three minus nine equations on the board. I huffed and put my head down.

Tiffany chuckled. "Stop laughing at me. I definitely do not understand anything that's going on." I said as I sat up and looked at the confusing equations written on the board. The rest of class I kept one eye on the clock and the other on the board.

Who made math classes mandatory?! I feel like who ever made it a regulation purposely did it to make fun of me. To embarrass me, and expose my stupidity for numbers. The school board sucks. Every math class I would count down the minutes until I could run out of the room and finally breathe. The horrible feeling in my gut is always instantly released once I exit the classroom.

"You can officially leave in four, three, two, and one! Run girl!" Tiffany smiled at me. I laughed lightly and closed my math book and notebook. "Thank heavens... See you later." I smiled at her. "Hey Eve, if you need any help, please let me know." Ms. Burns said with a helpful smirk. I always took her up on her help, but no matter what, I still end up sucking at math. "Okay." I replied. "See you later." she said. "Bye," I awkwardly said back to her.

I decided to skip going to my locker and just take my math book home. I quickly walked down the school stairs and went out one of the side doors and walked to my car. "Girl where have you been? I've been standing here for like ten minutes." Loren said to me while standing by my mustang.

Loren and I have early release from school, which means we are free to leave school at twelve noon every day. "Stop being so dramatic, it was less than five minutes." I replied. I smirked and pressed the button to unlock the car doors. "Have you seen him around here before?" I asked her gesturing behind her.

Walking towards us was a tall, mid length dirty blond haired guy. He had dark eyes and a pretty smile." He's cute." I mumbled. Loren fake choked. "To you." She said. I rolled my eyes at her comment.

"Hi there." the cute guy said as he finally reached us. "Hi." I replied. "I'm Parker Andrews, the new transfer student from Texas." He addressed. "Well it's nice to meet you Parker, I'm Eve Keller and this is my friend Loren Sato." I announced. Loren smirked at Parker and then took my car keys, letting herself in the passenger side.

"So what grade are you in? And if you don't mind me asking, what are you doing out here?" I asked him. Parker smiled at me. "First, are you an outside student cop or something?" He asked. I chuckled. "No, do I look like one?" I asked "oh wow you've got attitude... I like it." Parker said. I quickly turned my attention to Loren to semi hide the turned shade of pigment in my cheeks. I made an "are you serious? Calm yourself!" face at Loren who was getting annoyed and glaring at me from inside my car.

"You didn't answer my question." I said to him. "Oh I'm a senior and um I have early release." He said. "That's cool, so do I. How you like it out here So far?" I asked. "Um it's alright." he replied. Right before I was about to ask Parker another question, the horn in my car honked.

"Looks like I have to go." I said moving towards the driver's side of my car. "See you around?" Parker asked. I smiled. "Well you go to my school now, so it looks like it." I replied with the same smile. My stomach flipped when he smiled back at me. I got in my car and ignored the glare from Loren. "I see someone was getting her flirt on, how rare for you". She said. I blushed and ignored her comment. I drove Loren and myself to Burger King before dropping her off home, and then going home myself. Silently praying that I wouldn't have to put up with any nonsense from my family.

III

Winter at Fright Fest

I was happy that no one was home, that meant I would have peace and quiet, but I still hated being here. I'm Isolated from them, and kept in the nasty suffocating, basement. I hardly see my adoptive family, they are always busy and I'm always hidden in the basement. However when I do see them, it's like nails on a chalk board annoying. I only have two months left until I'm eighteen, and I can't wait to enjoy the freedom that comes with it.

At four thirty pm I took a drive to Loren's house, and from there we drove straight to Six Flags. The ride was kind of short only about an hour long and we preoccupied ourselves by talking about school and such. I tried to keep conversation to distract Loren from turning up the radio or changing the station from Z one hundred. I'm not a big fan of *her* particular taste of music. Listening to derogatory and the constant degrading in some music makes my ears bleed.

"Hey, thought you two would never show up!" David said when we met up with him and other friends in the Six Flags parking lot. "There was no time limit," Loren. said. I chuckled at her smart comment. "Yeah, yeah whatever lets go we are wasting time." He said. "And I wanna see your ass on a rollercoaster Eve!" He continued. "Yeah right Eve on a rollercoaster?" Josh laughed. Everyone knows how afraid of heights I am. Thankfully amusement parks aren't only about the coasters. I could go to the arcade, play a game, get food, or even watch a show.

The line to get into the park moved relatively quickly, and from the moment we actually entered the park, my alert radar went up. My shoes were tied tight, and my i.d, money, phone and lip-gloss were all inside my wristlet which was secured to my jeans. I was ready for anything.

"Let's go on the scream machine!" Loren shouted." No let's go on El Toro!" One of David's male friends yelled. "How about we start in the middle of the park, there's not many rides there." Josh said. I was getting annoyed of their indecisive bickering, and decided to take charge of the situation. "Ugh guys, let's start on the right first since that's the end of the park, and then move to the left and work our way back. We are wasting time being indecisive, it's already six and the park closes at nine. Everyone agree?" I asked. Everyone either nodded their head yes or mumbled their agreement.

Just as we all got ready to move to the right of the park, there in front of us stood four zombies ready to chase us. "Okay, on the count of three we all run together and head for the Batman ride okay?" Josh asked. Everyone either nodded their head yes okay or mumbled it "three, two, one run!" Josh screamed just before we ran. We were like balls being launched in a pin ball machine.

Within three minutes or less, we were by the Ferris wheel which was filled with people waiting to see a Halloween musical production. "Okay so everyone except for Eve is getting on right?" David asked as we stood in front of the Batman ride. Loren handed me her purse to hold, while everybody else agreed with David and then got online. I went to sit on an empty bench in front of the ride.

After a few minutes of Sitting there alone, basically in the dark and hearing chainsaw noises and screaming kids, it made realize that I needed to get up and move before something came to scare me. As I walked I came across a dark tent with *physic* written on it and I decided to check it out.

"Come in child." an angelic but also in my opinion creepy voice said. "I am Winter the physic. What would you like to know?" She asked. I looked at her. She was really pretty. She had short shoulder length auburn hair, and hazel eyes. She was dressed in an all-white gown, and sitting behind a table that had cards resting on top of it. "I guess just for you to read my palm, my future." I replied. "Okay, come and sit. When is your birthday?" She asked gesturing for me to sit in front of her. "December twenty third." I replied. "Okay let me see your palm." She said. I extended my hand to her.

Winter looked at my palm, and then quickly up at me. I could only see shocked or surprise written on her face. She made me nervous. "Well do you see anything?" I asked sarcastically, not sure if I believe in anyone's physic abilities or not. "Oh my God, for many years I've waited for this day." She said as she let go of my hand and smiled at me. "Eve." She smiled. I looked at her dumb founded.

"How do you know my name?" I asked her almost scared to hear her answer. "It is my duty to know. What I am going to tell you will seem weird but trust me." She said. Before she even began talking again I looked at her with wide eyes and a freaked out facial expression.

"In your blood and in your future lays royalty. Royalty that leads all things natural, realistic, and all things that require an open mind." I rolled my eyes, was she seriously feeding me this crap? In *my* future lays royalty, does she know who I am or where I go to sleep? She's obviously insane to think that someone like me can ever have royal blood. I sighed, this is why they say don't give a psychic your money. "What are you talking about?" I asked her no longer a little scared but just a tad bit curious.

"I can only say very little, my future queen. On the night you turn eighteen, your life will change. You will see and feel power that doesn't actually exist to earth roamers. At eighteen something wonderful will happen to you." She smiled. "Okay this is nuts, you sound more than insane right now but… what's going to happen to me at eighteen?" I asked, my curiosity getting the best of me. "Eve, have you wondered why you always feel like you are so alone, and almost completely lost? Like something is missing from your heart? Like no one gets you? This uneasy, unhappy feeling really kick started at sixteen, but soon, it will disappear." She said. I remained silent. She had a point with me changing at sixteen, I was at my lowest, and I've never told anyone about that. Okay so maybe this Winter lady has *some* physic abilities.

"This road that's coming will not be easy though, and you will have to be strong. You will have to embrace yourself; there are hidden secrets about your life that will soon be revealed. Some personal life questions that you have soon will be answered." Winter said. I just stared at her in worry and shock as those emotions had returned to me. What do you say to a physic who tells you a fortune that's a little scary, a little confusing and a bit accurate?

She then reached down underneath the table and handed me a partially heavy black drawstring bag. "What's this?" I asked her curiously. "This is for you to open up on your eighteenth birthday. Not a day more, not a day less. During the upcoming weeks of your birthday, you will notice changes within you Eve." She said as I stared at her blankly. "Your friends are now by The Haunted Mansion, wait outside there for them." She said while gesturing for me leave. "It was a pleasure to finally meet you." She said just before getting up and *bowing* to me. I got up and started walking out. "Okay, thank you." I awkwardly replied and finally walked out.

I walked to the mansion in complete silence. Surprisingly no hideous creatures ran after me, trying to scare the sense out of me. "Where the hell have you been Eve?" Loren asked me, while coming out of the mansion just like the physic said. "I was getting my palm read by a physic. What are you guys doing over here? What happen to the other rides on the right side?" I asked confused. "It's only been a little over an hour; we finished all the rides over there and had to move on from that section." One of David's friends Randy said to me. "No... It's only been like fifteen minutes." I replied in confusion. "It's been over an hour Eve." Josh said while placing his arm around my shoulders while we walked. "Wow... sorry guys, it's my fault for losing track of time." I said. "Where are you headed next?" I asked. "Scream machine!" Loren shouted. Loren led the way and we all followed behind her. "Hey what did the physic say?" Josh asked. I turned to look at him. "Nothing crazy, regular physic stuff." I answered.

The rest of our time at the park was fun. We got chased by weird dead zombies and clowns with chainsaws. We got on rides and watched the Halloween shows. However even though we were busy having fun, the meeting between Winter and I stayed in the back of my mind. I kept wondering about what was in the drawstring bag that was currently hanging on my back. Finally, it was nine pm and the park was clearing out.

"El Toro in the dark is so sick!" David yelled out in excitement. "I know right, that first dip had me though." Josh said. I laughed at their enjoyment. "Ugh well I'm out of here. See you later." I said giving them all hugs just before getting in my car. Since Loren lived closer to David, he would take her home. This would also save me some time from arriving home really late.

I drove home dreading what awaited me when I opened the door. My parents always try to start an argument with me any chance they get; it's their favorite past time activity. I walked into my house through the backdoor which I left open because I'm not trusted to have a house key. Just as I thought I was in the clearing as I made my way from the living room to dining area, the kitchen light was suddenly turned on.

"Where were you, do you know what time it is?" Mena asked me. Already annoyed by the sound of her voice I rolled my eyes. "Yes, its ten fifteen pm." I replied in monotone. "It's a school night Eve!" Lance said. Ugh they were like squawking duck trolls! All I wanted to do was go down into the basement, put a sheet over the couch, grab my pillow and blanket and close my eyes, and the trolls in front of me were preventing that.

"I know." I said. "Then what were you doing out so late?" She asked. I snorted. "It's not late." I replied. "You know what Eve, next time you do this; I will lock all the doors and keep you outside! Sleep outside or in your car or go to a friend's house, I'm not tolerating this anymore. You are so irresponsible." Mena barked.

Okay, now I had had enough. Was she seriously calling me irresponsible? Me, the one who only uses her for shelter, which sadly for me is in her dingy basement, is irresponsible? Has she gone stupid? "Really? I managed to buy myself a car, I pay for my own gas, pay for my own food. I even got myself good enough grades to get into college without your help, and you feel that I'm irresponsible?" I asked sarcastically. Lance and Mena went silent. There was nothing to say, besides the actual living situation, I'm pretty much doing everything on my own.

"Exactly, I'm going to my room...oh I forgot I don't actually have a room, I have a pipe leaking basement and couch waiting for me." I said. My point wasn't to make Mena and Lance feel sorry for me, they wouldn't do that anyway. My point was to make them realize that I'm a good kid. The responsible one who's doing everything on her own. While their biological daughters had their cars bought for them, food made or bought for them, allowance money given to them to spend every weekend. They lived like princesses and got everything they wanted and I do it all on my own.

People make me feel so bitter sometimes, which sometimes causes me to feel like I should become mean, and cause scenes where ever I go. Yell and fight with anyone that disagrees with me or dares to stereotype me. But then I think that would make people stay away from me. And even though I do feel a bit empty and alone, it's nice to talk to people even if they don't understand my personality or really care to get to know me. I bet it feels ten times worse to be unnoticed *and* alone.

I went down to the basement and sat on the tan couch and thought about the day I had, and then the life I had, which made some salty tears spill from my eyes. My living situation, crappy parents, made me hate life. Hate the beautiful world we live in. It sucks to think something beautiful like life is ugly and cruel. Life itself isn't ugly, just some of the people that exist in it are. And since their view of the world is ugly, they want everyone around them to share that vision.

However for me, no matter how much I cry or how my hatred grows for my family and sometimes life, that hatred gets burned to ashes every time I step foot onto the actual earth outside and look up to the sky, or at the grass and trees and wonder how they always grow even in the harshest weather. They always move forward and blossom for spring and summer.

I think how birds never worry about where they are going or how they are going to eat, they just live... and one day I would too. There's something wonderful out there in the world for me. Those thoughts burn in me greatly and burn out any hatred that keeps me awake at night. One day, this chapter of my life will be over and I will be happy. I just have to keep moving forward.

Just as I was about to hide the drawstring bag Winter had given me, my cell phone vibrated. I saw that it was a text message from an unknown number.

"Hey Eve how are you?"

I raised my eyebrows; clearly the unknown texter knew who they were texting.

"Umm hey, who is this?"

"It's Parker how are you?"

When I realized it was Parker my heart started beating out of my chest.

"Oh hi! I'm okay, what about you?"

"I'm great, feeling even better now."

"What do you mean now?"

"Well now that I'm talking to you I feel great, I like talking to you."

I couldn't think straight, all I could do was read his text message over and over again. When I didn't reply Parker texted me again.

"I hope you don't think I'm lame or creepy for telling you that. It's just you're the coolest girl I've met today; I mean you drive a Mustang for crying out loud. And to be honest you're actually the only girl that's really talked to me. Most others just stared, overly flirted or gave me one word answers.

I smiled. "No you're not lame or a creep, I think it's sweet."

We texted each other back and forth for about an hour. I like Parker but I kind of have my mind on other things at the moment. For instance this stupid drawstring bag. What's in it? And why can't I open it until my birthday? I sighed and put the bag under my clothes inside a storage bin. I put it there so I could basically forget about it. I took a quick shower and then closed my eyes, but not before checking the time.

It was twelve am and I had to be in class at seven thirty am. "Thank God for early release." I whispered to myself.

IV

Parker

Last night I dreamed of Parker, just us hanging out at the park together, and walking on the pier at the beach. Needless to say, I had a huge smile on my face when I woke up in the morning. I got dress, grabbed my things, and snuck out the back door so I didn't have to endure my family and headed to Starbucks before going to school. Over all I could feel that today was going to be a good day.

"So what's up? You *are* coming to my party tonight right?" David asked while getting out of his red Honda Civic. "I don't know David." I replied slightly annoyed. "Come on you have to come." he begged. I huffed. "If I go, I want to bring someone." I bargained. "Alright who?" He asked. "The new kid Parker." I replied. David looked at me not amused by my choice of guest to bring to *his* party. "What, I am just being a good new friend to him." I smirked. David folded his arms across his chest. "Alright bring him, if that's what it takes to get you there." David said. I smiled kissed his cheek and went to my first class of the day.

In my English class we were watching one of my favorite films, *"A streetcar named desire"*, the one with my favorite actress *Vivien Leigh*, and because I've seen it about 50 times and even knew the dialog, I decided that now would be an okay time to text Parker to meet me after school.

"Parker, you get out early today right?"

"Yes, what's up?"
"Meet me in the parking lot after your last class."
"Okay."
"What are you doing?" Loren asked sitting beside me. "Texting Parker." I replied. "Oh so you *do* like him." she smirked. I smiled and shook my head yes. "You're driving me home after class?" She asked. "Yes Loren." I replied. She chuckled and turned her head back to watch the playing film.

As Loren and I walked to the parking lot I saw Parker standing next to his black Camaro and that alone made my stomach and heart do that little flutter thing. "There's your man." Loren whispered to me. I handed her my car keys and she got in the driver seat of my car while I made my way to Parker. "Hey." he said hugging me. He smelled like the store *Hollister* and the scent made me tingly inside.

"Hi." I replied. "How are you?" he asked. "Great now, how about you?" I asked. "What do you mean now?" Parker asked me with a smirk, "and I'm good." He continued. I looked at him through my lashes. "Well, I like talking to you, and now that we are talking I feel great; I hope you don't think I'm lame or a creep for saying that." I chuckled, using his phrase from the night before. Parker laughed. "Nah your good. I think it's cute." he replied with a smile. I smiled back up at him.

"Okay so I actually wanted to talk to you about this party I want to invite you to." I said. "Cool when is it?" He asked. "Tonight, starts at eight, can you come?" I asked. Parker paused for a couple of seconds, and that made me a little nervous that he'd say no. "Sure, I'll come where is it"? He asked with a giant smile." It's at my friend David's house I can get you the address." "Wait...I will only go on two conditions." He said. "I'm afraid to ask." I quickly replied. Parker laughed before telling me his conditions. "one, you have to come to lunch with me and two, forget about giving me the address and lets go together." He said.

I stared at him in complete silence, unsure of what to tell him. Fact is looking at Parker; you would think that he would go for some surfer girl with a mind blowing body or an inspiring model, not the short insecure girl with no real sense of direction. You would think he would hang out with the most popular girl in school who has cantaloupe boobs, and drives an Audi. Not the ex-popular girl with apple boobs who drives a Mustang.

Also I don't know Parker, not enough to get in his car alone anyway. However something in my gut told me I could trust him, he wouldn't hurt me. Besides, if he did, I would surely return to earth as a ghost and haunt him in his dreams. "So?" Parker asked with hopeful eyes. "Okay," I answered. I chuckled as his entire face lit up. "I just need to tell Loren to take my car to her house and then to the party later." I said. Parker nodded his head in understanding. "Okay I'll be in my car."

I walked to my car and talked to Loren about what just happened. "Don't do anything I wouldn't do." she laughed. "You'd do anything and everything, I'm the pure one." I laughed, walking away from Loren and my car.

"Okay I'm ready." I said as I got closer to Parker's car and he opened the passenger side door for me. I smiled as my ears took in the beautiful lyrics of *Augustana's "Boston"* "This music okay with you?" He asked. "Yes! I love this song." I smiled. "So where are we eating?" "Where do you want to go?" he asked. "Hey you invited me, you tell me." Parker laughed. "We shall see where we end up." "Sounds good to me." I laughed at our indecisiveness.

Parker pressed five to change the song and turned his radio up. I started singing along to the next song that started playing which was *"Dani California" by Red Hot Chili Peppers*. Parker looked at me smiling. "You like *Red Hot Chili Peppers*?? My eyes widened." Of course I do, who doesn't?" I laughed. He let out a little laugh and started to sing along too. I was used to people being a little shocked by my music preferences along with my style, and even how I verbally communicate. Just some of the stereotypes a girl of my appearance gets, which is why I'm so misunderstood and sometimes feel alone. Being judged can turn a person's heart black.

Parker and I reached a familiar Burger restaurant, and like a proper gentleman, he got out of his car, ran to my side before I could get out, and opened my door. I don't know many guys that do that, especially guys around my age. I thanked him, and together we walked inside the retro restaurant. "How many?" The restaurant host asked. "Two please." Parker Answered. "Right this way." The hostess said before she led us to a table. Shortly a waitress came and we ordered our drinks.

This was my official first time out on a lunch date with a guy. As a matter of fact this was my first date ever, and I was a bit nervous and excited. Parker and I talked about each other's likes, dislikes, music and other interests. I also found out he got my phone number from Josh, who just so happened to see us talking in the parking lot after school. I decided right then and there that I would have to have a little conversation with Josh. Overall, Parker and I meshed well together, and I could tell that every moment I would share with him, would be easy, breezy and fun.

After Parker paid for our lunch, we started back to my house. "It seems you've learned your way around South Brunswick," I said. "Somewhat, South Brunswick isn't a huge town, there are just lots of back roads." He replied. "True," I said as I nodded my head in agreement. "Wow, you don't live that far from me, maybe ten minutes away." Parker said in surprise as we pulled up to my house. "Good, that means I'll be seeing you more often." I smiled. Parker smiled back." So the party starts at eight, what time should I be here?" He asked." Leave your house at eight and then come get me, oh and be careful it is mischief night." I said with a smirk. "For you I will be careful." Parker chuckled. I playfully hit his arm. "See you later." I said as I got out of his car.

Parker left but my butterflies in my stomach didn't. As I made my way in the house, I prayed that Mena would ignore me, and pretend that I was invisible. I opened the door and immediately saw her sitting in the living room watching TV. *As usual.* I thought to myself. I quickly but quietly made my way to the kitchen and down to the basement. I wanted today to be great, and her ignoring me added to the greatness.

After safely making my way down to the basement, I tore open my bins of clothes and tried on every piece of clothing I had until I found the prefect outfit. After trying on so many clothes I completely tired myself out, so I took a short nap. I once again dreamed of Parker. His smile, his laugh, his personality... he's perfect.

Later in the evening, I woke up, took a quick shower, made myself dinner and got dressed. "How come time only flies by when you have something planned?" I asked myself. I jumped when my phone suddenly rang and slightly scared me in the process.

"Hey I'm leaving in five minutes, you ready?"

"Yes, just waiting for you."

I walked out to Parker's car and noticed that Parker showed up wearing dark blue jeans, black shoes, a white t-shirt and a black leather jacket. While I wore black Brazilian jeans, black boots, a white studded belt and a white shirt with a pretty black cross on it, with leather jacket of course. We were matching.

I raised my brows to Parker. "Been window peeping me?" I asked playfully as he let me in the passenger side of his car. He laughed as he got into the driver seat. "More like we both just have awesome taste in clothing. You look great by the way." He smirked. "Thanks so do you." I replied blushing. I told him David's home address and he plugged it into his GPS and we began our short journey there.

We arrived outside of David's house and even from the inside of the car; Parker and I could hear the really loud house music playing. "Thank God he doesn't have very close neighbors!" Parker chuckled as we got out the car and walked up to the house. I knocked on the door and within a few seconds, David answered.

"Hey what's up, you two made it!" He said rather loudly. "Hey." I said giving him a hug. "Hello." Parker greeted. "David this is Parker, Parker this is David." I introduced. "Nice to meet you man, listen you two have fun, drinks are in the kitchen my house is your crib for a few hours." David said before taking a huge drink of whatever was in his red cup, most likely some strong, blended concoction of alcohol and juice.

Parker and I walked inside. "Want a drink?" he asked. "Bottle Water is fine." I smiled. I'm one of the few young adults out there that doesn't drink. Not that I'm anti drinking, I just never really had any interest in it.

The room was dark; the only light was coming from the kitchen and a pretty wave pattern on the TV that seemed to change shape as the music played. Everyone was there, well mostly every senior and even some college friends, which kind of made me, feel a little bit out of place. I was happy it was dark so it wasn't obvious I was actually there. In the dark could just blend in with everyone. While lots of people were dancing and talking in the living room, in another room there were two beer pong tournaments going on. I helped Parker make a few friends in David, Loren and Josh and David's friends and brothers.

After forgetting that I hardly talked with anyone at the party, I started to enjoy myself by dancing with Parker, Josh and Loren. "Thank you for giving my phone number to Parker, Josh." I said sarcastically. "No problem hun." He smiled before taking a sip of his Dasani water. I playfully huffed. "I love that you think it's proper to give a girl's number out to strangers." I continued with a little sarcasm. "Well he seemed harmless, and you need something new and exciting in your life, stop being so down, this year is all about you. Ms. Soon to be eighteen." I rolled my eyes and laughed.

"Alright, alright, if you're not staying the night here you gotta get out." David yelled out to the crowd of people. I looked at my phone and saw that it was three am. "Ugh Loren can I stay at your house, I didn't realize it was so late, and I really don't feel like getting into an argument at three in the morning." I groaned. "I was planning on staying here with the guys." Loren replied. "You can stay here Eve." David said. "And where would I sleep?" I asked, not interested or amused. "With me or one of my brothers or even Loren." I looked at Loren who had moved to a corner of the room and was making out with David's brother Greg.

"I would rather sleep on the floor." I said in a sarcastic tone. "Hey, you can come to my house." Parker suggested. I looked at Parker with raised brows. "Your mom would probably be upset if she found a girl in your house." I said. "Probably not, everyone is asleep and she has work tomorrow morning." He replied. I sighed. "Parker I can't, I feel bad." It's not that I didn't want to stay at Parker's house, I just figured it would be weird, having a girl he just met sleeping in his house. "Don't worry about it, come on." he said, ushering me to front door. "Well if you insist." I said lowly.

"Aw I thought I was going to see some Eve and Loren action!" David pouted. "Loren I need my keys." I said looking back at her, suddenly reminding myself that my car was parked outside. "As for you David, that's a lesbian scene you will never *ever* see." I smirked as I caught my car keys that Loren had thrown to me. David's' mouth dropped and Parker laughed. "Nice meeting you all." Parker said while heading out. "Oh and Parker, don't try anything funny with her." Josh said. "Yeah keep your hands to yourself." David added. I shook my head at David and Josh. "Don't pay them any attention, goodnight everyone." I said as I pushed Parker out the door.

"Well it seems your friends are quite protective of you." Parker said. I chuckled. "Josh… yes when he wants to be, David…only wants to get into my pants." I said honestly. "Are you gonna drive your car?" Parker asked. "Yes I am, and I will just follow you." I replied. Parker nodded his head in agreement and got into his car.

I followed Parker to his house, and my mouth dropped when I saw how huge his family home was. If I didn't know Parker, I would think some super rich snobby family lived there. I got out the car and stared at the huge white and glass house before opening the trunk of my car to get my bag of spare clothes. I always brought spare clothes with me for the fact that I hate being home and would rather sleep anywhere else except there. "Are you sure your parents won't be upset?" I asked. "Positive." Parker said while leading me into the house. Parker opened the front door and even though I couldn't see much because of the darkness I could tell his house was amazing. It was warm, and homely and kind of smelled like baked cookies.

"We have a spare bedroom but there are boxes to be unpacked in there, and I don't want you to sleep on the couch, so without any pressure, would it be okay if you slept in my room with me? I promise I won't touch you." Parker said holding his hands up in surrender. I chuckled. Of course he won't touch me, he wouldn't think twice about it. He probably sees me as every other guy has or does a friend or a little sister. "Sure it's not that big of a deal and for some reason…I actually trust you." I smiled at him with no worry in my voice.

Parker led me up the stairs and into his bedroom, which consisted of blue walls, a huge bed, a few jumbo bean bags and chairs, a nice TV, his own bathroom and his personal items. "So this is my room." Parker smiled and gestured to the space. "Wow, it's nice. I'm surprised it's so clean." I said. Parker snorted. "You're surprised that it's clean?" He asked. "Well most boys are messy." "Not me." He replied. "I can see that." I said letting out a small laugh.

"The bathroom is there, you can get dressed, shower or whatever if you want." He said pointing to an open bathroom door. "Do I have any other option?" I asked with a smile. Parker looked at me and a sly smile started spreading across his face. "I do enjoy shows." Parker said. "And I do enjoy jokes." I replied before sticking my tongue out at him and entering the bathroom.

Parker and I talked for a while before going to bed. He told me about his mom Nora and his six year old sister Amanda. I learned that he's actually Canadian and he even told me a little about his life in Texas. That's where he lived before he came here to New Jersey. I told him about my family situation, about being an adopted kid. Not that I wanted sympathy from him but because it's part of my journey, and I'm not ashamed of it, also just for conversation. "I'm sorry your family acts the way they do to you, you don't deserve it, and you're too special to be treated like that." He said. "Thank you Parker, but I am definitely not special, in any way shape or form." I replied looking up at him through my lashes. Parker pulled me in and wrapped his arms around me. "Yes you are, and don't let anyone make you believe in anything other than that." He said. Parker didn't touch me inappropriately, we just cuddled. It was nice and I felt comfortable with him. Probably the most comfortable I've felt in a while.

V

Trick or Treat

In the morning, I woke up alone in Parker's sun filled the bedroom. Even with Parker not in the room, I could hear his voice, and a little girl's laughter coming from down the stairs. I sighed when I looked at the time on my cell phone and realized it was twelve noon and decided that I didn't want to scare anyone, so it would be best if I freshened up and got dressed before going down stairs.

I went downstairs and followed Parker's voice into the kitchen. In the kitchen, Parker was carving pumpkins with a tiny brown haired girl. *I'm guessing that's Amanda* I thought to myself. "Hey you." Parker said smiling at me. "I got someone I want you to meet, Eve this is my sister Amanda, Amanda this is my friend Eve." Parker introduced. "Is she your girlfriend?" Amanda asked playfully. Parker's face turned a bright shade of red. "Not exactly no." he laughed. "Nice to meet you Amanda, what are you two up to?" I asked. Changing the subject and steering it away from an embarrassed Parker. "Pumpkin carving." Amanda said, showing me her little pumpkin. It had a partial happy face on it.

"Are you hungry? "Parker asked. "A little." I replied. "You know you're hungry, I'm going to find something for us to eat." he said. "Okay." Amanda and I said in unison. "Can you help me?" Amanda asked handing me a scalpel like tool. "Sure." I said moving to sit next to her. While carving with Amanda, out of the corner of my eye, I would catch Parker smiling and watching Amanda and I from time to time. *Creepy but cute.* I thought to myself.

"Parker honey!" a woman called as she opened the front door of the house. "Hey mom." Parker yelled back in response. "I just want you to know that I am going to be a little bit late tonight, and I'm gonna need you to take Amanda trick or treating tonight. I'm gonna run up and get a few hours of sleep and then go get some work done." She said. "First mom, I want you to meet someone, we are in the kitchen." Parker yelled.

Within a few seconds Parker's mom appeared in the kitchen. She was very pretty. She was tall and thin. Her brown hair reached past her shoulders and her eyes were a pretty brown color. I could definitely see the resemblance in her and her kids.

"Mom this is Eve, Eve this is my mom Nora." Parker introduced. "Hello, it's nice to meet you Ms. Andrews." I said. "Nice to meet you too sweetie, and call me Nora. She's cute Park." Nora said with a little laugh. Amanda laughed, and I blushed. "How did you two meet?" Nora asked. "We met at school." I replied. "Yeah, we have two classes together and we both have early release." "That's great." Nora smiled.

We talked a few more minutes before Nora started gathering her things. "Well you three, I would love to sit and chat but we have to save that for later. I own *XO magazine* and I'm also editor and chief, and I have so much work to do." She said. "Aw I love that magazine, and no problem, get some rest." I smiled at Nora. "Oh I like her." She said to Parker. "It was nice to meet you Eve." Nora said. "Likewise." I replied. "Oh Parker remember to get Amanda dressed and take her out." she said. "Yeah mom." Parker replied.

I didn't know I was holding my breath until Parker hugged me. "Relax." he chuckled. "Yeah relax." Amanda added. I let out a shaky breath and laughed. "I've never met anybody's parents or parent before except for Loren's. I haven't even met Josh or David's, I was nervous." I admitted. "It's okay, it went great." He smiled. "Okay, Amanda go get your costume on so we can go out soon." Parker said. "I want Eve to help me." She said. I pulled away from Parker and looked at her. "Okay." I smiled. She took my hand and led me up to her brightly painted pink bedroom.

"What are you dressing up as?" I asked her. "Ariana Grande." I didn't even really know who Ariana Grande was, but I knew she was on some Nickelodeon show. *She is on a Nickelodeon show right?* I asked myself. "Cool, she's your favorite?" I asked playing it off as if I knew who Ariana is. "Yes." Amanda replied while putting a red wig on. I smirked at her attempt to adjust the upside down wig before helping her with the wig and her costume.

Amanda and I walked back downstairs a few minutes later with her in a white dress, silver shoes, a microphone and her red wig pulled back into a ponytail. "Thanks for getting her dressed." Parker said. "No problem." I smiled.

That evening Parker and I bonded more as we took Amanda out trick or treating. With him it felt so easy, I could be myself and not pretend. Parker accepted me for me. We had the same interests and he didn't judge any comment that I made. For me, that was a breath of fresh air, I silently thanked Josh for giving him my phone number.

VI

Signs of Change

Ever since we first met, Parker and I have been close; it only made sense that we start dating. Sometimes I wonder why or how he ended up with someone like me. He didn't go for the current volleyball captain or cheerleader. I would bring this conversation to Parker telling him he was wasting his time on me, and he would call me silly. He would say I'm just right for him.

With parker, I gained a little more confidence in myself, and even a tad bit sense of direction. I've gotten so comfortable with him that I spend the majority of my time at his house; I even have some of my belongings there. I didn't move in or anything I mainly go there to get away from my family, and also to be with him and his own family. I find that if I am around happy, confident, positive people, I become happy, confident and positive. It's like what they radiate bounces off of them and on to me. Like attracts like. Parker's mother Nora and his little sister accept me and I love them like real family. They all give me sense of what a *real* family is.

Everything with me is somewhat good. However, every now and then I have these weird feelings and I've also been having strange dreams. Dreams I only tell parker about. They were Images of angels, some sort of God and other folk tale creatures like unicorns, vampires and witches. These dreams were sometimes beautiful and happy, and others were terrifying dreams or war and death. I snapped out of my thoughts about my strange dreams when my phone rang.

"Hey babe what you up to?" Parker asked. "Nothing, just thinking." I replied. "About what?" He asked. "Nothing really." "The dreams again?" Parker asked. "Yeah." I replied. "You still can't figure out what they mean or why they randomly appeared?" He asked. "Not a clue." I sighed.

"Look, I'm almost done getting dressed and when in done I'm gonna come pick you up and were going somewhere." Parker said. I could tell he was smiling through the phone. "Where are we going?" I asked, somewhat not amused. "You will see, get dressed." Parker said and with that, he hung up the phone.

Much to my dismay because I was seriously moody and wanted to be alone. Parker picked me up and took me to "IPlayAmerica." There, we ended up playing tons of games and rounds of laser tag.

Even though I was in a bit of a mood, during laser tag I started feeling comfortable in the dark. Something, some weird force began taking over my body and I could feel an internal change in me. A few seconds after feeling the change I could see very clear in the darkness and I also started to feel relatively competitive and primal. I wanted to tag everyone that was on the opposite team from me, including Parker.

Around the middle of our last game, I began to feel dizzy and even started hyperventilating. Thankfully Parker was on the same level as me and he saw me sitting with my knees pulled up to my chest on the floor. "Babe you alright?" he asked with a voice full of worry. I shook my head no.

Parker picked me up and carried me out of the laser arena area and into the dressing room, and then he sat me down on the bench. "Breathe babe, I'm gonna run and get you some water." He said. I nodded my head okay and closed my eyes tightly. The feeling of not being able to breathe is a scary feeling.

When Parker came back, I somewhat gained my composure. I took the water bottle from him and drank slowly. "You scared me." he said crouching down so that he was eye level with me and moving some hair out of my face. "Hey why are your eyes changing colors? It's like a purple color... and it's changing, it's turning back to your normal brown now." He said. As soon as Parker said the word brown, I dropped my water bottle and almost fell on him. It was like that something, that force that took over my body, had just released itself from me.

I began to feel like me again, no longer competitive, no special vision. Not even hyperventilating anymore all I felt was tiredness. "I'm tired." I said to Parker in a tired and raspy voice. "Come on then." Parker undressed my laser tag gear and then his own gear before he led me to his car.

After being in the car for five minutes, I could sense uneasiness between Parker and me. A Coldplay song was playing low, and Parker and I hadn't said a word to each other. I felt bad, like I ruined his night.

"I'm sorry for whatever it is that happened back there. Are you mad?" I asked. "No why would I be mad?" "Because I ruined your night." I replied. "You didn't." I huffed. "Because I've been a handful tonight." Parker snorted. "You can say that again." "Because I've been a handful tonight." I repeated. Parker stopped at the red light and laughed. He cupped my face and kissed me." I'm not mad at you babe, as long as your safe, that's all that matters. I was just worried." he smiled.

"Ever since those crazy dreams started, my world has been rollercoaster loopy. And now, I feel internally and emotionally different at times. I thought it was just moodiness. And then tonight happened. I don't know what's going on with me." I said to Parker.

Then it hit me! Winter, the physic I met at Six Flags said there would be changes happening with me. *Are these the changes she meant? Did that lady put voodoo on me?* I asked myself. I decided to tell Parker part of what Winter had told me, even though she said not to. Parker is the one person in this world that I trust. Even though I haven't known him for very long, he hasn't judge me, made fun of me or try to change me. He and his family accepted me for me. And if I have to go through anything, I'd rather it be with him, rather than going through it alone.

I opened up to Parker about what Winter told me and Parker being the guy he is, thought Winter was crazy, and the whole situation was stupid. Parker is very realistic, where as I have a mind full of imagination and my mind thought that maybe there was something supernatural going on with me.

After our talk, the tension between Parker and I floated out of the car and we were laughing the rest of the ride home.

I decided to stay at Parker's house, at his house I was guaranteed to get a great night of sleep. I got in and out the shower last out of the two of us and while I was putting my hair up into a messy bun, Parker was laying on his bed watching the movie *Legion*. "Come here." He said in a husky voice. I turned to him and walked up to where he was lying on the bed, which is when he pulled me on top of him. I bent my head down to kiss him, while my hands rested on his chest.

As our kiss deepened I could feel Parker's heart beating faster and faster. He then sat up and wrapped both arms around me, and flipped us over so that he was on top of me. He couldn't tell but I was nervous and obviously not ready. I didn't want Parker to see my body, not naked anyway. Not that anything is wrong with it; it's just not anything special. What if I disappointed him and his washboard abs?

Something inside me said not yet. Not that I'm saving myself for a specific reason, I just think when the time is right, I will feel ready. And I'm not going to have sex just to have it.

I sat up and pulled away from Parker. "I love you". He said. It took me by surprise and I was in total shock because no one and I mean absolutely no one has ever said those words to me. I looked deeply into Parker's eyes and never seen so much honesty in them. A warm feeling that I never felt before coated my heart and I smiled widely and kissed Parker. "Olive juice." I said whispering in his ear. Parker sat up and looked at me with an amused look. "Olive juice, it means I love you, without saying I love you." I said. "It's not that I don't love you, it's just that you're my first boyfriend and I've never said those words to anyone before. Saying those words make me nervous." I admitted. Parker smiled. "Okay, I'm not going to pressure you Eve, tell me when you are ready. But I want you to know that I do love you." He smiled.

If I had said those words to Parker, I wouldn't be completely sure if I truly meant them, and I didn't want to lie to him. I did feel bad for not saying it back but I couldn't bring myself to tell someone I love them if I wasn't sure if the correct feeling or emotion matched the words. Parker rolled down to his side and pulled the blankets from underneath us and snuggled with me. I was happy that he didn't take my non "I love you" response to heart.

My eyes were a glowing a fluorescent purple, my hair was in a high ponytail and I glowed in white light while wearing black boots, a dark purple leather cat suit with a gray tank top underneath. I looked different. In my opinion better. I looked at three men that were camping out around a bonfire, and walked up to them. "Hey! You guys started partying without me? You should be ashamed of yourselves." I said sarcastically. I smirked as the men gasped at my presence.

Before I knew it, all three men were facing me and that's when I noticed they were anything but human. They were hideous deformed creatures that grunted and made weird animal sounds. I stood there looking at them with not one ounce of fear in my body. "You three are the ugliest things I ever saw, I feel bad for your parents!" I said with sarcasm.

One of the creatures charged at me and from the palm of my hand I threw a white ball of fire at him. The next two came after me and we fought as well until two gorgeous guys appeared out of the north and east sides of the woods. The guys were so gorgeous that they could have been made from wax.

One guy was dressed from head to toe in black with his black hair pulled back into a ponytail. He had sun kissed skin and dark but brightly lit piercing eyes. The other guy had blonde hair and blue eyes and kind of a young *Nick Carter* look to him. He glowed in gold and wore dark blue jeans and a white button up shirt. They surrounded one of the creatures and grabbed his arms. While they were holding him, I walked up to him and slapped him across the face with a large staff. He fell to the ground, so I picked him up, and threw him into the large campfire.

I was now running, running very fast through the woods. I quickly looked up to the sky which was deep purple and then I focused ahead of me so that I wouldn't bump into any trees or brushes that I was running through. I stopped running when I reached a few feet away from a cliff. Standing at the cliff waiting for me stood a beautiful red haired girl. Her skin was a shade of olive and her eyes were bright green. We both were dressed in black from head to toe, and as I stared straight through her, she glared through me.

In the blink of an eye I ran at her, colliding with her. Both of us were rolling around until she flipped us over and ended up on top of me. While she was choking me, I somehow lifted her off of me and tossed her over the ledge of the cliff however not before she grabbed my foot and dragged me with her, making us both fall over the ledge.

VII

Feeling the Dreams

"Eve! Eve! Wake up!" I heard a voice calling to me. I opened my eyes wide and grasped for air to breathe. Parker pulled me into his arms and rocked me back and forth. "What the hell happened? You were crying, grunting and screaming in your sleep."

"I had a dream, a weird one again. I attacked these ugly monster things, and I was running through the woods, and then I reached a cliff and this girl was there. I ran after her and attacked her. We were rolling around and fighting before I pushed her over the cliff but she grabbed a hold of my leg and took me down with her. Everything felt so real. I could feel myself running and falling." I said with tears coming down my face.

"Are you serious?" Parker asked while looking at me like I had dumb written on my forehead. "That's it? I thought you were getting attacked by wolves or something." He said. I immediately got annoyed with him. So I hopped out of his bed and went to the bathroom, locking the door behind me.

In the bathroom I looked at myself in the mirror. *Am I over reacting?* I asked myself. It wasn't so much about the dream itself that scared me; it's the fact that I *felt* everything, like it was really happening. I jumped into the shower and let the hot water take over me. I seriously want to know what's in that bag Winter gave me. Ever since I met her my life has been so abnormal. Well abnormal for me.

I finally got out of the shower after twenty minutes, and as soon as I opened the bathroom door, Parker was standing right at the doorway with a plate of waffles. "What's this?" I asked. "I made you breakfast." "Thank you." I replied. "Can you forgive me, for earlier?" He asked. "I wasn't too mad at you, it's not your fault that you can't understand, I barley understand myself." I sighed. "It's just that everything in that dream felt real. All this scientific bull crap is just taking a toll on me." I said. Parker kissed my forehead. "This will all pass, it's all just some sort of phase. We'll get through it okay, I promise." he said. I took the plate of waffles and pecked him on the lips. Parker's words were only a little comforting, as what I was going through, wasn't a *phase* that everybody goes through. What was happening to me was unheard of. Everything going on with me... was just plain strange.

That afternoon, Parker had driven me to work. Working at the mall wasn't the best but working at my favorite store, *Charlotte Russe* was nice.

"Eve don't worry so much about that dream okay?" Parker texted me as I walked into the mall.

"I will try," I replied.

And I was being honest, I would try not to think about it, but with all the supernatural, freaky, crap going on, how it makes me feel, it's hard not to think about it. It's hard not to think that something is starting to happen to me. It's always scary when something is going on with someone and they don't have the power to control it or know how to deal with it.

I tried to block out all emotions or thoughts concerning the weird "changes" in my life and focus on work but it was no use. During the peak of my shift is where I began to get extremely tired. So tired that my coworkers Sasha and Andrew even noticed. I was yawning almost nonstop and my eyes kept watering. I counted down the minutes I had left in my shift, and then slowly walked to the main entrance to meet Parker.

"Baby you look so tired and completely out of it." Parker said engulfing me in a hug. "Thank you for the complement. You will be happy to know that I also feel like flesh eating zombie." I said sarcastically. Parker chuckled and let us into the car. "So where to?" He asked. "My house, gotta grab some more clothes to bring to your house." I said. "You should just move in already." Parker said. "Yeah I'm sure Nora would go for that, your mom has been completely nice to me but moving in, that's a whole other level." I said. "You practically live there now." He replied.

I sighed and rested my hot head on the cold window. I wasn't feeling up to having a debate, argument or even a general conversation. I honestly just wanted to sleep. "It pisses me off that I can't protect you from a few stupid nightmares." Parker said sadly. I looked at him. "Hey, I don't want you to feel bad that you can't. You can't protect a girl from everything Parker."

Parker looked at me with eyes that went from sad, to pissed off to understanding. "I'm sorry." Parker said. "I'm happy really." I said with a small smile. "I like that even though you feel like shit, and when your world is absolutely fucking crazy, you're so positive. I like that you keep your cool... most times anyway." he said. "Look I won't bring up anything that's been going on again okay. But I know you're not getting any sleep and its worse at home on that couch, and I like you sleeping with me. So please, stay with me for a little while?" Parker asked. I kissed Parker deeply and agreed. Truth was I did get more sleep at his place. It was peaceful there, and that in turn made me more at peace.

Parker and I reached the destination of my house. As usual I had him wait for me in the car as I went to grab a few pairs of clothes. I wasn't surprised when the door was locked, so I rang the doorbell and waited for someone to come open the door. I groaned, I definitely wasn't ready to hear any nagging, but whenever I entered this house, it was almost mandatory.

"Eve where have you been?!" Mena asked as she opened the front door. "out." replied. "I should *kick* you out! Coming in and out this house as you please. I almost packed up your crap and put it on the front porch, I'm not dealing with you anymore Eve!" Mena said. "Sadly you will have to deal with me until I'm 18." I replied. "Not really, you don't matter! No one wanted you when you were born, and honestly I don't want you now because of your smart mouth.

Since day one you have been a mess and we just so happen to be the ones stuck with you. Thank God your birthday is coming so I can be done with you." She said. "Thank God it is, you and everyone in this house are so miserable, that you want everyone miserable too. Thank God my birthday is coming so I can leave." I said calmly as I pushed my way inside.

"And where are you going to go Eve? Sleep on a bench?" She asked with a wicked chuckle. "Why does it concern you, I'm already sleeping on a couch. And if you shall know, I'm gonna go so much further than what you have accomplished in your entire life. Now if you'll excuse me, I have to pack some clothes so I can leave and stop interrupting your wonderful life." I said with a tired smirk.

"You're not going anywhere, you walked in here and you're not walking back out that door." She said. "I bet I am." I said now getting frustrated. "And I will call the cops and they will bring you right back here, and I will tell them that boy outside waiting for you, took you away against your will or my knowledge." She said. "For someone that doesn't want me, you are going through serious lengths to keep me here. You are unbelievably insane and I hope you know when karma is ready, she's going to bite you hard." I said.

I walked downstairs to the basement and texted Parker to tell him what had happened. He understood and told me to pack some clothes and just come over tomorrow after school. He always made unnecessary drama much simpler and tolerable. I agreed, put on my pajamas and tried to sleep.

While tossing and turning, I dreamed of myself lying down on a chair outside and looking up at two planets, the moon and the same purple sky from before. My eyes were closing as I was brading my hair. I wore a cream colored silk tank top and dark blue jeans, and I looked comfortable and completely UN worried.

The dream jumped to another scene and I turned my back to the window and I looked around at the beautiful room I stood in. It was a gold and royal purple room, with a large white canopy bed. It had a vintage glam look to it and it was absolutely beautiful. I walked to my bed and grabbed my iPod and sat on my chaise. Scrolling until I came across one of my favorite songs by *"The Red House Painters"* the impossibly attractive guy that was dressed in all black that I dreamed about before got up and snatched my iPod away from me.

"I'm sorry for not telling you about me being who I am, and about Scarlett...just stop acting like you don't care about me, and stop being stubborn and listen to me!" he commanded. "I am not being stubborn, I am being a smart future queen, you can leave Tess!" I yelled as I walked over to my mirror. The peace that radiated off of me when I was lying outside had vanished. Tess walked over and snaked his pale arms around my waist. I closely took in of our reflections in the mirror. His pale skin meshing nicely with my golden brown tone.

"I said I'm sorry Eve, what more do you want? And I'm not leaving, because I like you too much to leave." he said. I turned to look at Tess and I knew internally I had forgiven him. Tess kissed me softly and our lips sizzled. It felt so warm, the hot sun kissing the sand at a beach. I couldn't control myself, and pressed into him wrapping my arms around his neck. He wrapped his arms around my waist and lifted me up, holding me tightly against him. I dreamed of being intimate with Tess and enjoying every moment of it. It's usual to dream of a celebrity crush but it's a little confusing to dream about a normal human being that you've never seen before. However, with how beautiful Tess was, how his face looked like painted marble I came to the decision to forgo my confusion, and enjoy the dream.

After the intense dream ended, I woke up feeling sore all over my body. It was a mixture of feeling like I got my butt kicked and a burning sensation on my skin. I slowly walked to the bathroom and got in the shower, letting out a rather loud scream when the water hit my back. My back burned, it literally felt like desert heat mixed with alcohol on a fresh cut. I stumbled out and turned my back to the mirror, trying to see if any scratches or burns were the culprit for my burning.

I didn't find scratches or burns but I did see faint markings along my back. See, to anyone else my back would seem normal, but everyone knows their own bodies and I could see light faint marks. They kind of looked like marks that you get from resting on a certain body part for too long, along with a little red shade to them. Therefore I thought nothing of the markings, Perhaps the burning was from the shower water being too hot. I lotioned up and put some sensitive skin lotion on my back. I gently put my clothes on before grabbing my phone and purse and driving to school.

My back burned and ached against the seat of the car and I let a sigh of relief when I made my two stops for the day and had to get out of the car. Stop one was to Starbucks and stop two was finally to school. By the time I actually parked my car in the school lot, I only had fifteen minutes until the first class started. I smiled and waved at Parker, Loren, and Josh who were standing by Parker's car talking amongst each other.

"Good morning." Parker smiled as I got out the car. "Good morning, what's up guys?" I asked. "Nothing at all." Loren responded. "Morning." Josh said as he drank his usual morning tea. I went to kiss Parker, and he pulled me into an embrace, only letting me go when I screeched and tried to push him away from me. "What's wrong?" he asked. "I burned myself in the shower today; my back is still a little sore." I said. "I bet that's not the only reason why your back is sore." Loren chuckled.

I rolled my eyes. It annoys me that just because someone is good-looking with a great body, they are automatically in the "you're definitively not a virgin" category. Snap judgments and stereotypes are the enemy! But I let people think what they want, because they are going to think what they want anyway. "So, you still coming over after school right?" Parker asked. "Definitely." I smiled, and led us inside the school building.

I started internally freaking out because I forgot to do my math homework. Even though I was technically in my standards, *sick* over the weekend, I didn't know how Ms. Burns would react to my missing assignment. "Alright, see you guys later." I said as I grabbed my math book out of my locker and walked to math. I smiled at Tiffany who was sitting on the floor finishing up her homework.

"Did you do yours?" She asked. "No, I forgot to do it, and I left the book here at school so..." I said trailing off. "Hello ladies." Ms. Burns said as she approached us to walk into the classroom. "Hi Ms. Burns!" Tiffany and I said together. I got up and dragged my feet but followed her over to her desk. "Um Ms. Burns, I kind of missed doing the homework, I've been getting really sick lately and really tired from the lack of sleep I've been getting." I said. She looked at me and smiled. "Okay just have it on my desk tomorrow morning okay?" She said more than asked. "Okay." I agreed and then started to walk over to my desk.

"Remember Eve, if you need any help with anything or if you need someone to talk to you know where to find me, I will be happy to help." She said. "I will keep that in mind." I replied. "Just know this Eve, when your journey truly begins, which I'm pretty sure it has just begun...you turn eighteen very soon right?" She asked. I shook my head yes. "At that age, you will finally reach maturity and you will see the world in an entire new light. When that happens Just know you can come to me." She said. I nodded my head in understanding before saying thank you.

"Okay so everyone here?" Ms. Burns asked the class. Everyone looked around before saying a boy named Robert was missing from the class. Ms. Burns made note of it in her attendance book before proceeding to teach the class. "Okay, we are going to practice trigonometry and also have a review on the work we've done for this semester to get you prepared for the final next month." I groaned before resting my hands on my desk and banging my head against them. Math is the enemy! I sat and endured the familiar and yet majorly confusing lessons and practically ran out the room when class was over.

I got in my car and drove straight to Parker's house. "You okay?" He chuckled. Opening the door and noticing me out of breath. "Yes... I just hate math." I replied. Parker laughed. "Are mom and Amanda here?" I asked. "Nah, mom's at work and Amanda is at ice skating practice." "Wow, you didn't tell me she skates." I exclaimed. "Well you know since there's a rink close by, and some of her new friends go there, guessing she just wants to fit in." He said. "Doesn't everyone want to fit in?" I said more than asked. Parker shook his head yes. "We are ordering in Chinese tonight and we can watch a movie if that's okay with you." he said. "Sounds perfect." I smiled.

I laid my head on Parkers chest as my eyes drooped. We had finished watching *Avatar* and were now fifteen minutes into *Monsters vs. Aliens*. Sadly, for the fact that I started yawning every other three minutes, I knew I wouldn't be seeing the entire film.

"This year is going by quickly, what are your plans after school?" I asked Parker. "I'm going to Harvard!" he said sarcastically. I laughed. Seems my sarcastic personality was starting to affect Parker in a positive way. "No seriously." Parker sucked in a large amount of air before responding. "I'm not sure, I could go to college, but I'm not sure if it's for me you know. I'm thinking about just getting on my bike and joy riding for a year or something of that sort." I looked up at him.

"You're really going to ride your mountain bike cross country?" I asked trying to be funny. "Ha-ha...no my dad's Kawasaki is in the garage." He said. "You never told me he rode." I said. "Indeed he did. He was supposed to teach me before he died." I mentally slapped myself.

Parker told me dad had passed away last December, and that's why they ultimately decided to move away from Texas. To get away from the sorrow and memories. I hated bringing his dad into any conversation because it made Parker sad. I frowned. "I'm sorry for bringing that up. if you want to go exploring, sightseeing or whatever you desire to do for a year then you should do it. I'm totally for any decision you make." I smirked. "Thanks baby." Parker said before kissing my forehead. I rested my head back onto his chest, and within five minutes, I was in dream land.

VIII

Pizza Thanksgiving

"Morning Eve!" Nora said as I walked down the stairs of her house and into the kitchen. "Morning, Happy Thanksgiving. It smells nice." I said while rubbing my eyes. "Smells better than it looks." Parker said while watching his mom, who was trying to cook a turkey, but instead it looked like she was attacking it. "It looks absolutely disgust...." Amanda started to say but immediately stopped when Nora's uncooked Turkey ended up on the floor right in front of Amanda's feet.

"Oh my God I'm sorry you had to see that Eve." Nora said in embarrassment. Parker burst out with laughter and Amanda looked horrified. "No worries, how about we simply order pizza later, my treat." I suggested. "I want pizza! I am not eating that!" Amanda said while pointing to the turkey Nora was picking up from the ground. "I don't get why turkey is the signature dish for Thanksgiving. I don't even like turkey." I said. Nora sighed. "That makes me feel so much better. Maybe it was meant to fall on the floor then." She said. "It was fate." I smirked. "Well pizza it is then, I'm going to go get cleaned up." She said washing her hands.

Parker came over to hug me as Nora walked out of the kitchen. "Thanks for saying that to my mom, you know making her feel better." He whispered. "I only stated the truth. I actually don't like turkey." I replied. "Weirdo!" Parker called me. "Shut up!" I chucked as

I playfully hit his arm and then led him to the living room to watch the Thanksgiving Day Parade with Amanda. This Thanksgiving with Parker and his family was the most peaceful one I've ever had. This was the first Thanksgiving I actually felt thankful for something. I was sincerely thankful for meeting Parker.

"So Eve I can't wait for tomorrow it's going to be really fun! Just you me and Amanda." Nora said, now joining us in the living room. Tomorrow it would be us girls just shopping all day. And when I say all day, I mean all day. Nora had made plans for us to leave at dawn.

"I'm pretty sure it will be fun, all you're going to do is shop, bombard her with questions and tell embarrassing stories about me." Parker said. "I don't mind that." I laughed. "Park is just upset that he's not going with us. He's going to miss us so much!" Nora said in a playful voice. Parker rolled his eyes, and all the girls laughed.

I woke up at five am and prepared myself for the day. I smiled as I tip toed around a sleeping Parker's room. I went downstairs to the kitchen and let out a small laugh. Amanda had a piece of bacon in her hand that was aimed for her mouth, but she was still nodding off to sleep. Nora laughed at my small laugh. "I made waffles and bacon for us, we will need energy today. When we are all done eating we can leave." Nora said. "Okay." I replied.

After a short while riding in the car, I got a little nervous about what Nora and I would talk about. Even though she and I were close, we were never left alone together without Parker for a large amount of time. To break the ice I decided to ask the first question, and it was a serious one. "Nora, if you don't mind me asking, what exactly happened to Amanda and Parker's dad?" Nora hesitated and looked a little taken aback by my question." Christopher, Parker and Amanda's dad...was on his way to go see Parker's last football game, they were in the finals. Did you know Parker played football?" She asked. "Yes he told me he was a tight end." I replied. "Yes he was, and he was amazing on the field." She said, pausing before she continued. "Chris was pulling into the entrance to the school they were playing at to see the final game and a truck that was coming towards Chris, had swerved into his lane. I guess the driver took his eyes off the road for a second or something. He ended up crashing into Chris's side of the car at twenty five miles per hour. For a truck that's a lot." Nora said.

I really didn't know how to react to Nora's story. I felt so bad for what happened to her late husband, and I could only imagine how she, Parker and Amanda felt on the subject of Christopher. "I'm so sorry Nora." I said sympathetically. "It's alright Eve, it's actually nice that you asked. It shows that you care." she said.

Nora asked me questions regarding my future school plans, and asked a little about me not getting along with my adoptive parents. Other than that, we didn't bother with any more questions. I think it's because we both were too tired to think of good questions for one another. But she did tell me a few embarrassing stories based on Parker.

I learned that he sucked his thumb until he was nine years old, and that he didn't learn how to properly tie his shoes until he was thirteen. "It's not that he didn't know how, he just couldn't be assed with it; he used to be so lazy." she said.

We got home around three pm and I was beyond tired, yet again all I wanted to do was sleep. "So how was it?" Parker asked sitting on the couch with one of his headphones on one of his ears and the other headphone off. "Not bad at all, she didn't grill me like chicken at all." I said trying to be humors. But all Parker did was roll his eyes. And I laughed.

"I did learn that you sucked your thumb until you were nine." I chuckled. Parker turned red in embarrassment. "Mom! Come on, you can't tell her things like that. I wasn't sucking my thumb; I just liked to bite my thumb nails." He said in protest. Nora and I looked at each other before laughing at Parker.

IX

December

I watched the clock closely as it read eleven fifty-nine pm. It was one minute to twelve am. It was one minute from being December first. It felt like forever for time to go by, like it was playing some sort of game with me, making me wait patiently. It made me overthink what could possibly happen in twenty-three days. What would happen now on December first? I started getting frustrated, and then it happened. It was December first.

Nothing happened on December first, but you know they say everything takes time. Everything is a process. By the second week of December, I was feeling better than I ever had. Little changes in me started to surface. I was sitting on the floor doing the math packet homework assignment Ms. Burns had given us and it didn't fully hit me until I was halfway done with the packet, how easy it was for me to complete the assignment. It's like some form of clarity filled my eyes and my mind, and now the one subject that was difficult for me, was now very easy.

As time went on I noticed that I suddenly became smart. Not that I was ever dumb, but now I knew things. Any information on a world subject, a math problem, help understanding Spanish or French, or any information on an element on the periodic table, I knew. I knew it all. Sports became my favorite, a competitive edge transpires during every game, and I would find myself a little upset that it wasn't summer because I wanted to run laps around the track.

My sleeping pattern even began to change. I didn't need to sleep as much as I used to. Four hours was enough to keep me energized for the day. I only need four hours of sleep to feel like I have slept for twelve hours.

My voice had gotten a little more bass and authority to it, making me sound confident instead of the squeak toy I used to sound like. All of these new changes putting a confidence in me. Making me forgo questioning what was happening to me. At this point and time, I liked what was happening to me.

I woke up at six am on my birthday. It was the last day of school before break. But I wasn't worried about that. I was only worried about what would be happening to me later. Figuring that nothing weird would happen to me this early since I was born at eight thirty pm.

Boy was I wrong, I went to the bathroom and my reflection in the mirror horrified me. My skin was peeling all over. Think of severe sun burn peeling without the sun burn. It was especially bad on my back. I ran to my shower and scrubbed myself until I was almost in pain. I watched the peeling, dead skin fall off of me and go down the drain.

After thirty minutes I got out and walked back to the mirror. My face was acne free, and the curves to my body looked sharper than ever, any bit of flab or attribute that I thought was horrible, was now corrected and beautiful. My lips were always naturally a pretty shade of pink, but now the pink looked a bit brighter. My eyes were more open and bright. My cheekbones were also a little more defined. The hair on my head was thicker and about two inches longer. My apple boobs had even perked up a bit. I was sacredly amazed at the reflection that was staring back at me in the mirror.

The peeling had stopped and my skin was now glowing. My back was still a little dry and itchy, so I covered it in Victoria's secrets *endless love*. Yes it burned like hell, but it had to be done. I couldn't go to school and constantly itch myself every few seconds; people would think I had fleas! I grabbed some clothes and got dressed before heading off to school.

As usual I spotted Josh, Loren and Parker as I parked in my parking spot at school. Parker opened my door and gave me the biggest hug I ever received. "Happy birthday baby, you look so good." He said as he took my face into his hands, and gently pulled it towards him and softly kissed my lips. "Thank you so much." I smiled. "What happened to you? You look... weird." Loren said. "Weird how?" I asked confused. The confidence I had gained from looking at myself over and over in the mirror earlier had disappeared and suddenly I felt somewhat insecure. "I don't know, you're just shiny, glowly and stuff." She said in an almost disgusted tone. "She looks beautiful." Josh said. I smiled up at him as he gave me a hug. "Happy birthday." He said." Thank you." I replied.

Maybe my vision is distorted and I don't look the way I thought I did in the mirror. Maybe I got it all wrong. I thought to myself. Clearly I was confused on weather I looked as weird and horrible as Loren had made me semi believe, or did I look beautiful, like Josh said. With this confusion, I'd more so believe Loren's comment. The confidence I gained while with Parker and his family led me to believe that I'm not bad looking, but if I had to describe myself in any positive word to describe my appearance, it would be *cute*. I always pictured myself *at least* cute, but nowhere near beautiful.

"We are all gonna meet up and have a little get together dinner for your birthday." Josh said. "Aw thanks, but is that necessary?" I asked. I really appreciated them celebrating my birthday with me but I had business with a drawstring bag to take care of. "Yes it's necessary, it's your birthday." Parker smiled. I was just about to reply when the first bell rang, making us cut our conversation short. I kissed Parker once on the lips as my goodbye. "Ugh save that for a bathroom stall." Loren said. I rolled my eyes. "Get to class guys, see everyone later." I said before I walked to my locker.

When I opened my locker I found a large card signed by Parker, his mom and his sister. Behind the card sat a cute white teddy bear with a blue bow tie. I smiled as I inspected it. While looking at the bear, I had a feeling that someone was watching me, that someone was right beside me. I put the bear back and looked to my right. Standing right there in front of me was Ms. Burns.

"Oh my gosh Ms. Burns. You know a great way to scare someone." I said with my hand over my racing heart. "You've transitioned well, you're beyond beautiful Eve. Happy birthday." She smiled. "Thank you." I replied. "Today is a very special day for you and after this night, your life will be totally different. Eighteen is an age of new beginnings, and what was hidden in your past when you were a minor, is now laid in front of you." I just stared at her. In my mind I was thinking *this lady is more Looney than Bugs bunny.*

The final bell rang and she gasped." I better get to class. Enjoy your day and again happy birthday." she said as she walked away. I stood there in confusion before I realized I was going to be late to Language arts class.

School went by relatively quick since we did nothing but watch movies and ate bagels and donuts in honor of my birthday and the holidays. I met Parker in the parking lot and hugged him." Thank you for the bear and the card." I said. "My pleasure babe." He replied, kissing my cheek. "So I'm picking you up tonight at seven fifteen okay, so be ready by then." he said. "Sounds like a plan." I agreed. I got in my car, waved bye to Parker and then drove home.

Thankfully when I got home, not a single soul was there. Even though it's my birthday I didn't expect anything less from my family and besides I was happy to have a quiet and empty house to myself anyway.

In the basement I looked for an outfit to wear for the night. Seeing that it's my birthday, I wanted to look really pretty. For the most part I like to wear comfortable clothes, but when I have to get glammed up, I make sure I do it right. I pulled out a dark blue spaghetti strapped fringe top that had silver diamond embroidery going down the middle. I paired it with black skinny jeans a silver charm bracelet and silver heels. I then grabbed the drawstring bag out from the bottom of my clothes bin and put it beside my dress. I wanted to make sure I had everything prepared and ready to go.

Before getting ready, it took every ounce in me not to open the drawstring bag. It was my birthday after all! But I knew it wouldn't be right if I opened it before eight thirty. "I waited this long, mind as well wait a little longer." I mumbled to myself. I distracted myself by reading magazines, day dreaming, and listening to music before I went to the bathroom, to shower and get ready.

While I was curling my hair Parker had texted me and told me he was outside waiting for me. I added a few more touches to my hair and light makeup before grabbing my leather jacket, drawstring bag, purse and heading out to meet Parker.

He was standing by his car wearing his leather jacket, a navy shirt and light blue jeans. I smiled and walked up to kiss him. "You look beautiful baby." He whispered. "Thank you, but I am a little cold." I smiled. Rubbing my shoulders to gain some warmness from the cold December air. Parker chuckled and led me to the passenger side of the car before running to the driver side and sliding himself into the driver seat.

"You excited?" he asked me. I turned to him with a huge grin on my face. "I am. I haven't done anything special for my birthday in a really long time." I said. Parker took my hand and kissed it. "I promise from now on, your birthday will always be celebrated, your special Eve, and you definitely deserve it." "Thanks." I mumbled with a smile. "So, where are we going?" I asked. I noticed that the direction we were driving in wasn't a dead giveaway to where we could be going. We were headed in an area where there were tons of restaurants. "It's a surprise babe." Parker chuckled. I fake huffed. "Come on, I've been surprised enough, just tell me." I whined. Parker laughed. "No can do." He said shaking his head no. "Give me a hint." I begged. "No." he laughed.

He then turned the radio up, blocking out my begging and began to sing along to *Linkin Park*. Still with a smirk on my face, I folded my arms like a little kid and looked out the window at all the lights that were driving by.

After a twelve minute drive and a three minute search for a parking spot, I smiled as I read the large letters on the gold building that was somehow connected to the mall. "Oh wow, *cheesecake factory*, how did you know this was my favorite restaurant?" I asked with a giant smile. Parker laughed at my excitedness. "Josh suggested it." He shrugged. I got out of the car and took Parker's hand as we headed inside the factory.

Standing in the front by the hostess desk stood David, Josh and Loren. "Hey guys." I said giving them hugs. "You look nice." Loren complemented. "Thanks Loren... Josh, how did you know this is my favorite restaurant?" I asked. "I just guessed." He laughed and hugged me. I stepped back and moved to Parker, who was looking at his watch. He slowly removed his left hand to hold my waist and turned me towards him so that we were face to face. Parker smiled at me and cupped my face with his hands before kissing me deeply. "It's almost your birthday." he said with his lips brushing mine. I looked at the clock on my phone and saw that it was twenty minutes till eight pm. "Wow, time is going by fast isn't it?" I whispered to him. "Yeah, it is" he smirked. "Eve party of five! The hostess called out." I led the five of us over to the host where we shortly followed her to a booth and shortly ordered our drinks.

We made short conversation talking about what we were planning on doing over the break. Loren was going back to Hawaii to visit family. David would be in the Dominican Republic. Josh would be celebrating the New Year with family. Parker would also be around his small family, and I decided that I would spend my time either lounging around the basement or hanging out with Parker and his family.

After we ordered our food, I sipped my sugary and alcohol free special drink, and I smiled at the people that were surrounding me. They honestly did a better job celebrating my birthday rather than my own family. Yeah, it's only dinner, but I haven't done anything for my birthday since I was about nine. My adoptive sisters had a sweet sixteen, and for mine, I sat on the floor of the basement and cried. Mena said that a birthday is just another day, and ever since then, my birthday has been just another day, but my sister's birthdays were always celebrated.

After eating quite a bit of my food, I looked at my phone to check the time and when I saw that it was almost eight thirty pm and I almost choked. "Baby you okay?" Parker asked. I nodded my head yes. I took out the black drawstring bag that was sitting inside my purse and I excused myself and headed to the restroom.

My heart was beating so rapidly, that I was sure I could hear it.

My palms were starting to sweat too, all out of nervousness. I grabbed the black bag that Winter had given me, and then checked the time on my phone again. It was two minutes past my birthday, and I began to tremble. I decided I wanted to hurry up and get it all over with, to finally see what was in store for me. "It's time." I said to my reflection in the mirror. I locked the door of the bathroom and then I took a deep breath and opened the bag.

X

Permia

As soon as I opened the bag, the lights in the bathroom began to flicker. I looked around the empty bathroom before continuing to go through the contents in the bag. Inside the bag was a small plum purple box. Written on the box in pretty font was the word *Permia* I let my index finger scheme the writing.

I opened the purple box and came to find a locket. I opened the locket and found one photo of a beautiful woman holding a baby. She was beautiful, dressed in silver and purple. She had a lovely crown on her head and she was glowing. She had long curly black hair that reached her back, light brown eyes and a beautiful smile. The baby in her arms looked so small, sweet and innocent; she was dressed in a silver and purple dress. On the left, the man looked strong, and powerful, like a warrior. He was dressed like one, and he had a sword tucked away, enough for my warrior suggestion to seem true.

I've seen images of them in dreams I've had at the start of my change and I felt like I knew them. I felt some sort of feeling going through my body, a feeling I couldn't describe. Like a surge of electric filled my veins and I had too much adrenaline in my system. Behind the locket was a folded up piece of paper, with writing on it. I took a breather before reading the paper out loud as it instructed.

The time has come for me to leave
And return to the place I have to lead
Where the grass glows green
Royal skies are seen
Let it be, bless it be

I didn't understand what I had just read. Other than the fact the poem obviously rhymed. "Okay, this is a joke, so stupid. A friken poem." I mumbled to myself before the lights began to flicker, and the room began to shake. I fell to the floor, and closed my eyes tightly and then re-opened them to see if what was happening was actually real. When I opened my eyes, I realized all of this *is* real.

I began to feel over heated, and I actually started hyperventilating. I tried to get up, but came to a halt when I noticed my veins were turning fluorescent purple instead of the normal blue/ green everyone's veins are. I didn't know what was happening to me. All of the weird changes in me, had no comparisons to this moment right now, this was *too* much for me. *How does someone handle something like this?* I mentally asked myself.

The room suddenly stopped shaking, and I slowly got up. I threw my things into my drawstring bag, put the bag on my back and opened the bathroom door. I wanted to run to Parker and ask if he noticed anything weird had happened, but I couldn't, because when I opened the door, I was no longer facing the restaurant.

My eyes took in a beautiful snow white colored mansion that was sitting in front of me. The roof was flat, and it had about seven windows, two terraces and a huge but beautiful staircase that lead to glass doors that had a gold pattern painted on them.

Surrounding the house were bushes and trees that were glowing a bluish green color. An almost black purple color lit up the sky, highlighting the multiple planets in the sky. I shut the door, and re-opened it, hoping that I was only imagining it, but no I wasn't.

When I re opened the door, the same view of the mansion, and weirdly colored atmosphere was staring back at me. I walked out from the bathroom and into the glowing green grass, looking all around me, at my surroundings. I spotted, in the middle of the staircase; a pair of massive gold wings was spread out from a male body. And of course I reacted the normal way Eve Keller would, I screamed before I saw nothing but utter darkness.

XI

The Homecoming

When my eyes finally opened, I had a tiny headache and saw white spots everywhere. I looked around and noticed that I was in a room that I never seen before, and lying in a bed that I've never laid in before.

The walls of the room were painted gold, two white marble dressers were beside the bed and one was also across from the bed. The bed I was laying in seemed to be king sized and had gold posts, and white satin sheets.

I decided to get up but I lost my balance and fell to the floor. Shortly after my fall, a handsome blonde guy popped his head in from the door. I realized he had the same face as the guy I saw with the wings, at the top of the staircase outside, my heart automatically started racing. Instinctively, I crawled against the bed and brought my knees up to my chest, wrapping my arms around my legs. "Okay Eve, calm yourself...just breathe." the guy said as he walked closer to me. His voice was sweet and innocent, but I couldn't focus on anything in a complete calm or rational way.

"How...how do you know my name?" I barley whispered from the floor. "Well, we were expecting you." he said. He held his hand out for me to reach. I shook my head no and hugged myself tighter. "It's alright, I promise, I will not hurt you. You are safe with me." The stranger said again. He held his hand out again, and I reluctantly took it, and stood up. Trembling in the process.

When I stood up and really looked at the guy is when I noticed how beautiful the guy really was. His eyes looked like pools, his lips were a pretty shade of pink, and he was glowing. Not like glow in the dark but, I could see a shimmer radiating from his skin. He Kind of reminded me of Jesse McCartney in his *"right where you want me"* days. That's when I realized that this was one of the guys that *helped* me in the dreams I had.

"Who's we? Who was expecting me? and who are you?" I asked the handsome stranger. "My name is Bobby, and I'm an angel. A messenger Angel to be specific." he said seriously. I rolled my eyes before chuckling. This had to be the stupidest thing I've heard all day, and I have got to be in a deep sleep. "You really expect me to believe that? What do you think I'm insane, mentally challenged or something?" I asked.

Bobby sighed. "I am a messenger, and we are currently in Permia, a whole other dimension." he said. I looked at him like he was insane. "Here in Permia, the world is made up of different creatures. Angels, wizards, witches, centaurs, vampires, other creatures and you." he said firmly. My eyes widened. "Me?" I asked semi shocked and slightly amused. "Yes you, this is the world your mother, birthed you in. *Permia* is your home." he said. I narrowed my eyes at him. No one has ever spoken to me about my *mother,* and his comment about her made me annoyed and yet curious. I never met my mother, I haven't a clue about her and for the fact that a *stranger* was mentioning her to me made me confused.

How could a complete stranger to me know about me or my birth mother? "My mother, my birth mother? Okay, this isn't right; I think I need to leave." I said, frustrated. I noticed the wind was blowing the almost sheer curtains from a door the opposite of me, and I walked to it. I pulled the curtain back and gasped. My eyes connected to a deep purple sky.

In the distance, I could see two planets, the moon and stars. The grass and trees were glowing a turquoise like color, and it was definitely weird, but strangely beautiful. What I was seeing was totally unbelievable, and the only way you would believe it, is if you would use your imagination to see it.

"I get that this is strange, which is why I've asked the others for it to be just you and me at the moment, we will take it only a little slow." Bobby said from behind me. I turned to face him and was sure confusion was written all over my face. "Let's walk outside." he smiled. Bobby walked over to me and gently pulled me and led me out on a terrace.

To the left of the terrace were stairs that we walked down. I noticed Bobby kept peeking over at me, I guess to see how I was handling the atmosphere. I didn't say anything as we continued to walk, I acted calm, but on the inside, I was beyond freaked out. The terrace we had walked down from was in front of the house; therefore, there wasn't much to see except for the nature of the world and the Mansion itself.

We arrived to the large staircase I saw when I first arrived, which is in front of the mansion and it lead to two glass double doors with a beautiful gold vine pattern printed on them. I didn't want to surrender to the feeling in my gut, the feeling that something inside of me was telling me to trust Bobby. That he wouldn't hurt me and that all of this was real. I didn't want to surrender to those feelings, but I needed to at least pretend to, to get some possible answers. Seems like I've been relying on my gut so much lately, why not rely on it now?

Bobby and I sat in silence on the large staircase. It wasn't an awkward silence; it was more of a "wait for the moment before you speak and say the wrong thing" kind of silence.

When I was getting a little more comfortable with Bobby, when I knew I wasn't in danger, I broke the ice a little. "I recognize you... a little while ago, I was having trouble sleeping. I was tossing and turning because of a dream. A really vivid dream that you were in." I confessed. Bobby looked at me, clearly interested in what I was saying.

"What were we doing?" he asked. I sighed. "We were in the woods, and I was fighting these... these ugly monster looking creature things. You and another guy were there helping me fight them, before I ran off and fought this red haired girl." I finished. Bobby's eyes widened, the expression on his face seemed a little tense, but his voice stayed calm. "How long have you been having premonitions?" he asked. The only reason I knew what a premonition was, was because of all the *"Final Destination"* movies, I had watched over the years. Figures my life would have some similarity to a scary movie. *But wait, none of this is real right? Right! I mentally reminded myself.* "Only a few times for the past months leading up to my birthday." I said. "A physic told me I would see changes, and I started having weird dreams, that was just one of the changes that happened." I continued.

"Winter." Bobby said in more than a statement, than a question. "Yeah...wait a minute, how do you know her?" I asked him, totally confused. "She's a guardian of yours, she's inside the mansion as we speak." he said. I kept my mouth closed, because I didn't know exactly what to say. However internally, I was definitely freaking out.

Each moment that Bobby spoke, made it more clear to me that maybe all of this *was* real. I didn't tell him the name of the physic that I spoke to and yet he knew her name is Winter. How many physics are there in the world with the name *Winter*? "I want to give you a little history lesson about Permia, about your life. Everything that has been hidden from you for eighteen years." he said. I shivered at the *"history"* Bobby was going to tell me about. The hidden history of my own life.

Curiosity, fear, and a form of pain settled in my stomach. Did I really want to know what he was about to tell me? Well even if I didn't, I'm pretty sure he would tell me anyway. "Okay, teach me Yoda." I said

XII

The Reveal

Bobby took a deep breath and turned to me before speaking. "First off, Permia is the dimension also known as the invisible dimension, because this world doesn't exist to human eyes. Here in Permia, negative things can happen; negative people walk the grounds just as good does. But *we* the angels and royal council are to keep order and peace in this realm, and on earth. Our purpose is that, and to help people succeed in reaching their destiny's. To protect, honor and guide." He said.

"Even though we are not mortal, we have to balance the good and bad within ourselves, just like they do. We have to resist temptation, and vengeance. Here, in this mansion, lives the Archangel family The Caylan's. They are the true leaders of this realm and the highest to protect all humans and immortals in this realm and below. They also receive help from the high council, which consists of every species' high ranked leader. So we have the king and queen of the elves, the king of vampires, and warlocks, hobbits and other high ranked leaders of any species. Together, they keep Permia and the world below us, in order. Even though they are leaders in their own right to their own kind, the Caylan's rule over all. *You* Eve are a Caylan." He continued. My mouth dropped a little, but Bobby kept talking.

"There are elder angels as well as guides and messengers here to protect *you*. Which was a command given from your mother before her passing." he said. My eyebrows rose at his words. "Your mother Emirah Caylan was beautiful, and never saw bad in anyone, or any creature in the world. She loved everything, and radiated peace, and happiness. She spoke different languages, she was very wise. And her wings were a beautiful pair of gold shade. She was a beautiful queen that came from the line of three Caylan Archangel Sisters. She and your two aunts were destined to be queens since their birth." He said.

"They were created to bring peace, harmony and order to Permia and the dimensions below it. The oldest sister was Marnie Caylan. Marnie was beautiful, and always did what was right. She married an Archangel by the name of Atreus in which, Marnie had become pregnant with your first cousin Hannah. The middle sister was your mother Emirah; she protected Permia with all her might. And while protecting, she stumbled upon an injured warrior named Zion. She found out that he also fought for peace in Permia. He was large, and strong, but like most creatures, prone to injuries. Your mother tended to him, and they fell in love, and they became proud parents the night you were born." he said.

I continued to listen. Not wanting to disturb his story. "Your father to much of Emirah's surprise was a wizard, a wizard warrior. He had the power of premonitions, he could orb also known as self teleport, and he had the ability to react quickly in battle and used well powerful magic that protected the world. The bad attribute about him was that rules didn't always apply to him. Emirah liked to do things the proper way, Zion didn't mind cutting a corner or two, but Emirah loved him anyway." he said.

"Wait a minute; I'm a friken Harry Potter? Are you serious?" I asked Bobby in a shocked tone. Bobby laughed at me. "Well, not exactly, your half wizard and you are half Archangel Princess, one of the most powerful beings of Permia." he smirked. I shook my head in disbelief. Bobby smirked before he continued.

"That brings me to Kara, the last of the three Archangel Queens, and also the rebel of the three. After being banished for practicing wicked magic and cloping with a warlock, she converted herself into a witch. She had no desire for peace; she wanted to rule Permia in her own way, which obviously is not allowed if there is an ounce of darkness in your heart. Darkness began taking over her, and Emirah, and Marnie, felt it was wrong, and ridiculed Kara." He confessed.

"After you were born, it sparked for a war; Kara had gotten upset that she had been banished from the mansion, and for the fact that she would never rule Permia. She raised up an army of dark creatures who's mission was to crucify your mother, Marnie, your cousin Hannah, the other angels and council, anyone fighting for good including you." he said. I stayed quiet and took in everything he was saying.

"This started a huge war. Good versus evil and family verses family. To keep you safe, Emirah had you shipped down to the Earth Dimension, away from the evil here, and she made a spiritual promise that you would return, if not right away, than on your eighteenth birthday. She made the elder's promise to take care of you, to watch over you, and to help you rule Permia, and your powers were to be binded until you reached your eighteenth birthday, which is today." He said. Bobby noticed that I was only going to keep quiet, and listen so he continued with the story. I just wanted to hear everything he had to say before I came up with my own scenarios and conclusions.

"They prepared for battle, your mother and father stood together, side by side, but tragically died one after the other in that battle. Your mother was stabbed by Kara who was using the *white fire dagger,* the most powerful and deadly dagger in all the realms, and your father surrendered himself, choosing not to live without her. As Kara's punishment, she her powers binded and was killed by Marnie. Marnie had ruled Permia for sixteen years after the war." Bobby said.

"That sixteenth year anniversary of the war, Marnie had been murdered, and we didn't have any suspects. After Marnie's death the elders along with Atreus, raised Hannah to be queen. Turns out, Kara had a daughter of her own; a sixteen year old named Scarlett. Half Archangel, half witch, and she confessed to killing Marnie, Practically bragged about it, she said it was for her mother. A life for a life." He said.

"For almost two years, Scarlett had been in light contact with Hannah, trying to get her to turn dark, but Hannah, being the pure and young Archangel she was, resisted. This lead to Hannah and Atreus getting captured by Scarlett and her friends, and ultimately lead to both of their murders." he continued. A single tear escaped from my eye as I listened to what had happened to my family. "We learned that soon after you were born, Scarlett was born as well. You in December, she in August, and once she turns eighteen, she plans on ruling Permia, with no worries of you or any living creature." he continued.

"There was discussion about going down to Earth to get you, and to simply raise you here to be queen, but the elders decided to not just *steal* you away from your Earth family or also risk your life. If they would have brought you here as a baby, you would have been a target just like the others were."

" Before your cousin Hannah died, she wrote a letter to you explaining how she wishes for you keep Permia safe, and rule it the way that your mother's had done previously. It's in your room if you want to look at it." Bobby said. I got up and found myself down the front of the staircase and still walking. I didn't know my destination but I just needed to move.

I shortly ended up sitting on the grass in the middle of the field in front of the house, and looked at the oddly purple sky before looking down, and pulling at the fluorescent turquoise lit grass. *How could this happen to me? Why me? Out of all the time's I wished for something amazing to happen in my life, I get this! I get told by a hot guy that I am some freaky Archangel Wizard thing that is supposed to protect and rule an entire dimension, and earth. Right now, I just wish to be normal again. To be the closet loner and confused girl that I naturally am.* I thought to myself. I sat there thinking about everything until I felt a presence behind me.

"Hey, you okay?" Bobby asked. I didn't look at him, I only kept looking down. "Yeah just peachy." I replied sarcastically. He chuckled at my sarcasm and sat down beside me. "Okay, now that I think about it...that was a stupid question to ask. I'm sorry for springing all of that on you, but you needed to know the hurtful but honest truth, to feel the pressure before you can start to move and breathe easier." he said. I stayed quiet. "I can't imagine how you must feel; I know it's a lot to take in." Bobby said.

"So what will really happen if I say no, if I don't want to do it?" I asked still peering out. "Honestly, I'm not sure; royalty is in your blood. This is the reason for your being." he answered. All of this news was clogging my brain and I know longer could think straight. "Maybe the title to reign will go straight to Scarlett, so far she's been making a name for herself, causing destruction wherever she goes. She walks into the mansion like it's hers. She knows about you, but I'm not sure if she's even been worried about you returning or not." he said.

I was angry; I had begun feeling a fire fuel in the pit of my stomach. Right then and there, I decided that I hated Scarlett, and Kara, for destroying our family. For making me an adopted child, for me missing out on my real life, for destroying my parents. If that stupid war didn't happen, my mom and dad would still be here, and my entire life would have been different.

I strangely didn't have any fear if Scarlett came after me, I decided I would destroy her if she came after me or not. Forget the crown, forget ruling and being queen for a moment, at this point and time, my focus is all about getting redemption on Scarlett for her and her mother's destruction. "How do you know all of this?" I asked Bobby. Bobby stared at me and ignored my question. "What?" I asked him, annoyed at his stare. "Your eyes are purple.... what are you feeling right now?" he asked. I gave him a confused look. "They are definitely not!" I squealed, while moving my eye balls from left to right and blinking my eyes.

I wish I had a mirror to actually see what he was talking about. I couldn't sense any change in my appearance, only the feeling of fury. "I am feeling angry, angrier then I felt in my life." I confessed. Bobby sighed. "Breathe... I didn't want to upset you; I just needed to let you know the truth." He huffed. "I know all of this because I am a little older than you, and I was fond of your mother, she would look after me, and guide me. Your mother, and my mother Elsa, were very close." Bobby said. I kept my mouth closed and looked at the grass. "To lighten up the mood, you look almost identical to Emirah." he said.

    I smirked at Bobby. I felt a little jolt of happiness in me when Bobby said I looked like Emirah, my mother. But still, inside, I felt angry. We stayed in silence until we heard the front door creak open.

XIII

The Angels

I turned to look at the door that was now cracked open and gasped. "We have given you enough time alone with her; we need you two in the dining area." A familiar face said. Bobby grabbed my hand, and helped me up. We walked over to Winter and I smiled at her. "Eve! I am so happy you are here, and I apologize for our first meeting, leading you only halfway through to your new life, but it was forbidden, for me to expose myself to you until this night of your birthday." she said. She hugged me, and I wrapped my arms around her in return. "It's okay, no harm done; you were doing what you were supposed to." I said.

Winter smiled. "You are going to be a great queen." she said. I smiled at her in reply, even though I wasn't sure if I would be right for this job. *Me rule an entire dimension? Seriously?* I thought to myself. "We don't want to overwhelm you Eve, you already have had quite the day." she said. I smirked at her. "You have no idea, but I can handle it, just tell me everything now so I can get it all over with, I adjust better that way." I confessed. Winter nodded her head in agreement.

We walked inside the *Caylan* Mansion, and it was beautiful. Right at the entrance, my eyes caught the shiny white marble floors, and two large semi spiral staircases. Hints of gold were all round the room and a beautiful chandelier lit up the foyer. To the left I could see a sitting room. The floors were gold, and the couches were solid white. There was a large gold fireplace, and beautiful paintings hanging up.

We walked down one of the many hallways where I noticed the same two colors, Gold and white. Gold and white patterns were on the marble floor, the chandeliers that lit the hallway, and all the doors we passed were white. It was a very classy house, obviously with a royal and peaceful feel to it. "I know this place seems huge, and it will take some time to get used to, but you will figure it out, it's not impossible." Winter said. I nodded my head in understanding. We stopped at two gold double doors and Winter looked at me. "Ready?" she asked. "Yes." I replied. She pushed one of the doors open, and I stepped into yet another gold and white room.

The room itself was very large. It had a huge long table that had 14 chairs around it, and it was beautiful. Sweet gentle harp music played in the background and beautiful people dressed in light tones stood around, conversing with each other. Winter wrapped her arm around my shoulder and smiled. "Everyone, she's here...this is Eve Caylan!" she said. I smiled at everyone. "Hi." I said nervously. The music shut off and the entire room went quiet. A toothpick could have dropped and it would have seemed incredibly loud.

Within a few seconds, I was greeted with Happy birthday's and welcome home's. Some *angels* were young looking having baby faces, and some others looked a little bit older. No one looked old though, everyone appeared almost young. "I am happy that you are finally here, you will be a wonderful queen just like your mother was." An older guy with dark short curled hair and blue eyes said to me. He was dressed in tan slacks and a brown vest shirt, and he looked immortally handsome.

A woman dressed in a beautiful white gown gracefully walked over and stood beside him. She had black hair that fell down to her waist, with a beautiful pair of emerald green eyes. Her aura was peaceful, and I could sense that she was gentle and wise. "Eve, this is Marius and my mother Elsa. They are two elders that are here to watch, protect and guide you, a promise they kept in honor of your mother." Bobby said.

Elsa put her hand over her heart and then engulfed me in a tight embrace. When she pulled away I noticed tears were in her eyes. "I was the one that brought you down to earth; I was the last from Permia to see you, your mother and your aunt Marnie altogether. It would be an honor to serve you dear." Elsa said embracing me in another hug. This time I wrapped my arms tightly around her. It triggered a sensitive and sincere emotion in me for the fact that she was the one who last saw me with my mother. Anger also hit my heart. *She* was the one that brought me to earth. But how could I be mad at her if she did what my mother asked her to? With that question in mind, I suppressed the anger.

"How long have you been in Permia?" I randomly asked the two elders. "A century before your birth." Marius answered. I could feel my mouth drop. They were so old and yet they looked so young. "Angels never age after thirty." Marius smiled. "This gathering is all for you welcome home and enjoy yourself, I'm going to go get some air, and it's wonderful to see you again." Elsa said with more tears in her eyes as she walked away.

Marius looked at me. "So now that Bobby has filled you in, what are your thoughts?" he asked. I looked around and caught the eyes of two young girls who looked around my age. Bobby looked at me and followed the direction I was gazing to. "That's Chaska." Bobby gestured to. He pointed to a beautiful tan girl with really long chocolate hair. "And Destiny." he also gestured to a pretty young girl with mocha skin and hazel eyes. I smiled and waved at them. I felt a little at ease for the fact that they looked similar to my age range. I would have some females my age to relate to.

"I don't know what I think, besides that all of this is a bit overwhelming and definitely seems unreal." I confessed to Marius. "Scarlett has been working hard to gain the role as the new queen of Permia. If Scarlett takes over Permia, any good, any peace that exists, will vanish. Our world is in palm of your hands. Everyone else in your bloodline has passed; this leaves only you and Scarlett as the only connecting line to the Caylan Archangels. You two are the only archangels left here in Permia, and are the true royal caretakers." he said.

"So you want me to rule an entire planet? Rule in a world where people hardly know me and yet actually may want to kill me?" I asked. "Quick question, if Hannah would not have died, would all of this still happen to me? Or am I here because you need me?" I rambled and asked. I was getting frustrated. I know I said give it to me all at once, but they were throwing too much at me *at* once, and all I could feel was pressure weighing me down like a ton of bricks. Being told that a world is in the palm of your hands, and basically your hands alone is hard to swallow.

"Yes you would have been here regardless if Hannah passed on or not, Permia is your birth right. It's who you are, and you cannot change that. The only difference is that you wouldn't have been thrown into a ruling position so quickly. You would have gotten to understand life here better, and comprehend what's expected of you in an orderly way." he said. I looked at him straight into his blue eyes as I impatiently tapped my foot. "As for the killing you, no one specifically has you as a target, no one knows if you will show up here or not, no one knows how powerful you are or how powerful your aren't." Marius said. "If Scarlett gets defensive, you have us, your guardians and other creatures and the council around. You have powers in you that no one, not even you know about yet. You have to practice and train hard. It is not going to be easy, you are not going to be some, master warrior princess overnight... but it will be worth it in the end." he said.

I cocked my head to the right, and rolled my eyes. *His speech was boring.* I thought to myself, not wanting to hear what else Marius had to say. "So, will you Eve Caylan...will you accept your birth right, and accept your role as Queen of Permia?" Marius asked. I didn't realize I was even holding my breath until I spoke. "Um, I don't know." I choked out. "What?" Marius asked in a shocked tone, as if he was expecting me to say *yes* right away. "Excuse me." I said as I went through the double doors we came from and walked out the front door, and accidently bumped into someone in a purple hooded cloak.

I stumbled back from the figure that appeared in front of me. On the inside, I was screaming to run from the hooded figure, but my feet wouldn't move. The unidentified hooded figure removed the hood of the cloak, and my eyes, popped out of my head. "Ms. Burns? Really?" I asked my Math teacher. She smiled. "Hello Eve, I am so happy you made it here, I told you, your birthday would be a special night for you!" she gushed. I couldn't believe that my math teacher was here in front of me, in a totally different dimension from Earth.

"Yeah, but I didn't think you meant this…and wait… what are you? Do you live here?" I asked her. "Don't be upset, or scared. You have nothing to worry about tonight. Tonight is all about celebrating you. I am a wizard, not as high ranking as you, but I do have powers. And yes, I do stay here, and I go from here to Earth, and reverse as I please." she said. I couldn't believe what I was hearing.

"I just came here to welcome you home. How are you dealing with it all so far?" she asked. I rolled my eyes and shrugged my shoulders. "Obviously freaked out a bit, wasn't expecting anything this drastic." I replied. She smiled at me. "You will get used to the idea of there being another dimension and one for you to actually lead. It will get better, I promise you that." she said. I looked at her and relaxed a little. "I hope your right." I replied just as the front door opened and Bobby walked out and over to us.

"Hello." Bobby said. "Bobby this is my earth math teacher Ms. Burns, I just found out that she is a wizard." I announced. "Everyone in the land of Permia knows everyone that lives inside the Caylan mansion. Kind of like everyone knows the president of the United States and his entire family. I know Bobby even though he may not know me." Ms. Burns said. Bobby didn't look amused. "I was a friend of Zion, I've been keeping an eye on Eve as she's grown up over the last four years." she said. I smiled at her, as we all stood in an awkward silence. "Well, I am glad that you are here, and I will see you at school. Happy Birthday Eve. If you ever need anything, let me know." she smiled as she hugged me. "Will do." I smiled back at her. I watched a dark purple glitter color wrap around Ms. Burns, and within a few seconds, she shimmered away.

"Sorry for disturbing your conversation with your teacher, I just wanted to make sure you are alright." Bobby said. I smiled at him. "I am alright." I said. I could tell that my answer wasn't all that convincing to Bobby. I sighed. "okay, this is all too much, none of this makes sense, none of this is real." I huffed, and realized that everything that was happening seemed to be real, so I had to stop saying that this world wasn't real. Even if I didn't want to believe that it was real. I had to realize and accept that all of the good and evil creatures we read about or see on movies are real. Ghosts, zombies, vampires, angels, fairies... all of them are real, and make up the population of this realm, and I'm supposed to lead it. I stomped the ground before speaking again.

"Okay, so even if all of this fairytale, bed time story crap is real... I don't want to be part of it! I don't want to be an archangel wizard princess thing. I think you've got the wrong girl. I said trying to convince not only Bobby, but myself as well. Was I born with a twin that just so happens to have the same name as me?" I asked in a slight sarcastic tone. Bobby shook his head no.

"Eve, this is your birth right, and all of this *is* real, and not as bad as it seems. I will prove it to you." Bobby said. "How? By telling me what kinds of powers I have?" I huffed. "Sorry Bob, but I need a little more action rather than just hearing speeches about me being this, and being that. I *need* you to show me. Show me and prove to me that I am this *magical being.*" I said annoyed. "You sure you want to know?" Bobby playfully asked. I nodded my head yes, and he smiled.

"So let me tell you a little about us angels. we all have great hearing, and vision, we can also read minds and block our thoughts. You being part royal Archangel, have more powers than the rest of us here on Permia, except for Scarlett, since she is half a royal Arch as well. You can read minds; possibly speak all languages just like your mother. It seems that you already have premonitions." Bobby said. You probably have tons of powers inside of you, that we just have to figure out." he continued. "Archangels can create faster or slower winds can change the temperature, start or end fires, create tsunamis. They have complete control over the elements. Regular angels can manipulate the elements, but not as extreme as an Archangel. It only depends on what element you are blessed with to control, check this out." Bobby continued.

Bobby held out his hands in front of himself, and then rubbed his hands together. After a few seconds, he slowly separated his hands, and a clear watery ball appeared in between the space of his hands. "Wow!" I said in awe, looking at the ball. Bobby then tilted the watery ball so that it was now in his left hand. He through his arm back, and then threw the ball at a tree across from us. When the ball and the tree connected, there was a low but powerful splash. "So your element is water, that's awesome!" I smiled at Bobby.

"That was an element ball. Each angel that has an element and can make them. We use them for necessities, like to make a fire, make fresh water, anything really that requires force from an element. They are also used for battles. If you're ever in a battle, or a war, you can bet that you will see some of them being thrown around." he said. I sat quietly as I listened to him speak.

"We should find your element!" he suggested excitedly. "Um, I don't know how to do that?" I asked as he walked towards me. "That's why I'm going to help you." he replied. "We are going to try Earth first. Close your eyes, and hold out your left hand." he said. I unsurely stood up and did what I was told. "Now imagine the feeling of grass between your toes. Visualize dirt, and the large tree tops that almost touch the sky, concentrate on those images. Focus and reach out with your mind until energy washes over you." he whispered, standing behind me. After a minute of nothing happening, I started to feel like a complete idiot.

"Okay, Earth isn't working now is it? Let's move on to another element." he said. "You're not proving *anything* to me Bob." I smirked as I turned to look at Bobby. "Okay, okay." Bobby laughed. "Keep your hands out, and imagine wind. Imagine how your hair blows through It." he said in a low voice. I shivered at the feeling of the warm air coming from his mouth on the back of my neck. Then I sighed and imagined the annoying wind making my hair blow. Once again, after a minute nothing happened and Bobby quickly moved onto the next element, so that he wouldn't hear me complain about looking like an idiot.

"Visualize campfires, cooking with the fire, imagine feeling heat...focus." Bobby said. I smirked and peaked my eye open. "Yeah, yeah why focus if it's not gonna work?" I laughed. Bobby sighed. "Eve, just do it." he said growing annoyed of me. "Alright, alright." I replied as I closed my eyes again. I visualized a fire place. I imagined being kept warm by it and it started to feel like I was really being warmed up by a fire. "Open your eyes." Bobby whispered in my ear. I reluctantly and slowly opened them. "Oh my gosh! It's like... like fire in my hand...why isn't it burning me? It just feels warm!" I rambled to Bobby, but kept my eyes focused on the fire in my hand. I started moving my hand from left to right, clearly freaking out. Bobby laughed at me. "It's your element, its purpose it to help you, not harm you." he simply said. I nodded my head in understanding while looking at the almost white fire ball in my hand.

"Okay, so how do I put this thing out, how do I put it out?" I asked in a shaky voice. "Just close your hand." he replied. I looked at him like he was insane. To close fire in your hand would definitely cause major damage. I once burned myself with an iron, and it was terrible so I can only imagine the pain level of this! "Go ahead, just close your hand." he said. "It's going to hurt!" I whined. Bobby looked at me sternly. "Eve…do it." he demanded. I closed my eyes and breathed really deep, and then, I closed my hand.

It didn't hurt; the warm feeling in my hand only increased, and then slowly started to decrease. "See, that wasn't so bad, was it?" Bobby asked. Now Bobby had me, after making fire in my own hand, I now had no other choice but to believe that all of this was real, and that I was a wizard archangel princess thing. I opened my eyes and smirked at Bobby. "Not at all, what's next?" I asked.

XIV

Wings and Orbing

Bobby laughed at my new change of heart towards the reality of what I am, of what we are. I didn't care what he thought though; I just made fire out of my hand! In this moment I felt like a really expensive magician.

"Archangels as well as other types of Angels can also sense emotions, and we also have the power to heal. You heal someone through your hands, by pressing your hands on the wound or injured area, and letting the power inside of you take over your mind and body, willing for a healing and then the wound to be healed. You can also heal yourself at will, when you are hurt or wounded. But obviously you will have to practice that on your own or when someone needs your help." Bobby said. "That doesn't sound hard." I replied.

I was getting into everything Bobby was teaching me. The fire in my hands had been the key to making me believe that all of this *was* real, because no human could do that. "Next are your wings. Now since you are half wizard you can probably orb teleport like a wizard, as well as fly." Bobby said.

I quickly remembered the weird burning sun burn sensation, peeling and faint markings that I felt and seen on my back earlier in the day. "Earlier, as in this morning when I woke up, my skin was peeling and my back felt badly burned. After I showered, it all went away and my skin started to kind of glow, but I did notice weird markings started to form on my back. They weren't so visible that anyone else could see, but I could see them. What's all that about?" I asked Bobby. Bobby smiled. "Well you are an angel. Like all angels, when your wings are stored away a marking, or tattoo in the shape of your wings will replace the actual wings you have." he said. *"Stored?"* I asked clearly confused.

"when your wings aren't in use, when you aren't flying, your tattoo will replace the wings, that's what *stored* means." He said. "We all have a specific pattern marking on our backs when the wings are stored. The peeling was for your new skin to be prepared for your new change in DNA. It had to happen so you and your body can both adapt to the environment, preparing your body for your ability to orb, heal and use any powers that you have." Bobby said.

"Think of a vampire, if their skin was attached to their bodies whenever they would move fast it would hurt. So when they become vampires, their skin detaches." he added. I nodded my head in understanding. "The burning you were feeling were your wings in preparation for your birthday, which is the day they would become fully developed." he continued

Bobby got behind me and put his hands on the hem of my shirt. "Do you mind?" he asked. I hesitated before answering, and I relaxed when I remembered I had on one of my cute bras, a hot pink one that had little bedazzled designs on the front, and got comfortable with Bobby for the fact that he wasn't being forward. "Not at all." I replied. Bobby lifted my dark blue shirt so that my back was visible to him. "wow." he said as his hands traced my back. I shivered against the coolness of his fingers.

Have you looked at your back again since the first time you've looked?" He asked. I nodded my head no. "You have a tattoo. The pattern of wings on your back....they are beautiful. Come and look." he chuckled as he led me inside the house and into a nearby bathroom.

I lifted my shirt again and saw my back had been covered by a big beautiful tattooed pair of angel wings. The wings started as a dark purple color at my shoulder blades. The purple color got lighter as the feathers flowed nicely down my back. As the wings ended at my tail bone, they faded into a shimmering Gold. "Wow, they *are* pretty." I muttered under my breath. I always wanted a tattoo, and now I got one, and I didn't have to go through massive pain to get it, even though the process did hurt a little.

I turned to face Bobby. "Can you show me how to fly?" I asked almost quietly. Bobby nodded his head yes and walked out the side door to the mansion, and I followed. I stood in front of Bobby and watched him take his shirt off, and slowly unfold and open his wings. When they were fully exposed, I noticed how huge they were. They were silver white, and beautiful. "They are amazing." I told him. He smiled at me. "Thank you." he replied. "How do I do that, *unstore* my wings?" I asked, saying the word *unstore,* as if it were foreign.

"First, your top has to come off unless you want it to rip." He replied. "Um, I really like this shirt, and I don't want to ruin it." I said. Bobby chuckled. "Okay, then I will stand behind you, I promise I won't look." I nodded my head in understanding and took my shirt off. "Close your eyes, envision yourself surrounded by the sky. Imagine yourself in the air and everything is peaceful where you are. Focus on the fact that you can fly. Command yourself to fly. Let go and let the energy take over your body." Bobby said. I believed everything he was saying.

I felt him extend my arms out, and then move away. I heard and felt a non-painful rip behind me, and I then felt a little discomfort into my back. It didn't hurt; it was just an all-around *different* feeling. Like something was extending to my body. You know that feeling when you have to crack your back or a muscle in your body and after you do it; your body feels so good and less tense? That's what it felt like. I felt a cold breeze come from the middle of my back, up to my shoulder blades, but the coolness was shortly subsided by a warm fiery, comfortable feeling.

"Open your eyes." Bobby said. I opened my eyes, and let out a squeal, when I realized my feet weren't touching the ground anymore. I happened to be floating in the field, five feet in front of where I was just standing. "Oh my God! How do I get down! Bobby!" I screamed. Bobby laughed. "No, just follow me." he said. I watched him and his beautiful wings, gently and gracefully align with the sky, and somehow willed myself to follow.

Okay, so clearly flying wasn't my thing. It felt like no gravity was on the earth and I could face plant on the ground at any minute. I didn't like the feeling. It felt like I was on an airplane *without* the huge chunk of metal protecting me. I felt afraid of the height, and the fact that if I wasn't careful I could fall hundreds of feet out of the air. However, even with me being scared, I couldn't help but notice the beautiful view of Permia.

Our single mansion stood amongst the glowing grass. The tree tops all glowed and the deep purple of the sky made the stars, earth, moon and other planets look extremely bright. This was a totally different world that I was used to living in. A different but beautiful world.

"Come on this is your own terrace and your own room. Think down, push yourself down and bend your knees when you touch the ground to keep your balance." Bobby said as we landed on the large terrace. Bobby opened two white double doors and flicked up a light switch that was next to the terrace door, and the lights in the room switched on. I walked into the room and saw the same colors and room settings that I saw in my premonition dream.

The room was huge, and had gold walls with a hint of purple designs that looked like little diamond shapes. It had dark purple carpet, and a large white canopy bed. A long vertical purple mirror and a purple couch accented the room. Dressers and crown molding in my room were also painted gold. I walked into the bathroom and admired the odd color it was painted, which was a deep purple, and gold. A gold bath tub, deep purple shower and sinks. It also had a TV and deep purple chandelier. Clearly I couldn't believe that this room was real, nor that it was all mine. I wasn't use to living this way.

Bobby laughed at my shocked facial expression. I looked at the long vertical mirror and admired how my wings automatically folded behind me when I stopped flying. I put my back to the mirror and touched my large pair of wings. They were soft to the touch, almost feeling like cotton. Deep purple poured at the top which turned into a lighter shade of purple before finishing off in gold, just like my tattoo.

"Told you they are beautiful." Bobby smiled. I smiled but didn't take my eyes off of my wings. "To store them, concentrate on them getting smaller. Visualize markings on your back instead of your wings." he said. I did as he said and shortly after, I had the feeling of something being injected into me. The feeling was a bit annoying, like a pebble stuck between your toes or something of that sort. I could hear nasty non-human sounds, which kind of sounded like cracking bones, coming from my back, but I was too afraid to look.

After a few more seconds, I could feel air around my back; I could feel that my wings were no longer there. I also felt lighter, and kind of empty. I finally looked back into the mirror behind me and saw the tattoo of my wings.

A breeze made me shiver, which is when I finally realized that I was standing in front of an angel who is basically a stranger to me, in only my hot pink bra. I covered myself and looked to Bobby. Bobby looked as shocked and nervous as I did. "Sorry forgot about that, we males don't need shirts." He said nervously.

"Um to orb, or self teleport like a wizard, you pretty much visualize the place you want to go, focus on it, let the force you feel take over and just let yourself go. Oh and you can let someone enter your mind, or mute your thoughts to shut everyone out." Bobby said as he walked to a closet. "Mute my thoughts?" I asked as I watched him search through various clothes." yes so that no one is capable of knowing what you are thinking." he said handing me a tan shirt to put on.

"To mute your thoughts, you stop thinking for only a moment, think of nothing. You want to free your mind. It's like meditation. Then after a minute, your head will start to feel a little heavy that is a shield of force that binds your thoughts. This will take practice." he smiled. I put on the shirt and then looked at him knowingly "I bet it will." I said sarcastically. I silently thanked Bobby for his rambling as a *cover up* to dispute the tension and embarrassment of me having had no shirt on. It definitely cut the tension and embarrassment.

"Just practice. As much fun as I want to share with you here in Permia, you are going to have to work hard. Creatures from here are going to test you, and we don't know what angle Scarlett has. You have to learn to protect yourself, even with *us* guides, and elders to help, *you* need to learn." Bobby said. "What is a guide or a guardian specifically?" I asked him. "Everyone has a guide; it's like a mentor or a really good friend that's positive in life. They will help you make decisions, help you with needed information to keep order, and to help you rule. Being a royal, you will have quite a few guides." He replied.

    I sat on my new bed in my room and processed what Bobby was telling me. "On a lighter note, you can orb from and to both worlds. I'm pretty sure your still in school, so you'll have to find balance until you graduate, then you can do what you want." Bobby happily explained. I rolled my eyes and huffed. "It's not that bad. Your part Arch, I'm sure you will be if you're not already, smart as a computer. Over time, you will train, get to know Permia, and more importantly, get to know yourself." He said. I remained silent.

    You should try to orb right here, right now." He suggested. "How?" I asked. Bobby stood up and walked outside to my terrace and turned around to face me. "Close your eyes, picture me right here on your terrace looking at you. Focus and will yourself to come to me. Don't be afraid of what you feel, just let your powers guide you Eve." he said. I took a deep breath in and then let it out before I felt myself gently being lifted.

    It didn't feel like I was flying with my wings, *that* was actually a bit scary. This was just a gentle lift. It actually felt quite peaceful. "Open your eyes." Bobby whispered. I opened my eyes and found myself sitting on the ground by his feet and starring up at him. "Why the heck am I on the ground?" I asked in a little raised and surprised voice. "Because that's the position you're orbed from. You were *sitting* on your bed." Bobby chuckled. He extended his hand and helped me up.

    "I like when you orb. You look beautiful, peaceful and comfortable. You have a light that surrounds you unlike any others I've seen; it's a light shade of lavender and gold. You are your parent's daughter," Bobby smiled. "It *felt* peaceful. No offense to you angels, but I think I will stick to orbing, that's more comfortable to me." I said with a smirk. "None taken." he laughed.

"How come everything is purple? My orb color is purple, my eye color, the sky, my veins and wings?" I asked. "It's not just purple. But also gold and silver, those are your parent's colors. Wizards are magical beings, and often their magic is purple or a purple like color. As Angels, we represent royalty and purity, which are white, silver and gold. Witches, warlocks and vampires are usually red, black and white.

In our world eye color, veins and wings and the color of orb really depends on your species and genes. You've inherited traits from both of your parents just like humans receive genes from their parents. From what my mother has told me. Your father's veins were purple because of the magic that ran through him. His eyes changed from natural brown to fluorescent purple when angered or focused. His orb was also purple. And your mother was unnaturally beautiful and her wings were a shimmering gold. So you've inherited their genes. The sky has always been shades of purple, just how on earth it is blue." he answered.

"You being part Arch, and part wizard will be a little challenge, it will create you to have new senses and urges, a change in behavior." Bobby said. I looked at him confused. "What do you mean a change in behavior?" I asked as I went to sit down on the large bed and I watched Bobby sit down beside me. "The wizard in you, will make you want to live a little on the edge, have a need for thrill. While the Arch in you is a peaceful, headstrong goddess. More passive but not completely. You were lost on earth, very passive and indecisive. You will not be that way here. Here you will come into your own, find clarity and inner peace and your strength. But you will have to find a balance between the two in yourself. Everyone has good and bad in them, in Permia it's just more upfront." he said with a light chuckle.

I noticed that I hadn't really said much in comparison to Bobby's constant talking in all of our conversations. *Well, I am just learning.* I thought to myself. However, I *do* feel like I could have asked more questions. I guess the passiveness in me was more present than ever tonight.

A few hours ago, I was at a dinner party with my boyfriend and friends, excited about being at the cheesecake factory. And now, I'm here talking and learning from an adorable Angel, in a world that I am supposedly from, and supposedly to rule called *Permia*. Oh and I have powers! Yet I have nothing to say. It's not that I have nothing to say, it's just... what do I say? What would you say when your world has been turned upside down?

    I suddenly started to become a little tired. I could tell that my eyes weren't going to keep open for much longer. "Bobby, what time is it?" I asked. "A few minutes to 1:30 AM." he replied. "Are we in the same time zone as Earth?" I asked. Bobby nodded his head yes. "I don't know what I'm going to tell my friends when I see them again." I said in a whisper. Bobby laughed. "You will figure something out." he smiled. "Well, I think you should get some sleep. It's going to be a long journey Eve, oh and that is your closet, where all your necessities are. Clothes, toothbrush, toothpaste, products for girls" he added. "Sounds good, thank you for everything." I said giving him a small smile. "No problem, goodnight." Bobby said. "Goodnight." I replied as he walked out of my room. I was finally alone in an entirely new bedroom and planet. Now I knew what people meant when they said "overnight things can change."

XV

Orb

When Bobby left my *room* I decided to look around. My dressers were already filled with undergarments, and my huge walk in closet was filled with assorted shoes and light toned shirts, dresses and bottoms. I held up a gold satin tank top and shorts pajama set and laid it out on my new bed before walking out to the terrace. I watched the earth, amazed that it actually looked the way it did in text books and pictures on Google, before my mind came across Parker.

    I wondered what his thoughts of me currently were and what he could possibly be doing right now. Thoughts of him flowed through me, resulting in me deciding to orb down to Earth to see him. However before I even orbed away fear sliced through me *what if something where to go wrong?* I thought to myself. I took a deep breath. "Nothing is going to go wrong, you've practiced a little, just do it, just go Eve." I said to myself. I walked away from my window and moved to stand in front of my bed. I closed my eyes and concentrated on Parker's foyer at the entrance of his house.

    In only few short seconds of concentrating, I felt myself lift and gently be placed down on a solid ground. I opened my eyes and saw that I was still in front of my bed. "Okay let me try this again." I said to myself getting annoyed that my orbing didn't work. Once again I concentrated and now wished to go, I wished to move and arrive at

Hidden

Parker's front entrance. I felt myself lift and I opened my eyes to see that I was surrounded by lavender and gold sparkles. I couldn't see exactly where I was, only the two beautifully blended colors that were surrounding me.

When I finally could see, it had been because I landed and was now standing right by the entrance door inside of parker's house. It was dark inside the house, but the light to the kitchen was on. With my new super bionic hearing, I could hear voices and I could tell that they were Parker's and his mother's.

I tip toed to the kitchen entrance, and placed myself against the wall trying to camouflage but horribly failing, and listened. "Still no sign of her?" Nora asked "Nope and no one we know has seen her either." Parker replied. "What about her parents?" "I don't talk to them and they wouldn't tell me if she was home or not even if I asked nicely. Heck I doubt that they even noticed that she is missing." Parker said. Nora sighed. "Don't stress too much Parker; she will call when she can." Nora said.

Parker sighed and he got up Nora embraced him and he held on to her. "Try to get some sleep honey." she said. Parker nodded his head in agreement, and let go of her. He lifted two cups off of the island counter and headed to the sink. While doing so I took a chance to orb from my current position, to go up to Parker's room.

I safely orbed into his room and deeply inhaled. I let his scent take over all my senses. I missed the smell of him, the comfort and familiarity of being with him and his family. Even though it hasn't even been a full day without him, the unusual and unfamiliar atmosphere I had been surrounded in for a few hours, made me miss him more.

In Permia, yeah something inside me told me that being there was right, that I was home. But I wasn't in my comfort zone. Parker, Nora and Amanda, being with them is my comfort zone. Sleeping In parker's bed was where I usually laid peacefully.

I took in every familiar object that was in Parker's room and smirked. I sat on his bed and looked at a picture of us hugging and laughing in the school parking lot before sighing. "I can't believe I just snuck into Parker's bedroom. What the hell am I doing?" I asked myself with a quiet chuckle. But before I had a chance to *respond* to myself I heard footsteps coming towards the bedroom.

I put the picture of Parker and I back on it's secure spot on his dresser, bolted into his closet and tried to remain silent. I was so scared that I began breathing a bit harder than normal. I could literally hear my heart beating out of my chest. Parker walked into his room and sat on his bed and looked at his phone. He then sighed and went to his bathroom.

As soon as he closed the door I ran out of his closet and tried to orb back to my room in Permia. But before I could actually orb I heard the bathroom door knob and watched it turn to open, so I ran for the closet once again. Parker looked around as he seemed to feel a small bit of air or even a presence around him. I began to orb but not before accidentally bumping my foot on one of Parker's shoe boxes. I closed my eyes tightly after seeing Parker make a move towards the closet. I quickly imagined my canopy bed and gold walls in my new room and I began to lift.

Within seconds Parker opened his closet door and I had successfully arrived in my bedroom back in Permia. I knew my boyfriend had to see something, but I honestly didn't care as long as he didn't recognize me. Hopefully he would blame it on his sleepiness. "I'm so stupid!" I whispered and sighed to myself as I changed my clothes and went to bed.

XVI

Unexpected Visitor

The day after my birthday, I woke up to the sun beating my face with its rays. I opened my eyes expecting my entire Permia experience to be a dream. But as soon as I sat up, and looked around, I realized I was lying in a comfortable canopy bed and not my dingy couch or Parker's bed. Permia wasn't a dream after all, it is definitely real. I went out on the terrace and looked out at the world. The lilac like colored sky was filled with white clouds and the large field was a perfect shade of green.

After a while of enjoying the view I took a quick shower I changed into a white tank top, brown khaki shorts and black cargo boots. I also braided my hair into a ponytail. I walked out the doors of my bed room and walked down the long white hallway. In the distance I could hear voices, and since I didn't know where I was going, I made the decision to tune in and ease drop on the conversation while walking to the voices.

"She is royal by bloodline we simply just have to train her proper." A strong voice said. I could tell by how strong and familiar that it was that the voice belonged to Marius. "Does she know Archangel ways? She could go down a dark path now that she knows the truth about herself and her parents. She could turn now knowing what Kera and Scarlett have done and by the way she's no match for Scarlett! We should ship her back to Earth where she belongs and rule this land ourselves." An unfamiliar male voice said.

The only dark path that I was on was the path I was walking to, which was to the voices. The unfamiliar male's words triggered an angry emotion in me. I could kill him the way he undermined me. Completely no faith in me. I hate being doubted by anyone, but especially strangers.

I put my anger off for a moment and kept listening and walking towards the voices. "We can't just take over here that is not destiny. Permia is *Eve's* purpose. To be queen is her birth right! We are going to help her make the correct decisions. Teach her all things good, the good that died with her mother shall be restored with Eve." Marius said "And what about her father, he was a wizard, we have never had a mix breed rule Permia." A woman's voice spoke. "That is her source for strength. Yes Eve will have desire to practice magic, use spells and even see in a different way than us, she is half breed. But it does not mean she is evil, we have to teach her. She will unite us all." Marius said.

Now I was a few paces away from the voices, standing behind the door that the voices were coming from, I had heard enough of the stupid conversation in which the topic being me. I pushed open two gold double doors which led me to walk into the room of voices that I previously heard. I looked around the beautiful large white and gold room. People sat in rows to the left and right sides. Right in front of me were two beautiful and large gold chandeliers and just below it was a gold and purple throne.

I stood in the middle of the room and looked at everyone sitting down. They were all staring at me and usually I would feel nervous with all eyes on me, but in this moment I didn't. I felt a new confidence in me that I never felt before. I felt in control, I felt ready to lead. Where did these new feelings come from? I don't know, but I definitely felt them.

"I would like to add my two cents to the conversation before I end it, first, Good morning." I said with a smirk while looking at everyone. "Hope you don't mind that I join in on the conversation you are having about me." I said. "We think you need to be placed back on

Earth that's where you belong." a dark haired male Angel said. I could tell that was the one that had doubted me from before. "No! Alan, is the only one who believes that, everyone else wants you here Eve." Elsa said.

I looked at Alan with a straight face." I believe I am going to ignore your stupidity and erratic comments of me. If I were evil you would have known that by now, especially when I walked in this room, you making remarks like that, I could have killed you as soon as I saw your face." I said sternly. *Wait a minute; did I really just say that?* I mentally asked myself. That authority is not a normal characteristic of mine. "You're not fit to be queen." He said. I narrowed my eyes. "And I'm starting to believe that you're not fit to stand alongside anyone in this room. Perhaps you are unfit to be on the council. I find it rude that you don't know me and yet you're already judging me. You already had an opinion of me before we even met one another." I replied through gritted teeth.

I could feel my heart starting to beat quicker and my blood boil. The room gasped and I looked around clueless. Bobby and Destiny stepped forward and handed me a mirror. The reflection looking back at me was normal. Everything was normal except for my eyes, they were now an almost glowing purple. "That must have happened out of anger." Chaska said. I looked at her and then back at myself in the mirror, touching my face to believe I was me. I *was* the one I was staring back at me in the mirror.

"Bravo sweetie that was a wonderful speech you gave to poor Alan. Stupid Alan." A voice from behind me said. It was a sweet but solid voice. Almost angelic, but failed due to the sneering and hissing found at the base. I turned around to face a girl I recognized. She looked around my age, had deep red hair, olive skin and bright green eyes. She was beautiful, too beautiful to be real. As she walked towards me I felt even more put to shame by her in the looks department.

"What do you want Scarlett!" Marius yelled rushing to my side. "How did you get in here?" Bobby asked stepping in front of me. "Hi

Marius, how ya doing buddy? Oh and you know there's nothing an Archangel Princess can't do dear Bobby boy." she smiled while pinching his cheek and then lightly smacking him. Bobby made a scorned face to her. "What do you want?" he asked. Scarlett sighed. "To see my cousin of course, I heard she was finally in town, and I just wanted to say hello. It's about time we met, don't you think?" She chuckled. Bobby backed up in front of me a little bit more, standing in a protective stance.

"There's no need to protect her, I'm not going to hurt her... yet." she added. "But I do have to ask you all, since *everyone* from the council is here... why should she be queen when in fact until yesterday she didn't even know about our people. She doesn't know our ways, we don't know her temperament. I think she should be killed, preferably skinned alive." Scarlett said. I huffed. I just officially met her and I was already irritated. "Well, it seems like everyone already knows your temperament Scarlett and obviously it sucks. The only thing you should rule over are sewer rats and earth worms." I replied with a smirk. Scarlett narrowed her eyes and I continued talking.

"I was created to bring peace and protect this world and earth from evil and I will defeat anything that tries to stop me from fulfilling that task and that includes you. This is my world now *not* yours, so why don't you see yourself out?" I asked almost politely. "Why don't you see yourself dead?!" She yelled as she levitated in the air. My mouth dropped!

Suddenly the girl that looked my age had started to look older and powerful. She looked confident and predator like. Four angels flew into the air floating across from Scarlett as Marius and Bobby took a tighter solid stance in front of me, ready in case Scarlett made a move to attack. "What? I only want to give my cousin a proper *Permian* welcome." she said.

Before I could even register Scarlett had appeared behind me and back hand slapped me across the face. Scarlett grabbed my neck and began to squeeze. Subconsciously I balled my right hand into a fist and hit her in the jaw. A lightning bolt from behind me zapped at Scarlett hitting her in the chest making her scream and let me go. I dropped to the floor and scooted away from her.

Scarlett gained her composure, launched herself at Marius and lifted him up into the air by the neck. I looked up to see the four floating Angels and saw that they were securely bounded to four large posts, and all other angels and council were frozen in place. Right then, I realized just how powerful Scarlett *really* was. She was definitely ballsy enough to walk in here alone. "Now Marius, I know you're a bit old and quite *dumb,* but you should know better than to try to hurt me. I am the most powerful being here in Permia. I can end you right here and now!" she said to him with gritted teeth. "Don't!" I said walking towards her. "You want me... this is between you and I. Of course Marius is going to protect me I'm pretty sure your psycho friends will do the same for you." I said. Scarlett slowly took her eyes from Marius and looked at me. "You sure do talk a lot of shit for a princess that doesn't even know how to use her powers. You're weak and pathetic. A waste of Archangel. And a tiny little bullshit obstacle in my way to get *my* crown, and royal glory." She said Tightening her grip on Marius's neck.

"She just got here Scarlett what do you expect?" Bobby asked. Scarlett dropped Marius to the floor. "Bobby, Bobby, Bobby my have I missed your weak link ass, long time no see. So you're saying that's why Eve is no challenge for me, because she just got here." She smiled and said more than asked. "Hmm...That may be true so I will give her a little time. Eve is right too though; this battle is between her and I." Scarlett said. "I'm done for now. I just wanted to see my competition, and it seems that I have nothing to worry about. However, I suggest you teach her a few things Marius, maybe like how to flap her wings and sprinkle pink fairy dust on all the pathetic mortals in the other realm. You know, she doesn't stand a chance of living long if she's going up against me. Just let her play with her newly found magic while she can. Nothing is going to stop me from owning this land." She said flying up to a window in the room. "I'll let myself out. I'll be sure to tell everyone about my beautiful big cousin, I'm sure they will want to see you before your death." she said punching and breaking the window and flying out. "Oh and big cousin, welcome to Permia, I'm sure I'll be seeing you around, when you least expect It." she smiled as she peeked back inside, and then finally disappeared.

    I sighed a relief. "Some of you make sure she leaves, someone please take care of Marius and anyone else that is hurt." I said as I walked out the room. "Where are you going?" Bobby asked. "I need some air." I replied looking at him and then walking out.

XVII

The Difference

I walked out the mansion and went to walk around the gardens. It was filled with large shrubs and bushes of flowers. I was pissed and I wanted to kill Scarlett, or anything I could get my hands on at the moment. Anger seared through me and I had to take a few deep breaths to gain my composure. I stood by a large water fountain and stared down into the water, concentrating on trying to find my *Namaste* until I heard footsteps coming from behind me.

I turned around to come face to face with Bobby, Chaska, Destiny and an adorable curly brown haired guy. His skin was alabaster and his eyes were a shade of ocean blue. "Hey you okay?" he asked? "Fine." I replied. "Eve this is Eli he's a messenger for you." Bobby introduced. "Okay so what's the message?" I asked. Eli laughed. "There isn't any message right now and all that means is that I help give you clarity to any purposeful situation you end up in and don't understand." He said. "Oh well than it's nice to meet you." I said almost lowly. "Likewise, you sure you okay?" he asked. "Yes." I confirmed.

"So obviously we need to work on your powers, so next time we *will* be ready, no one knew Scarlett was going to show up." Bobby said. Honestly from Bobby's comment, I was getting even more pissed and upset. I just got here and already I was part of the motion to battle, make war, or be ready to fight. I wanted to focus more on the "your here to create peace, spread love and heal unicorns" part of my new job instead of the "protect the worlds from evils" why couldn't I at least enjoy this at first? Why couldn't I at least have a week to settle? "This is so much...why me?! I didn't ask for this. Yesterday I was a normal 17 year old nobody." I yelled. "And now you're an 18 year old young woman, but also an Archangel Wizard princess. Don't fight your destiny Eve." Bobby said. I crossed my arms over my chest and pouted. "How come Scarlett has her powers, and *so much* power and I only am at the start of mine?" I asked curiously and yet annoyed.

"Scarlett has never left this dimension; she's been learning and maybe even practicing, probably since she could walk. If you didn't get sent to earth or have your powers binded, you would have had some of your powers and also would have been learning as well." Chaska said. "However Scarlett turns eighteen in some months so her powers aren't at their full capacity. An advantage you can have over her if you work hard and train." Eli said.

"Creatures and breeds of all kinds would love to bring Permia into a new time, possibly evil and darkness. And most including Scarlett, want to combine earth dimension humans with our dimension species. She wants to rule both worlds." Eli continued. "Um that can't happen, it would probably start wars, and not to mention it would be like Halloween every day." I said now chewing my thumb out of frustration. "Exactly!" Eli replied. I sighed. "This is so much pressure."

I sat down on the edge of the fountain and tried to mute my mind. I focused and tried to put a shield around my mind. Slowly I felt a force of energy spread and slide in the front of my head. It was like a sheet covering my body on a cold night.

I am the difference. The difference from evil. And I am the only one that can prevent it in two dimensions. But how could I be a somebody here in Permia when at home, I easily was a nobody. To rule this place and protect earth, will be hard...but life is hard in general isn't it? I asked myself.

"Fine...help me with my training." I said, now looking at the four angels that stood to the right of me. My new friends and housemates cheered. "We have to plan your crowning ceremony. "Destiny said. I looked at her confused. "On that day you will be Crowned queen and it will be official you'll be the ruler, Queen of Permia." "Oh well go get things sorted and fill me in later." I smirked at them. Destiny Eli and Chaska happily flew off. I looked up at bobby. I watched him closely as he remained silent.

"It doesn't feel like Christmas Eve." I said breaking the ice. "Sorry about today." Bobby said softly. I snorted. "Sorry about what? Me getting my butt kicked?!" I asked. Bobby nodded his head from left to right. "I guess." he said. "It's whatever, all that means is that when you guys start training me, I don't want you to take it easy on me. I want you to push me, really hard." I said seriously. "We will do that." Bobby smiled at me. I figured he was probably envisioning me getting a major butt whopping since I didn't say anything worth him smiling about.

"I like that you've learned to mute your mind already, fast learner." Bobby said. I looked up at him and smirked. "Oh Bobby, do you know where my bag is? I had it when I first came here." I asked. Bobby smiled and I watched him close his eyes and my bag suddenly appear in his hands. "Thank you." I said as he handed me the bag. I looked through until I found my phone. I clicked unlock and immediately saw sixteen missed calls from Parker, his mom and even one from Mena.

XVIII

Reunited

That night I orbed home back to my basement. When I got there I instantly felt sad, out of place and slightly like a caged animal that just wanted to get out. "At least in Permia they actually care to give me an actual room." I mumbled. I looked at my blue bin where the keys to my car were. I grabbed the keys and then headed upstairs.

"Eve Where have you been?!" Mena screamed. "Sheesh you could at least say hi first." I said sarcastically." I was at Parker's." I sighed. "And you didn't think to let us know where you were going?!" She asked. "I didn't know how long I would be gone and I didn't have my phone to call you. And besides that's the best part about being eighteen, I don't have to tell you a thing." I said. Mena looked at me like I had stupid written on my forehead. "You know what Eve; I have had enough of your mouth! I want you out of my house! Go live in a hotel!" she said. I rolled my eyes. "You want me out of your house? Fine, that's not a problem. As of now, I won't be living here anymore." I said smiling, grabbing my keys and heading out the door. Out of all the times I had been kicked out of my house, this time I was actually happy about it. It meant that from now on I wouldn't be in a cage, or alone in the dark. I would be free.

I got in my car and drove to Parker's house. When I parked in his driveway, I decided to text him, making my return to him a little bit more dramatic.

"Parker." I texted
"Eve where are you?! Are you okay?"
"I had a surprise delivered to your house, open your front door please."

I stood in front of parker's front door and within two minutes I heard footsteps walking towards the door. "Wow my hearing is like supersonic." I said to myself. Parker opened the door and I just smiled up at him. "Oh my god Eve!" He said as he grabbed me and hugged me tightly. "Where have you been?" He asked. I rested my head on his chest and listened to his heartbeat. "Gosh Parker, you make it seem like I've been gone forever." I chuckled. "You randomly disappeared on me. What was I supposed to think, I was just worried about you babe." he said. "I know, I'm sorry and I'm okay." Parker kissed my forehead and then my lips before he invited me inside the house.

We walked into the living room and I smiled as I watched Nora and Amanda laugh as they watched frosty the snowman. "Look who's here," Parker announced as we stood at the front of the living room. Nora and Amanda's heads whipped around and Amanda called my name with a little squeal before running up to me and giving me a hug. "What's up munchkin?" I asked hugging her back. "Hello Eve." Nora said waiting to embrace me. "Hi." I replied as I wrapped my arms around her. "Let's talk in the dining room yeah? Amanda I'm gonna talk to your brother and Eve for a second, you keep watching the movie okay?" Nora said. "Yes mom." Amanda replied. We watched her run to sit on the couch before us three walked into the kitchen and sat down.

"It's great to see you Eve, what happened?" Nora asked. *Sheesh, she cut right to the chase, gotta come up with a good and realistic little white lie. Could angels lie? Or would that be a bad thing? Whatever.* I thought to myself. "It seems that my family was in the mall, that's connected to the cheesecake factory. They saw us go in, and when I went to the bathroom, I basically got dragged out, and went home." I said. "Really? That is so uncalled for." Parker said. Clearly frustrated. "Yeah... sorry for scaring everyone. I've been home sleeping with my phone on silent by accident." I said. "That is no way to spend your birthday, I'm sorry that happened to you." Parker said.

Okay so I lied, but what else was I supposed to say? That I passed out and went to another dimension? Yeah right, they would send me to a nut house in Switzerland if I answered truthfully. Nora and Parker knew how my family was so the little lie was a perfect cover up for Permia. Besides, if I were found in that restaurant by the Keller's, I'm sure I really would have been dragged out.

"It's okay." I replied. "No it's not." Parker said hugging me and kissing my forehead. Nora nodded her head in understanding as if she comprehended and believed my story of what had happened at the cheesecake factory. "Well I know you two have some things to talk about so I will leave you two. Amanda and I will be down here watching Frosty." Nora said. "Okay." I replied for parker and myself.

Parker and I walked upstairs and entered his bedroom. I walked to his window and peered out. It's so weird that there's a whole other dimension out there that we can't see. It's also weird that from here, everything seems so ordinary, natural and small. From Permia, everything seems bigger, supernatural and special. Like anything in our wildest dreams can happen there.

"I missed you." Parker said wrapping his arms around my waist. "A day without you seems like forever." he continued. Parker pulled my body around so that I was now facing him. "And that was no way to end your birthday." He whispered in my ear. "Oh, so how was it supposed to end?" I asked curiously. Parker had grabbed my waist and pulled me closer to him. Our lips met and with them still attached Parker pushed me to the window. I shivered as the cold from the window connected with my warm spine. From Parker's kiss I automatically felt a fire that was beginning to blaze in the pit of my stomach. "Talk about being hot and cold." I said pulling away from Parker.

I wondered if Parker would like the *new* me. The wizard angel princess, warrior version of me. Those questions would never be answered, because my true identity would forever be hidden from Parker. At that moment of realization, any passion, love or heat I had felt in my body had started to diminish. How can you continue to love someone you have to lie to? Parker wouldn't know *me* anymore. He would never know the *real* me.

"You're so beautiful." Parker whispered. I looked into his eyes before kissing his collarbone. "I'm kind of tired." I whispered. Parker took my hand and led me to his bed. He took my top off while I took off my pants, leaving me in a tank top and boy shorts. I climbed into his bed and watched him get undressed. Shortly, he joined me in bed. I wrapped my arms around his waist and he wrapped his arm around my shoulder. We cuddled in silence, reveling in being together. I wondered how much longer he and I would last as a couple. With everything happening in my life, it was a fact that I was embarking on a new identity, life and future. Nothing would be the same again.

XIX

Happy Christmas

Christmas morning, I woke up beside Parker, who was sitting up looking at me. "Ok, it's kind of creepy waking up to someone eyeballing you." I said adjusting my eyes. Parker laughed. "how did you sleep?" he asked." Good, you?" "Like a baby." he replied. "What time is it?" I asked noticing that it was still a bit dark outside. "It's six thirty a.m." Parker said. I groaned "Why are you awake?" "Guess I couldn't sleep anymore." he replied.

He lifted my face up towards him and gently kissed me. "Merry Christmas baby." he smiled. "Aw, Merry Christmas babe." I smiled back at him. "Sadly I have to be home by eight. I don't want the family to freak out." I told him. "I don't want you to leave, I just got you back." he whined." Hey don't worry; I won't disappear on you again." I said cupping his face and looking into his eyes. "You sure, you promise?" "Yes." I said to him.

I seemed confident in my verbal answer to Parker but on the inside, I wasn't so sure if what I said was true or not. I'm not sure how the balance between my life in Permia and my life here was going to work. "I got a gift for you." Parker smiled. He got up and walked to his dresser in front of us, and pulled out a tiny box wrapped in snowflake wrapping paper. "What is it?" I asked. "Open it and see." he said handing me the box. I removed the wrapping paper, and stared at the tiny black velvet box. "What are you waiting for?"

he smiled. I looked up at him and rolled my eyes. I took a deep breath and opened the box.

Inside were two silver and brown leather bracelets. On the insides it had our names, along with the date we started dating November thirteenth two thousand thirteen and the word forever written on it. "Aw it's beautiful!" I smiled up at him. "I love it, thank you." I said reaching up and giving him a hug. "One is yours and the other is mine." he said. I looked up at him and smirked. "I kind of figured that." I said sarcastically. Tracing my fingers on the engraving of the large and small bracelets. "My gift for you is in the car, come with me to get it." I said. Parker nodded his head okay, and I put my clothes back on and headed down to my car with him.

I opened the trunk to my car and grabbed one white bag that contained the Christmas gifts inside. "Open it now." I said to him while handing him a large red box. Parker opened the box and stared at the item. "Are you serious? How did you even afford this?" he asked. "It's no big deal, try it on." I told him. Parker first hugged me, before trying on the Harley Davison leather jacket on. He looked like a true biker boy with the jacket on, he lost a bit of his country, beach boy look, and it was replaced with a "bad boy" type of vibe. "I have to take these to your mom and sister." I said gesturing to the white bag. Parker took my hand and led me back inside.

We walked by the living room and saw Amanda sitting on the floor by the Green Christmas tree. "Look what I got for Christmas Eve!" Amanda said while looking adorable in a Santa hat. "What did you get?" I asked her. She held up a brunette Barbie for me to see, and then pointed to a pile of new toys on the floor. "Here you go!" I said giving her a small silver box. Amanda tore through the paper like an insane child, and her jaw dropped once she unveiled the actual gift. "Thank you!" she gasped holding up the Ariana Grande charm bracelet. "You're welcome." I smiled and handed Nora her gift from me. She smiled and hugged me when she noticed she received the latest Dolce and Gabbana perfume.

Amanda ran from me and back to the Christmas tree and then back to me with a medium size present in her arms. "It's for you, from us." she said. I took the box and shook it. "What could it be?" I asked. I opened the wrapped box and gasped. I eyed the purple and black zipper *Hashtag One Three Seven* handbag. "Oh wow, it's beautiful thank you so much ladies!" I smiled at Parker's mother and sister. *Perfect colors* I thought to myself.

"Well I better get going." I said hugging Parker's family one last time. "I have to celebrate with the *family."* I said sarcastically. "Good luck." Nora smiled. I smiled at her and headed to the door with Parker following me. "Call me when you get home." he said hugging me. "I will." I said kissing his cheek and then walking to my car.

I parked my car into the parking lot at home and then walked through my backyard and into the woods. I closed my eyes and imagined they Caylan mansion in Permia. I felt myself lift and felt the energy flow throughout my body, and I knew I *orbing* home.

After appearing at the front door of the mansion, I walked in and started looking for Bobby, however, I found Chaska instead. "Hi Eve! What's up?" she asked. I smiled at her. "Well, I want to officially move here, and I was wondering how do I get my earth items here to Permia?" I asked her. "Just orb your things here." she said. I looked at her puzzled. "Okay...how do I do that?"

"You have to hold onto the item that you want to bring here, and just orb up to your room." she said. "So I can just hold onto a pair of shoes from home, and then orb here and they will appear here with me?" I asked trying to clarify. "yeah." Chaska replied. "Just like that?" I asked not totally convinced. "Just like that." she assured me. "Cool, I'll try." I smiled.

"Ugh... this is so much to take in Chaska. I can't believe I'm a who I am, daughter of an Archangel Queen and a wizard. One day I was an ordinary girl who lived in a basement, and lived with my evil adoptive parents and sisters, and now... I'm not." I said. "Sounds like a real life Cinderella story." Chaska smiled. "Yeah but I'm *no* Disney character." I replied. "No you're not, but weird and wonderful things happen to people that deserve it. You better start moving everything in your castle princess." Chaska smiled. "It's going to be a long productive day." I said more to myself than her.

"Wait what am I going to do with my car?" I asked out loud. "Orb it here." Chaska suggested. "But how will I get to school?" I asked.

"Orb to school." She said. "Yeah but people will notice I don't have my car." Chaska and I heard footsteps coming towards us and my senses took in the scent of the incoming person and automatically signaled through me that the person walking towards us was Bobby. "Hey what's up ready to move in?" Bobby asked. "Zoning in on peoples conversation isn't attractive Bobby." Chaska said. I laughed. "Almost, just trying to figure out what to do with my car. It has to stay on earth." I said. "Well why don't you talk to your teacher Ms. Burns about it. Maybe she can help come up with a solution, like you can keep it at school or something." Bobby suggested. "That's a great idea, thanks Bob." I chuckled. Bobby narrowed his eyes at my nickname for him.

"I was actually coming to tell you, your crowning date has been dated for February sixteenth. Tonight after you are done settling in we will start your training." He said. "Roger that master chief!" I joked. I saluted Bobby and then orbed home. In the basement I put on some house music and quickly got to work. Hoping to be invisible to my *family*.

XX

Moving In

I had gone through my two blue bins, two pink bins, a green one and my giraffe printed suitcase. I ended up with two piles on the floor. Pile one was clothes, shoes and accessories to give away, and the other were ruined clothes to throw away, while my bins contained the items I would keep.

Six times I took a bin into my hands and orbed off to the purple skied dimension. With all my earth belongings sitting in the middle of my new room, I took a moment to really look at my room. It was beautiful. It had an edgy, glam, royal feel to it and I adored it. I chose not to say goodbye to my earth family, it would be better if I just left. That's what they would have wanted it anyway. I firmly believe that it will take them six months to notice I'm not even living there anymore.

Once back in Permia, I noticed that it was ten a.m. The sky blended with the bright sun beautifully and I couldn't help but smile at the awesomeness that had suddenly and randomly appeared in my life. I unpacked my things and designed my room how I wanted it.

By the time I got done fixing everything up, it was one thirty p.m. and I was tired and decided to nap. I dreamed peacefully. No visions, no premonitions, or anything scary. Just darkness and peace.

XXI

Magical Practice

Around six p.m. Bobby woke me up and we went to the large backyard. I took in the scenery and inhaled deeply. It was starting to get dark outside and the grass, trees and bushes were beginning to glow. "It's so beautiful here. Hard to believe that evil exists here." I said. "There's evil everywhere." Bobby replied. "Okay, let's start." He said. Bobby had laid out a blanket full of weapons and I gasped at the sight. "I only see these kinds of items in movies; I didn't think they were real." I said to Bobby as I picked up a large steal shield. "Yeah, well they are real." Bobby laughed.

I sat on the grass and listened to Bobby explain each weapon before we actually got up and used them for practice. Swords, stakes, staff's, chakram's, daggers and even my own hands. I practiced using my fire element ball, and even how to move items around with my mind and hands. All in all practice was actually fun, what tired me out was the quick and severe staff training. There is a lot of technique and footwork that goes with that kind of play. To be honest, that tired me out more than the three mile run Bobby had me do.

My favorite weapon to use, were definitely the daggers. They fit well with my sort of small hands and I found myself having great aim when it comes to striking targets with them. Clearly this would be my weapon of choice.

After about three long hours of training, Bobby decided that we had practiced enough and that it was over for the day. I walked over to a glass table in the backyard and picked up my phone. I swiped my phone to unlock it and notice I had a missed call and two text messages from Parker. I decided to call him back, and explore the grounds around the mansion.

I ended up by the pool, and began to take my shirt off, that is until I felt like I was being watched. I listened to the phone ring, and then Parker's voice from his voicemail. I hung up the phone without leaving a message. I looked around and decided *not* to swim. Instead I sat on the edge, and stuck my feet in the water. I sat there quietly and watched my feet glow under the water.

I looked up towards the trees because I thought I heard something ruffling the bushes, but the wind was also gently blowing, so I decided to ignore the creepy feeling. Still sitting there, I felt eyes on my back. I turned around to find Eli standing a few feet away staring at me.

"What are you doing here just staring at me like that?" I asked. He smiled and walked closer to me. "Just checking on you. Since you're so new to all of this, we have to watch and protect you. Anything can happen to you right now, there are many evil doers around and they would love to destroy you." Eli said. I snorted at his comment. "Well thanks for checking up on me. I have been practicing you know." I said. "I kind of already figured that ugly weird things were gonna start trying to kill me after I met Scarlett. Figured she will start to send her minions after me soon enough." I admitted.

Eli sat next to me and began putting his feet in the water. "Yeah but you have to be prepared on both worlds, who knows when, where or who will attack you at any given chance." Eli said. "Why would they attack me on earth?" I asked. Eli furrowed his eyebrows. "Even though you really just got here, you have a list of enemies already. Individuals and clans that hated the Caylan's. They can and will attack you at any moment, and even anywhere." Eli said. "They can and possibly will attack you on earth to catch you off guard." He continued. I stayed silent and thought about what he just said.

"some evil beings are so wicked, that they will go anywhere to find you, some are willing to hurt themselves, not caring if they get killed in the process, as long as in the end, your dead too. They will try to kill anyone who they feel will try to stop them from running the world, they are kind of like terrorists." he continued. I huffed. "That is so lame, I mean, it's like they know if they come after me, they know they are going to die, but they still come anyway, it's like running down the green mile." I said. Eli splashed his foot in the water.

"They will do anything as long as in the end, the enemy is no longer a threat. Think of it this way...wouldn't you sacrifice yourself if you knew that if you died, the entire world would be promised peace?" he asked. I couldn't answer Eli's question, because it seemed like a trick question. Of course I want the world to have peace, but I don't want to die either. Does that make me selfish?

"I get what you're saying." I said to Eli trying to avoid straight up answering the difficult question. I quickly turned my body to the right and looking at the woods. "Did you hear something?" I asked. Eli looked at me with a confused expression on his face. "Nope, just the wind." he said. "I have a feeling that I'm being watched or something." I confessed. "Maybe we should go inside." Eli said getting up. He put out his hand for me to take and I reached for it and stood up. "Thank you." I said, and he smiled.

XXII

Downtown

I could hear voices from inside the mansion clearly while being outside and more than fifty feet away. As Eli and I got closer, so did the voices. "Hey." I said walking in the door with Eli, and spotting Chaska and Destiny in the living area. "What's up?" Chaska asked. I sat down on the couch opposite of them. "Okay, I'm gonna go and let you girls do your *thing*, I guess." Eli said walking out awkwardly. All of us chuckled.

"Nothing much really, just getting used to things around here, what are you two up to?" I asked. "I was trying to get Chaska to go Downtown with me, but she's being a lame." Destiny said in a whiney voice. I smiled at them both. "I have to study!" she said. I looked at her clueless. "I'm training to be a messenger, and a guardian. Angels have different jobs to do, along with being your helper." Chaska said. "Wow, I thought that you were just born being messengers and guardians and all that, I didn't know you had to study for it." I said.

"Yes we have to train to do our jobs properly. Kind of just like when you have to go to school and gain knowledge to graduate and get the job you want, it's just as that is." Chaska said. I nodded my head in understanding. "I get it, you being a messenger and guardian is a huge deal, you should study." I smiled at her before turning my attention to Destiny. "What's downtown?" I asked her. Destiny smiled. "Downtown is definitely whimsical; it's where everyone including all the *cool* people hang out. That's where all the shops and restaurants are. People have parties and throw concerts there, and not to mention *Immortal U* is there." Destiny said. I looked at her kind of confused. "What's Immortal U?" I asked both girls. Destiny lightly laughed. "It's our only college." Destiny said. "Immortal University, has classes such as battle strategy, power control, wizardry, witchcraft, there's pretty much any class available for any need. They even teach human history and classes, so some of us Permian's can graduate and then go work on Earth." Chaska said. Some "people" you see working everyday normal jobs down there on earth, are actually from Permia." she added. "Like my teacher Ms. Burns." I whispered to myself.

I was intrigued about going downtown, from Destiny's description of it, it sounded fun. I smiled and turned my attention back to the girls. "Well downtown sounds cool, mind if I join you if you go?" I asked Destiny. Destiny's eyes lit up. "Um, yeah! I don't mind being see with the future queen, let's go now!!" she squealed.

Destiny took hold of my hand, and pulled me outside. Destiny stood in front of me and spread her arms out, and before my eyes, a beautiful pair of white wings appeared and blended beautifully with her white strapless dress. "So, I'm sure you know how to do this right, Bobby taught you?" She asked. I nodded my head yes and took a deep breath before closing my eyes and focusing on unstoring my wings.

Thank god I wore a tank top, I thought to myself. I felt a little heat sensation and pressure to my back and my wings unfolded just above the strap of my tank top. Destiny's mouth dropped. "Wow, your wings are like really pretty, and I don't use that comment on anybody's wings but my own. How come you get beautiful, large multicolored wings?" She said more then asked while folding her arms across her chest. "I'm actually jealous!" She huffed. I just stood there with a stupid little smirk on my face. I didn't know exactly how to respond to her.

Destiny turned her back to me and looked up to the sky. "Follow." She said just before she took off into the air. "Oh God, here we go." I mumbled before I began to rise into the air and follow Destiny. I held my stomach in and kept my eyes on Destiny's wings refusing to look down.

Being a princess and moving to Permia definitely had its perks, but for me, flying certainly isn't one of them. I looked up ahead at some tall buildings Destiny and I were about to fly past and I realized, we were entering a little city like town.

Destiny and I landed in a spot surrounded by trees. We stored our wings, and then walked towards the bright lights ahead of us. I smiled as I saw the town was lit up by stores, buildings and even modern cars. The city was filled with mostly young Permian's out to have a good time.

Destiny pointed out to some cool clothing stores, book shops, restaurants and even pubs that we came across. And every so often we even walked into a store to look around. We made a pit stop to the ice cream shop *"Tommy's sweets"* before we walked by a huge old building that I soon realized was a college. Walking by it, I got an eerie feeling.

The school was humungous and made from old brick. The shape of the school was like a large eighteenth century castle, and in my opinion, it was creepy, even making me shudder. "Dest, is this Immortal U?" I asked her. She took a lick of her vanilla ice cream and sprinkles, and looked at the school. "Yup, this is it. Kind of creepy isn't it?" She asked. As we walked by the school, I felt like I was being watched again. "You okay?" Destiny asked me as she looked over my shoulder after I had stopped walking with her. "Yeah, just looking around...this school is huge, and you're right it *is* creepy." I half replied. Destiny smiled and then looked forward to the street and started walking again. I followed behind, until I caught up and started walking beside her.

We continued walking in silence until Destiny smiled and broke the quietness. "Look up!" she said. I did as I was told and looked up to the purple sky. "Wow..." I said as I realized for the first time since we'd been walking, that the sky was just as filled as the downtown street was. Wizards were orbing from place to place, witches were flying on their brooms, and other creatures flew into the purple night sky.

Destiny and I walked to the end of the little city, and we came in front of a little pub called the *Brown Ridge*. Permian guys and girls were hanging outside sipping on drinks, and rocking out to current alternative music. For some reason I was drawn to it, and my feet started leading me in the direction of the entrance. "Um, where are you going?" Destiny asked me, pulling me back. I turned my head to look back at her and pointed to the pub. "No, that's a bar...angels, we don't belong in places like that." she whispered. "Hey...I'm only half angel, remember?" I asked her with a smirk on my face. Destiny looked a little annoyed, and walked towards me. "Okay, it's time to go. I don't even think your old enough to go in there." she said pulling my arm. "Oh boo!" I whined before cooperating with Destiny, and walking with her.

Once again, I got that "being watched" feeling, I turned my head back towards the pub, and I caught the shadow of a guy who was standing by the entrance of the pub. His body was turned towards mine, and even though I couldn't see him clearly, I knew he was watching me. To be honest, it kind of weirded me out. But I chose to ignore it. I'm new to Permia, and I'm supposed to be queen, I don't want to make a dramatic scene on my first night out.

Destiny and I headed back in the opposite direction of the pub and walked to a spacious area. "Thank you for coming with me." Destiny said as she spread her wings. "No problem." I smiled. "But um, I think I am going to orb back home, flying is for the birds." I chuckled at my own stupid and lame joke. Destiny raised her eyebrows. "You can orb too? This is not fair!" She said stomping her feet on the ground. I laughed at her childishness and watched her expand her wings and head into the sky and become one with the night.

I noticed a handful of Permian's around my age started walking towards me, but stopped a few feet short and went down some stairs. My curiosity got the best of me and I had to ask a question. "Hey, what's down there?" I asked a cool looking girl with pink and purple dyed hair. *"The underground."* She replied. I gave her a blank expression. "It's a club called *The Underground;* it's down inside the tunnels. I can tell you're new to the nightlife." She smiled. "I am." I smiled back. "Cami Jane, come on!" A guy called out to her from down in the tunnel. I peered down into the darkness, and saw a pair of glowing purple eyes staring back at me. *A wizard.* I thought to myself.

"You should come down sometime; I'm Cami Jane, the owner. We're open every night starting at eight p.m." She smiled. "I'll remember that." I smirked back. "See ya." Cami said and walked down the stairs and into the tunnel. I contemplated about going down there and checking out the club, but to save myself from embarrassment and loser status because I would be showing up to a club alone, I decided to hold out and comeback when I'm either not alone or more confident in my loneress . I closed my eyes, and orbed home.

As soon as I got in the door, I walked up to my room, and checked my phone. I realized I had forgotten all about it, and didn't check it in hours. I wasn't surprised to see missed calls and texts from Parker. What surprised me was the one from Mena. I quickly sent Parker a text saying sorry for the late reply, but I'm really busy and I will call him tomorrow. As for Mena, I deleted her phone number. I figured, Permia will be a fresh start, I could start all over again, and my new life wouldn't include my *family.*

I made a mental note to ask Ms. Burns if it would be possible for her to get all my school mail, and hold it for me instead of sending it to my home address. "Time for a new start." I mumbled to myself as I lay down and got comfortable in my giant sized bed.

XXIII

December Thirty-First

I continued my intense training with Bobby and even added in some boxing with Marius, gymnastics and healing training with Elsa. I also got some help on wizardry with Ms. Burns. Ms. Burns and I have become quite close, she even lets me keep my car parked at her house, so I can orb to and from there to get to Permia and to school. I now understand that she was always looking out for me, and she's always there to talk or give me advice.

I trained daily until Friday which just so happens to be December thirty first. I had been so busy training that I never even called Parker like I said I would. Honestly, I wasn't too excited to go back to earth; Permia was starting to feel like home. I began to have more clarity about everything including my life. I also got adapted to the plan of me being queen. My true self was starting to emerge and shine and I wanted to stay in Permia forever. But there was only one reason stopping me from actually making that huge move. I couldn't just leave Parker behind.

After training, I orbed down to Ms. Burns house, and got in my car. In my car, I called Parker, and told him to meet me at my job, soon as he could. I looked at the clock on my radio and groaned that it was only eight thirty four a.m. I groaned not because I was tired, but because I had to be at work at nine a.m., and that didn't leave me with much time to talk to Parker.

Even though I was frustrated with the time, I knew I had to talk to him, and I wanted to do it right before work. However, Parker had different plans. He texted me back saying he would be at my job in thirty minutes. "That's the time I start work." I said groaning to myself. I became a little used to Permian's orbing or flying to me, appearing quickly whenever I needed them. I couldn't expect Parker to drop everything and meet me in ten seconds flat; he's only human after all.

After parking my car in the parking lot, I got a bad feeling in the pit of my stomach, a feeling that I started to rely on, because that instinct inside of me was always right. I had the feeling that something was wrong or that something was going to go wrong.

I got out of my car and heard a loud inhuman growl coming from the left of me. I turned my head and found a tall, muscular, dark skinned guy wearing brown and black leather, standing in the middle of the field across the parking lot, and he staring at me without blinking. He looked like a gladiator, and just by his appearance, I knew I was gonna have to fight, and fight quickly before Parker showed up, and before I was late for work. "The feeling in my stomach is always right." I said to myself.

I orbed in front of the Permian gladiator, and caught him by surprise before quickly punching him in the face, and then running deep into the woods, leading us out of sight of humans. I waited for the gladiator to come after me, but he didn't, or so I thought. I didn't hear anything coming towards me, but I heard a twig snap in back of me, and before I knew it, he had me in his grip.

He raised me in the air, and I felt as if I was as high as the leaves on the old trees that surrounded us. I wrapped my legs around the gladiator's neck and squeezed the air out of him. He tightened his grip on my neck and I began kicking him in his temple, in which he finally let me go. Dropping me to the ground, and I quickly sat up and glared at him.

"I really appreciate you dropping me like a hot potato but you could have done it more gently sheesh." I said sarcastically. "And you're supposed to be a queen? Stand up and fight or crawl on your knees and bow down to Scarlett!" he said. I immediately got angry. At the fact that he was sent to earth by Scarlett and because *no one* tells me to bow down to anyone. I will never bow to anyone on either of these dimensions, let alone my own sick and sadistic cousin.

Scarlett was making me even more furious, over the past few days, she had been sending her little goons to attack me, and one by one, they all fell at my feet. I'd like to thank my fellow angels and math teacher for my wonderful battle skills. "Do I have stupid on my forehead? Cause if I don't, what makes you think I will ever be stupid enough to bow to someone as dumb as you or Scarlett?" I asked while standing up and muttering the word *nutcase.*

The gladiator got upset at my comment, and charged at me. Suddenly a little tired to physically fight, I decided to use one of my favorite and most simple defense moves I've learned. The element ball. The gladiator ran up to me, I closed my eyes and concentrated on releasing the element from my hand. Within a few seconds, my hand started heating up, and white fire appeared out of my right hand. I threw my hand back and struck the gladiator in the face with the ball. I watched him scream and try to rub the fire off of him, but the rubbing didn't work, he fell to the ground holding his face before he burst into fire then ashes and then dust right before my eyes. I sighed out of tiredness, and began walking back to my car.

"Hey, what were you doing in the woods?" Parker asked getting out of his car. I was so out of my mind that I didn't even notice that his car was parked next to mine, and he was sitting in it waiting for me. I widened my eyes, as I thought of a quick lie to tell Parker. "I um, saw a weird animal, and I wanted to see what it was, so I went to look...but it ran away." I said not looking into his eyes. Parker chuckled. "Such a silly girl. I miss you, where have you been?" he asked, taking me into his arms and wrapping them around me tight. "I miss you. And I'm sorry for the lack of time we've been spending together... family has been driving me insane." I whispered. Even though it wasn't the family Parker knew, I considered the angels that live with me, my family. And with all of my training and practice going on, they really were driving me insane.

"Wait, what time is it?" I asked parker while pulling away from him. He looked at his phone. "Nine fifteen." he replied. "Holy fudge,

I'm late!" I yelled as I speed walked inside the mall, happy to hear footsteps behind me, indicating that Parker was following me. I ran into Charlotte Russe, greeted my coworker Sasha, and then ran to the back to put my things away, leaving Parker and Sasha alone. In the back, I smiled at my awesome sense of hearing. I could hear Parker and Sasha's casual conversation as clear as if I were standing right beside them.

"Sorry I'm late." I said to Sasha. "No problem, there's nobody here, chill out chica." Sasha said. I nodded at her and then turned my attention to Parker. "How's your family?" I asked him, interested in knowing what Nora and Amanda had been up to. "Never better, they miss you." he said hugging me again. "I miss them too." I said sadly. I honestly did miss Parker and his family, but this was my life now.

"How are you? You've been acting a little weird ever since your birthday." he whispered in my ear. I knew I had been acting *weird* to him and everyone else on Earth for that matter. But since it would be too hard to explain myself true fully, I decided to play dumb. "Weird like how?" I asked. Parker sighed and pulled away. "well, you've been MIA, you disappeared on your birthday without saying a word, and I've been trying to contact you and you don't reply...or if you reply, it's days later. What's wrong? Did I do something wrong?" he asked looking deep into my eyes. "No, no! You've done nothing wrong at all, your perfect." I assured him.

Honestly, what I was doing to Parker was breaking my heart. I had been neglecting him, and had been being a bad girlfriend in general to him. But that's one of the downfalls in my new life.... neglecting Parker, and my entire life down here. I sighed. "I know, and I'm sorry. I'm really sorry; I've been trying to balance being taken seriously as an adult and dealing with everyone at home. It's been really crazy." I said sadly.

Parker pulled me into him and wrapped his arms around my neck, and I wrapped mine around his waist. "You know you can always come over to mine if they stress you out." he said after kissing the top of my head. "I know, and I feel bad that you feel neglected. How about we spend New Year's together, just you and me?" I asked looking up at him. I watched Parker smile and a huge grin form, which made me smile in return.

"Sounds good, I'm definitely looking forward to that!" he said kissing my forehead. I smiled at him. "Maybe, just maybe we will end up in New York." he grinned. I squealed in excitement, New York on New Year's is seriously crowded, but amazing, and the fact that I would be alone with Parker added to the amazingness! He laughed at my reaction. "Okay, well I'm gonna go so you can get to work, promise to text you later." he said. I nodded my head in agreement. "Sounds like a plan!" I replied. "See you later." he said. I waved goodbye to him.

I turned my head and found Sasha staring at me with a huge smile on her face. "What?!" I asked while turning away to hang up a pair of jeans, and also to hide the change of pigment in my cheeks. "You two are like an adorable married couple." she laughed. I shook my head, and continued with my work.

XXIV

The Inherited

After my shift was over, I brought my car to it's secure location, and orbed back home to Permia. There, I found Marius and Elsa standing at the top of the staircase by the front entrance. "Hello." I said to them. Elsa hugged me, and Marius bowed his head. I had to get used to their friendliness, as well as all these unnecessary royal gestures. "How was your day princess?" Elsa asked me. I looked around and thought about the day. "Well, first I got attacked by a gladiator demon thing or something, he was very strong, but he was nothing I couldn't handle and then I had a very normal teenage life." I replied. I watched an expression I didn't recognize appear on Marius's face.

"Eve, we have to discuss your wellbeing on earth, we cannot let you roam earth without any protection closely watching over, you have to be careful." Marius said. I huffed. "Okay, I get the whole I need protection thing, but I don't need anyone to watch me closely, it's not like I need someone to help me go potty." I said getting annoyed of his suggestion that I need a *babysitter.* Marius's eyes widened in shock at my comment.

"I'm sorry, but there has to be some line drawn. Ms. Burns is there with me when I'm in school and no one has attacked me when I'm with friends. Only when I'm alone or at work so far..." I trailed off. "Eve, you are still learning, you are learning something new about yourself every day and I don't want you to fall into a trap and get hurt. It is bad enough that you've been going out looking for Scarlett;

you're looking for more than trouble. When you're with your friends it's fine. It's just when you are alone that worries me." Marius said. "Marius, I don't appreciate how it seems like you have little faith in me. Also, I *will* get my hands on Scarlett, for everything that she has done to my family; some sort of justice has to be served. She and her mother destroyed the family, and altered my life, and you think I'm not going to go after her? Boy you're not smart for an elder." I said in a semi serious tone.

Marius looked down at the ground. Yes I was a bit harsh with my reply to him, but it is the truth. Scarlett would get what's coming to her, and it doesn't even matter when or where I just knew it would happen. I could feel it in the pit of my stomach.

"I think you should quit your job." Elsa said. My jaw dropped. "What?! And how will I provide for myself with no income?" I asked her. Elsa smiled. "You are the future queen, you have money. Plenty of it, your parents left you." she said. "Where?" I asked. Curious about this *money* my parents left for me that I didn't know about. "In a safe, in the back of your closet on the right side." Marius answered. I sighed. My closet was huge and I did adjust things around the way I wanted to in there, so I didn't think to look for anything let alone a *safe* in the back of it.

I closed my eyes. "If quitting my job is the right move for me to make then I will do it, and if not, then I won't. Right now, I have things to do, and this discussion is over." I said just before orbing straight up to my room. I wasn't being mean, and if I seemed rude, I wasn't trying to come off that way. It's a leadership bug that has bitten me, being a future queen and being in charge, and not being passive or letting others use me as a doormat was now in effect. I also had to show everyone here including the elders, that I am right for the job. I couldn't let just anyone walk all over me.

Once in my room, I dropped my purse, took off my shoes and went into my closet. I walked all the way to the back right and saw a large vertical floor length mirror. I looked around for the safe before I pulled and lifted up the mirror. Behind it was a large gold safe. I put the mirror to the side, balancing it on my rack of shoes and looked at the safe. It required me to press my pointer finger on a scanner to open it. I placed my finger on it, and watched the scanner light up, and then pop open.

I slowly pulled open the safe door and peered inside. A bright white light came on and as I stepped inside the safe, my mouth dropped. All along the walls of the safe consisted of stacks of money of different countries, states and continents, and in the middle of the safe were papers. I reached for the papers and noticed that it was my mother's will.

It stated that if I were to become Queen of Permia, I owned the land. More importantly for me, I owned this home. This made me feel at peace, knowing that I would always have a home of my own. I kept reading and then came to a stop when my eyes came to the final print at the bottom of the papers. "If I pass away or pass my title of queen, everything would be given to the next family member, *Scarlett Caylan.*" I read in a whisper to myself. I closed my eyes, and breathed deep, trying to control my anger. There is no way in heck that she's getting to rule Permia and turn it into something wicked and dark.

I folded up the papers, before a small picture fell out from the bottom. It was a picture of my mother, my father and I. Not the same picture inside my locket, a different picture. My father really looked like a warrior, he had curly black hair with a strong jawline, and he wore a gladiator style outfit. He had a happy smile plastered on his face. To the right, sitting on his lap was me, a tiny baby, wearing an all gold dress with a purple jeweled headband on. Beside me, was my mother, she was beautiful, wearing a gold long-sleeved sheer dress. She had her long straight hair parted in the middle and it traveled down her back. We all looked like a really happy family. *This* is why I was doing all of this, for my parents.

I wiped the tears that were coming from my eyes, and wished my parents were here. I wished I was just a normal girl with a normal family and upbringing, but I guess being *different* is what makes us *special.* To the side of the safe, I noticed a small purple and silver pen that had a point on one side, and a round crystal on the other side. I lifted it into my hands and it suddenly and randomly unfolded into a large staff.

It was the same staff that my father had been holding in the picture of us. "This must be his." I mumbled to myself. I put the picture and papers back into the safe and locked it up. I carried the staff with me, and laid on my bed, thinking about my parents until I fell asleep.

XXV

The New Year

I woke up at six thirty p.m. and went out on the terrace. I heard voices coming from below so I peered down. I could see that there were caterers carrying trays of food and beverages out from white catering trucks and heading to the backyard. Letting my curiosity get to me I decided that after I took a nice hot bath, I would go downstairs and check out what was going on.

Even though my strength and pain tolerance has way increased, my body still gets a little sore after fighting ugly ghouls, demons and evil creatures. Right now was proof! My back and shoulders were seriously upset, they ached whenever I moved. I sat in the extremely hot bath and daydreamed.

I was relaxed until I thought I heard a thud come from my bedroom. I stood up from the tub and wrapped a towel around myself, and looked out and into my bedroom. "Hello? Is someone there?" I asked. I tried to hear for any thoughts, movements or any sound in general that were close enough to be inside my room. I stayed quiet and listened for a few seconds, but I could hear nothing in very close range.

I walked out to my room, and looked around. There was nothing out of the ordinary. "Okay Eve, now you're getting paranoid for no reason." I said to myself. I went to my closet and picked out a silver sequined tank top with a pair of black jeans to put on with my black combat boots. I looked at my clock and realized that it was almost seven thirty and quickly got dressed.

I had just pulled up my jeans when Bobby's voice entered my brain. "Eve, it's seven fifty four p.m. we have a party that you need to attend, come outside please." I huffed and mentally spoke back to him. "I promised Parker I would spend New Year's with him Bobby." It only took a second for him to enter my brain again. "Just come to dinner, and then you can leave. You will get to him by nine." Bobby said. I sighed and made my way downstairs while texting Parker telling him I have a surprise for him and to go straight to the hotel, I would meet him there.

"Hi!" Destiny said as she came out of her room. "Hey." I smiled at her, putting my phone in my back pocket. "So this is a New Year's party right? Tell me how this entire thing works." I told her as we walked together. "Well, it's actually really fun. First we all talk and have dinner outside. After that we usually just celebrate the coming New Year. We have food, music, games, and the pool. Then we all sit in front of the house and watch fireworks." she said. I looked at her in surprise. I thought it would be some sort of boring gathering, where there are teachings and boring stories.

"Angels can have fun too!" she said. I looked at her in semi shock when I realized I didn't mute my thoughts, and she actually heard them. "Sorry." I smirked. "It's fine, come on then." she smiled while grabbing my hand and leading me outside to the backyard.

When we got outside to the backyard, the first person I recognized was Bobby. He was standing at the bottom of the staircase looking at the almost black purple sky, with the moon and the planets shining brightly. "Hey you, why are you standing at the bottom of the stairs, staring up at the sky like a statue?" Destiny asked him. Bobby turned his head to look at us. "I can't look at the stars?" he asked. "Everyone is around the dinner area, having fun and you're the only one over here. What are you having a *moment?* You need some Bobby time?" She asked with a smile, while making her way down the stairs to him. Bobby laughed. "No, No... I'm good, you two look very pretty." he said. "Thank you, but I already knew that I look gorgeous." Destiny semi joked as she twirled in her white baby doll dress. With a cute little smile, she dashed off and joined the others.

"You gonna come down here or just stay up there?" Bobby asked me. I laughed and shook my head. "So this is New Year's in Permia?" I asked as I walked down the stairs. "Yeah, you really look nice Eve." he smiled. "Thanks, you don't look too bad yourself." I said, finally reaching the bottom of the stairs. "You excited?" he asked as we started walking towards the crowd of angels and the council. "I guess... more curious than excited though. It's so beautifully set up." I beamed at the sight in front of me.

There were Gold lit lanterns and candles used as lighting on the tables, as well as lanterns that were hanging in the air, as support light. The tables were all white, and the chairs were spray painted gold. There was a dance floor in the middle of all the tables. There were also ice sculptures, and a huge projection system that was used for music. It was beautiful.

At the dinner party, I was introduced to other angels, and members of the council that lived in or near the mansion. Some of them were closer to my age, others were guides and elders that were ancient but didn't look over the age of thirty. I had a huge grin on my face after meeting a hilarious twin pair of angels named Jay and Joy, until a familiar face caught my eye. "I'll be right back." I said to them as I made my way over the familiar face.

The tall guy with the angelic face and shaggy brown hair caught me staring at him and immediately smiled. I ran up to him and hugged him tightly. "What the heck are you doing here? How? When? Why didn't you tell me?" I asked in a rush. He laughed. "Well, as for what I'm doing here, it looks like I'm enjoying the New Year's party. And as for why didn't I tell you, it's because I wasn't supposed to." he smiled. I blinked my eyes a couple of times to see if I was dreaming, but *Josh* appeared every time I opened them. I kept blinking as he laughed. "Yes, I'm here, this is real" Josh laughed.

"This is unbelievable, what else don't I know?" I asked more to myself than anyone else. It may seem like I'm handling this "Permian Princess" bull crap really well, on the outside. But on the inside, I was going insane. All of this was mind blowing crazy, too much to adapt to in such a short period of time. "Are you okay?" Josh asked. "Yes, I just can't believe you're an angel, wait you are an angel right?!" I asked. Josh laughed.

"Yes he is, and I allowed him into your world, to look after you, he is one of your earth guides. He's been watching you since you first became friends." Marius said. "That was in the seventh grade!" I almost screeched. "Hello father." Josh greeted Marius. "Now I felt like I really needed to sit down." I groaned. Marius laughed at my wide eyed expression. "Let's get this party started before you pass out, shall we then." Marius suggested. I nodded my head yes unable to speak.

Knowing that Josh was now part of this new experience I was going through, made me feel better. Being around a familiar face takes the edge off of new situations and being in new environments. Now, I had someone on earth that I could talk to about all of this. Not that I didn't talk to Ms. Burns, but it's different when you have someone your own age, and someone you are totally comfortable with to converse with.

I didn't have to keep my entire life a secret or feel like I was hiding all the time while at school anymore. I was so happy finding out that Josh is an angel that I could have made a fool of myself and did the happy dance right there in front of everyone.

We walked to our assigned tables and Josh pulled out a chair for me, which was located in the center of the main table. Bobby and Destiny sat to the left of me, and Josh and Chaska sat to my right. I stayed quiet as I watched Marius move to the right head of the table.

"Welcome all. This is a celebration of the incoming New Year, and the celebration of a new era, with a returning member of our family. Our future queen, the Archangel Princess, daughter of the beautiful and late Emirah Caylan, I give you Eve Caylan. May our world be bright, at peace and filled with a new force of powerful love, good and light, cheers." he said holding up his gold painted glass. Others followed his lead, and held up there glasses before drinking.

I looked down into my cup and looked at the red liquid. "Oh God." I whispered to myself. I side eyed josh as I heard him chuckle at my reaction. I blew out some air before bringing the cup to my lips and taking a small sip. I was surprised and relieved to find out that I was drinking food colored cider and not some type of weird Permian concoction. I liked that Marius called me by my *rightful* name. *Eve Caylan*. I even loved how it sounded together. Way better than *Eve Keller* in my opinion.

I sat my cup down and looked behind me and into the woods. The irritating feeling of *being watched* appeared…again and goose bumps appeared all over my body. "Guys, how come I've been feeling like I've been being watched? It's kind of freaking me out in a weird scary way." I asked my angel friends. Bobby turned to look at me. "What do you mean." he asked. I thought about how I could explain myself better before responding.

"I literally feel like someone is watching me. It's like someone's behind me, watching me right now. I need eyes in the back of my head to see who the creep is." I said. "Maybe you're just being paranoid. Being new here in Permia and everything probably has you a bit mind freaked." Chaska said. "Well, you are future queen, maybe someone is watching you…When did you start feeling like this?" Josh asked. "I don't think someone would just watch her, and *not* attack or acknowledge her." Eli replied before I answered Josh. "I guess ever since I changed I've felt this way. Or it could have started right after Scarlett first attacked me, I'm not sure of accuracy." I said while standing up.

"Where are you going?" Destiny asked. I looked back at her. "Into the woods, don't worry I won't go too far, I just need to convince myself that no one is actually there, that this feeling is all in my mind." I said. No one except Bobby looked satisfied with my reply. "We will be listening out for your thoughts, just to make sure you are alright." Bobby smirked. "I'm sure I will be fine, got the daggers in my boots." I smiled back. I turned my back to them and walked into the woods.

Honestly if the wind wasn't blowing it wouldn't have seemed so scary. I was captivated by the dark purple from the sky, and how the grass and tree tops lit a neon blue green color. There were no animal sounds, just leaves rustling and the party behind me. I walked further, deeper into the forest and came head to head with a little stream. I stopped to observe it, until I felt like I had been being watched again. "Who's there? Hello?" I called out. Nothing, not a single sound except the sound of trees blowing in the wind responded to me. I decided to head back to the party and upon heading back, I heard movement and felt a breeze on the back of my neck.

This wasn't a normal breeze feeling; it felt someone was breathing on me. I shivered at the feeling of the warm air, and turned around, and faced no one. No one but trees, brushes and the little stream. I silently walked back to the party with my arms folded across my chest. "Did you find anything?" Chaska asked. "Nope just me, some creepy wind blowing thing and a cute little stream." I replied. Bobby smirked. "Yeah, that's Pia's stream. It's healing waters, and it's quite a romantic setting if you are with the right someone." he smiled and looked at Destiny, who blushed in return.

I looked at both of them and smiled at their little flirtatiousness before wondering if it was allowed, were angels allowed to love each other? Or did marriage and relationships only not exist in the realms above us? "Ahem, thank you all for joining in the dinner portion of our celebration. I hope you all have enjoyed your evening as much as I have, thank you all for attending, and now let the fun begin." Marius announced. We all clapped and whistled while the lights dimmed lower and the projector began to glow and waves started to appear on the screen.

Instrumental background music began to play, and I bobbed my head to the bass. Tables of "people" continued to converse in casual conversation. As eaten food was taken away on trays and new trays filled with deserts replaced them. "I love this part of the party, food, music and fireworks!" Eli clapped. "And a heated pool to enjoy with friends." Destiny added. "So um yeah, what we are doing still sitting down like losers we should be having fun, let's go!" Chaska laughed. The five of us along with Josh, Joy and Jay first headed to the desert table and then walked to the pool. "I dare all of you to jump in the pool!" Eli shouted. "We don't have bathing suits on fool." Chaska looked at him confused. "Well, I will do it, if Bobby does it." Destiny smiled. "And I will do it if Eve does it." Chaska added. "Okay, we all have to do it together. Deal?" I asked. Everyone agreed. I took my phone out of my pocket and laid it on the concrete floor next to the pool. We then grabbed each other's hands. "On the count of three!" I said looking to my left and right. "One, two, three!" I shouted before we all jumped in.

XXVI

Forgetting Parker

The fun really started after we all jumped in the pool. We had glow sticks, and waved them around as we danced and laughed. We filled the hours with swimming, telling jokes, dancing, eating and laughing and honestly, it was one of the best nights of my life. I sat on the ledge by the front of the pool and watched my friends have fun in the pool, dancing and just being happy. I felt at peace, I felt like I could *finally* belong somewhere, even though this life is crazy, and definitely not ordinary, it's amazing. And besides, it seems better to be unique, what's the fun in being ordinary?

"Hey, you good?" Josh asked me while sitting down beside me. "Yeah, just watching all the craziness. I never would have thought that angels could have fun like this!" I confessed. "Well obviously, there are no drinks, except for the tiny glass of wine the elders had with dinner. There isn't anything provocative going on, it's all harmless fun. And it's not like we behave this way every day." Josh said. I nodded at him, indicating that I was listening.

"We were placed here to create peace, and bring positivity and clarity to others and the world. To steer them in the right direction. However, we also have to find ourselves in this world, and resist temptation. We all have reason for being, and we all have missions in our predestined life. Even though you are half good and kind of somewhat half bad as we all are, you were created to be a leader. To unite everyone on Permia, and to help innocent people. You were also made to destroy evil, and help Permia maintain peace. Yeah you will have bumps along the way, but that's all part of it." he continued. "Like this Scarlett issue, honestly Josh, I want to rip her to shreds. Finding out about what really happened to my parents, it all makes me confused. Confused about what I should, what I could and can't do about it. I have to balance handling that with school, work, being here, and getting crowned." I said almost angry. "Yeah, it's a lot to take in, just know I'm here if you need someone to talk to or something." Josh said. I smiled at him. "Thanks Josh." I replied with a slight smile.

"Hey, why are you two just sitting here looking so serious? This is supposed to be a New Year's Eve party, come on! We have five minutes before the fireworks start." Chaska said in a giddy voice. Josh and I stood up, and we made our way to the front of the house. We sat at the top of the large staircase with the rest of the angels.

Bobby was being very tentative to Destiny, which made me wonder if they were into each other. That made me question, how would they even work out in a relationship, since angels can't behave in the sort of way you're supposed to in a relationship. *Are they even allowed to hold hands?* I asked myself. I would have to ask Bobby about this later. My thoughts were interrupted when Joy started speaking.

"Okay guys, twenty seconds until the New Year begins!" she cheered. I looked into the field, and noticed that tons of Permian's were sitting in the field, waiting for the firework show, and the New Year to arrive. Something inside me felt wrong, like I wasn't supposed to be here. But I brushed the feeling off when everyone had begun counting. "Seven, Six, five, four, three, two, one... Happy New Year!!" everyone shouted, Katy Perry's *"firework"* started playing as a bunch of fireworks began to light up the plum purple sky.

It was amazing to see the purple sky, the moon, the planets, the glowing grass and tree tops, blend with the fireworks. It was also amazing to see how happy people were for the start of the New Year. I could tell this year meant a lot to the Permian's. This year was the beginning of a new life for everyone. The dawning of a new era. They would crown a new queen, and this world would change. The feeling of love and happiness was in the air, it made me notice how much I wish I could have had someone I really cared for, to enjoy this moment with, and that's when it hit me like a ton of bricks.

"Oh my gosh! I forgot about Parker!" I shouted. Josh looked at me confused. "What?" he asked. "I had plans with Parker, and I totally forgot, and he's going to be so upset...I'm such a bad girlfriend." I said sadly as I covered my face with my hands. Josh frowned at me. "You know it's going to be impossible to date him, he's a human." he said. I shrugged my shoulders. "What's wrong with dating a human?" I asked him. "It's just never happened before, we are different species, and how can an immortal be with a mortal?" he asked. I didn't know the answer to that question, so I kept quiet.

"You aren't a bad girlfriend; you've just been busy with your new life." Bobby said coming over to hug me. "Yeah...well, I'm gonna call him or something." I said more to myself than anyone else. "Well, there's really no point in getting to him now, it's kind of late now." Destiny said. I rolled my eyes. "Better late than never." I murmured before orbing off to the backyard.

Once in the backyard, I picked up my phone from where I left it on the concrete floor by the pool and then orbed to my bedroom and changed my clothes, choosing to put on blue skinny jeans and gold off the shoulder sweater, followed by my black peat coat and black gloves and beanie. I grabbed my phone and saw that Parker texted me hours ago immediately after I first texted him telling I had a surprise for him. He texted me that we were to be staying at the "Times square hotel" in Times square, which had the best view of the ball being dropped. And we would be staying in room eleven twenty-three. I sighed out of sorrow and pictured the familiar hotel before I orbed to the hotel in the city.

XXVII

New York

After getting to the city, I became really nervous as I walked to the hotel room door. Once at the door, I hesitated before knocking on it. My senses were shouting at me telling me that something wasn't right. I had an overall bad feeling. I took a deep breath and knocked on the door. "Who is it?" Parker asked right as he opened the door. I stayed silent. "Eve, what are you doing here?" he slurred. My eyes widened. "Parker are you drunk?" I asked already knowing the answer. The smell coming off of him was enough to tell me, he was trashed. And with my new senses, the alcohol smell radiating from him was stronger than ever. It took all I had not vomit.

I pushed Parker out of the way and walked into the hotel room. "I thought you weren't coming." he slurred. "Okay, so since you *thought* I wasn't coming, you decided to drink yourself to this extent?" I asked looking around the hotel room. I found a beautiful king size bed, and flat screen television.

Through huge windows, you could see the lights of the city. It really was a great room and I felt so bad that I wanted to cry, because I had forgot and ruined it. On the table I found a bouquet of roses, which aren't my favorite flowers because every girl like's roses. I like exotic colored flowers, and ones that don't smell like roses. I also found Parker's keys, his jacket, sushi takeout food and three huge bottle of alcohol, one and a half being empty. My sadness was replaced with a short lived anger. I wanted to yell at parker for doing this to himself. But I knew I couldn't. If the shoes were on the opposite feet, I know for certain I would be upset, and want to erase the lonely start of the New Year too. But I don't think I would do it by drinking a bottle and a half of Captain Morgan.

I looked at him with sad eyes. "I thought you weren't coming." he repeated, standing away from me, half slouched. I could tell that he wasn't really *here*. "sorry, it was hard for me to get here, and I know it's my fault, I ruined our night together and I am truly sorry Parker, I really am. But you didn't have to drink yourself like this." I said to him in a low voice. Parker huffed. "Why are you here? You never have time for me anymore...go away!" he slurred. I walked over to parker and hugged him, even though he wasn't hugging me back, I continued to hold on to him. "I'm sorry, I promise things will go back to how they were, my life has just been complicated since my birthday." I admitted.

Parker pulled away and sat down on the floor. He covered his face with his hands. He looked like he could both cry and pass out at any time. Like his body was going to stop functioning at any moment, it honestly scared me. "Okay, let's get you into bed; you need to sleep this off." I said to him, while picking him up from off the ground. He literally weighed almost nothing to me, and if I wanted to, I could take Parker's entire body into my hands, and lay him in the bed, but I didn't know how out of it Parker was, and I didn't want to take a chance on freaking him out with my super strength. While trying to get him to the bed, he didn't even fight me off; and my upsetting him drove my spirit down.

After actually getting him *in* the bed, I cleaned up the room, poured all the alcohol down the drain and then checked out the view from the window. It was a perfect view to see the ball drop. My head started pounding, and even though I wasn't tired, I decided to nap, hoping that when I woke up, Parker and I could talk like the young adults we are. I got on the left side of Parker, and pulled the Duvet over my head and went to sleep.

Parker was calling me late at night and for some reason I didn't answer the phone. He got upset, and drove to my house, only for my adoptive dad to tell him I had moved away, and that he didn't know where. Frustrated, Parker drove home, and punched the wall closest to the door and fractured his hand. Darkness filled my vision but shortly came to an end when I saw Parker asleep in his bed. I looked at the clock, and read the time being six minutes past three a.m. The window was open and the moon was shining through. I walked over to his bed...and then...

XXVIII

The Talk

I woke up. "I hate dreams that don't continue." I whispered to myself while sitting up. This seemed more like a dream rather than a premonition. I didn't feel shaky, scared, or like I was really there. But, anything can happen, and the dream was unfinished, so who's to say that it's not an actual premonition.

My thoughts about if my dream had been a premonition or a dream, were interrupted by a thought that appeared out of nowhere. *Was my dream telling me that I should tell Parker that I moved away before something bad happens?* Well, that's what I decided it meant. I looked at the clock and read six thirty one a.m. I stayed awake from then until eight a.m., when Parker was only half asleep. I decided now was the time to tell him.

"Babe, I don't live at home anymore." I whispered. Parker opened his eyes, but still rested his head on his pillow. "What?" he asked confused. "I don't live at home anymore." I repeated. He flipped over from his side, to his back, and placed his hands behind his head, and rested it on them. "Where do you live?" he asked amused. I took a huge breath before answering. "I met some of my *real* family. They live a couple hours away." I lied while giving him water and two Advil's that I had in my clutch. I had to lie, if I had to tell him the truth, what would I say, *well Parker, I actually live in another dimension, none of us are completely human, I have ugly demon things that come after me, oh and I am a future queen!* I don't think Parker would be able to handle that nicely or take it seriously.

Weather I liked it or not, the more I get into my life in Permia, the more Parker and I didn't have anything in common, there wasn't much to talk about anymore. It seemed like I was just using him to have some sort of comfort, or connection to Earth. But being in Permia, I feel more myself than ever, I don't have to hide anything in Permia. There, I feel somewhat free.

"When did you move?" he asked me, breaking me out of my thoughts. "A short while after my birthday, about two days after. Which I guess is why I've been acting *weird* lately, and I'm sorry for that." I said. "It's okay, why didn't you tell me?" Parker asked. I looked down at my toes before looking into his eyes. "Well, we haven't been in school, so I've been getting to know my family. I wanted to do it at the right time, and Mena and Lance don't know about it, and this is something that I don't want them to ruin. Not that it matters now because I *am* eighteen." I replied.

"I understand." Parker said. I had to leave out the major parts of my story otherwise, I knew Parker would start to ask more questions, and I couldn't reveal my true self to him. Not yet anyway. "Baby, were you here with me all last night, as in for the New Year?" He asked with a giant smile on his face. I looked at him. "You don't remember?" I asked. Parker shook his head no. I decided that I didn't want to dim his happiness and even though it is wrong to lie to your boyfriend or girlfriend, some situations have purpose to tell small white lies.

"Yes I was. And you drank an entire bottle and a half of Captain Morgan." I said pointing to the garbage with the bottles in it. "Oh God, and that's why my head is pounding." Parker said as he got up and swallowed both Advil's.

For the next two hours Parker and I cuddled, watched a movie and ordered room service as we talked and laughed. I missed moments like these between the two of us. It felt like old times. After those two hours Parker changed his clothes and we both freshened up before we got into his car and drove the hour and fifteen minutes from Manhattan to his house in South Brunswick.

While on the journey I texted Ms. Burns and asked if she could pick me up from Parker's house, and I was thankful when she said *yes*. The only problem with lying is that you have to be able to keep up with them. It's easy to get caught up in your own web of lies.

I stayed quiet as I made my way up to Parker's room after he let us inside his house. "Everything good?" he asked me. I smiled up at him. "Yeah, I do have to get home soon though; my new and real family isn't used to me sneaking out late at night to surprise my boyfriend." I smiled. Even though I did have to get home, I was really feeling the effects of lying to Parker. Guilt filled my blood, and left a sour taste in my mouth. Parker laughed.

"How naughty of you to do that?" he said before taking me into his arms and kissing me firmly. I pulled away from him. "I feel bad that I have to leave you like this." I confessed. He hugged me. "It's okay, I'm happy you spent New Year's with me, even if I can't remember it." he said with a forced smile. I looked at him and rolled my eyes. "Don't ever get like that again, you scared me." I said as I moved away from him and put on my coat. "I promise, I will spend so much more time with you, I just have to balance everything out with my family and the distance." I continued.

Parker just sat on the bed staring at me. I walked over to him and kissed his cheek. "Keep your phone on." I said to him. "I will, I love you." Parker said. "I love you too." I replied. I felt like crap. What kind of girlfriend was I? I had been somewhat ignoring Parker, ignoring his texts and calls. I've also been lying to him, and *then* had the guts to say that I loved him?!

I truly want to make it work, make it better, make us better, but it was obvious our relationship wasn't going to go so smoothly anymore. My phone started vibrating and that's when I looked at my phone and saw that Ms. Burns had left me a text message.

"I'm here, parked in the front."

I sighed and looked up at Parker. "I have to go, my aunt's here." I internally cringed at yet another white lie that I had now told him. I could see a sad flicker in his eyes, but he tried to mask it with his perfect pearly white smile. "I'm sorry, I promise to find the balance babe." I said hugging him tightly.

It felt good because he actually hugged me back, and even though his strength wasn't bone crushing or could even be possibly considered *manly* with my new powers, it still felt good. It felt good to be with someone that cares for me and proves it over and over again. "I'll see you later." I said kissing him and starting off towards his door. "See you later." He waved. I blinked my eyes once, opened his bedroom door, walked down the stairs and went out the door.

I opened the door to Ms. Burns car and slid in. "My, you look sad. What's wrong?" She asked. "Just afraid Parker and I will be over soon, life is getting complicated." I replied. "It will get better, right now you are just settling in, your new to all of this, everything will be fine in time." she smiled. I gave her a little smirk in response. "Thank you for saying that." With that, Ms. Burns drove the five minutes to her house, and I orbed myself to my bedroom. I went straight to the bathroom and took a bath. I needed to relax and think. Think about how I was going to balance my life on Earth *and* on Permia.

After twenty minutes, and not coming up with a single solution for my problem I actually felt a little bit refreshed and charged. I felt less stressed, and more focused and even a bit angry. Angry because my life was altering in front of my eyes, and there wasn't a thing I could do about it. I got dressed in a forest green tank top and black sweat pants; I needed to have a judo session with Bobby.

"You ready to get your butt handed to you?" he asked coming into my room with a smirk on his face. "Yeah, we'll see whose butt is handed to whom." I chuckled. I watched Bobby's face expression go from angelic, to serious in a spilt second. "Let's work." he said leading the way to the back yard.

XXIX

Reoccurring Dream

That Friday January third, school finally restarted after winter break. That was the day I decided to quit my job at the mall. I loved that job, but I had to give something up in order for me to function. Training, school, orbing from Earth to Permia and reverse, watching my back for danger, saving the innocent, working, focusing on Scarlett, and trying to devote some time to Parker, was killing me.

"Hey!" Josh said running up to me in the gym. He looked at me in my blue jeans and white shirt as I sat on the floor "not participating today?" he asked. I shook my head no. "I am so beat, and it's crazy because now that I'm immortal, I only need four hours of sleep, and usually with the four hours and coffee, I feel like road runner, but now, I'm just tired, really tired." I confessed. "Well what's got you so stressed? Angels aren't supposed to get stressed out, and we are not usually tired, what's wrong?" he asked while sitting down next to me.

I shrugged my shoulders. "I guess it's because I've been training really hard, and I've got a feeling something is going to happen soon. I've been hunting for Scarlett, saving the innocent, and even going out to look for demons to practice on, but no one has attacked me since that gladiator I found by my job. It's too quiet; it's like the quiet before the storm." I said to Josh. "Eve, you're not playing? What's the matter? Are you sick?" my gym teacher asked. I looked at her. "I feel so stressed and tired out, I'm afraid that if I play I might pass out, or fall asleep in the middle of class." I replied to her. She nodded in understanding and continued to take her attendance. "Okay, my neck is hurting; I'm lying on your lap." I said smiling at Josh, while picking my head up from off the gym floor, and resting it on his lap. "Anything for the future queen." he chuckled.

"Ugh, don't remind me, and my crowning is coming rather quickly, this is too much to take in already, I can't imagine how I'm gonna feel once I am crowned." I said. Josh laughed. "You will adapt, I promise, it won't be as bad as it seems." he said. I wanted to believe Josh, but that feeling in the pit of my stomach wouldn't let me. It was telling me that it wouldn't get better, it will only get worse. Within a few minutes, my eyes were closed. I dreamed of myself sitting in the field in front of my house in Permia. I was at peace.

I was peacefully dreaming until Josh started talking. I didn't want to get up; I groaned and asked for five more minutes. "Parker and the two followers are coming over here." he said. I opened my eyes, to see Parker leading Loren, and David over to Josh and I. "Wow, now don't they look really hardcore, and gangster!" I said sarcastically, causing Josh to burst out with laughter. Parker gestured for my hand, which I gave him, and he helped me get up from the floor, he gave me a hug, and then glared at Josh, who wasn't paying the least bit of attention to us.

"What's up guys?" I asked. "Nothing much, what's up with you girl?" Loren asked. "Nothing new, just really tired." I replied while rubbing my right eye. There was a little awkward silence before David decided to speak. "Are you messing around with Josh?" he asked. My eyes widened. "What?" I asked. "Do you like Josh?" he asked again. I cluelessly looked at David. "Not at all." I replied and looked towards Josh, who looked just as confused as I did. "Are you sure? You're looking really cozy on his lap." David replied. I chuckled at David's stupidity. "We've all known each other for years David, and you know I'm not into anyone but Parker. I'm tired, and I'm just lying on my friend's lap, like I do to all my friends." I said. David crossed his arms. "You don't do that to me." he replied. I smirked. "That's because that area of your body can't handle that much pressure. I don't want to end up with a lawsuit on my hands for breaking your tiny bones." I said sarcastically. Everyone around us, who had been listening to our conversation, laughed. Truth was, yeah I was being sarcastic, but I was also being serious. With my training, being immortal, and my powers... I'm sure if I were to lay on him I would feel like I'm made out of a ton of bricks.

"Well, I wanted to know if you would like to get some food after class, I'm willing to skip fourth today." Parker told me. While Parker was asking me to go out, I was thinking about how tired I was, and I actually didn't want to eat. All I wanted to do was sleep, but I had word vomit and heard myself say. "Yeah, that would be nice." I mentally groaned as one of the male gym teachers interrupted my train of thought, and was shouting at kids to start walking. "See you later." Parker said as he kissed my cheek. I gave Parker a little smile, and then went back to lying down on Josh's lap.

I dreamed of a guy and I. It was the same guy I saw in the dream I had of him Bobby and I fighting those ghouls. He was handsome, with dark hair, and pretty brown eyes. We were walking down an eerie path downtown in Permia. We were staring into each other's eyes, and we were just happy. His arm snaked across my waist, and we orbed on top of Immortal University. We looked out at the view of the world that was technically owned by me, the world that I was the queen of. But we didn't talk about me being a queen; we didn't talk about Scarlett either. We only talked about each other. We were at peace. The dark purple sky surrounded us, and we just felt so free and comfortable with each other. We got away from it all, we got away from all the drama, and it was now just him and I.

My peaceful dream was interrupted by the sound of a bell, signaling the end of class. My eyes opened and I popped my head up, looking at my phone for the time. "Yeah, you slept for the entire class. It's good that you got some sleep though." Josh said to me. I smiled up at him. "Thank you for letting me sleep on you." I chuckled. Josh shook his head and laughed. "No problem, you needed to sleep. I better go, don't want to be late for class, see you at home." Josh said as he started walking away. I watched him walk away before texting Parker, and telling him that I would wait for him inside my car.

After walking to my car in silence and tiredness, I sat in the driver's seat and nodded off while waiting for Parker. I hoped to continue dreaming about the hot guy and me, but I didn't. Instead I dreamed that dream again. The one about being in Parker's bedroom.

I walked into Parker's room, and looked at his clock, which read six minutes after three a.m. Parker was sleeping and his room was lit by the moon that was shining through his open window. In my gut, I felt that something wasn't right. I walked over to Parker's bed and...

My dream was interrupted by Parker knocking on the car window. "Sheesh! You scared me!" I yelled while unlocking the door. "Wow you really are tired, and you're starting to look it. You're getting deep dark circles around your eyes. You're looking rather raccoonish." Parker smirked. I quickly looked into the mirror and groaned at the sight of my face. "Well, thank you that's the best compliment I've ever received from you." I said sarcastically. I scooted over to the passenger side of my car so that Parker could drive; I figured it would be better if he drove. If I drove, there would be a slight chance of a car accident.

"So, where are we eating?" I asked him. I kind of already knew the answer before he even spoke. I shouldn't have even asked. Parker is always indecisive when it comes to where we are going to eat. "Where ever your car takes me." Parker smiled. I chuckled. "Indecisive." I whispered. "So are you." He stated. I kept quiet because he was right, I am indecisive. "Why are you so tired, I've never seen you like this?" he asked. It was frustrating talking to Parker about *me* now, because I couldn't be honest with him. Practically everything I've been recently telling him has been a lie, or some twisted up truth.

"School." I lied. School was easy; I knew all the answers to everything now. Instead of my schoolwork being hard like it used to be, it now felt more like preschool work to me. "Family." I continued. That wasn't so much a lie, but the actual definition of *what* family, kind of was. Parker would probably be thinking I was referring to my adoptive parents and siblings, when I wasn't. I was talking about my *real* family, my angel and immortal family. "Regular adult stuff and I also quit my job." I added. Regular, was anything but me now, so that was a lie. And I did quit my job, I just had to. I couldn't focus on being a future queen, going to normal mortal school, train for a battle with

Scarlett, have a boyfriend, worry about Parker, manage to cover everything up etc. something's had to give. I could barely get the full four hours of sleep that I was required to get.

"What?" I asked at Parker who was just staring at me. "Why'd you quit your job?" he asked. "I'm tired, and it seems like life is just getting harder and harder, I had to let something go." I confessed to him. Parker took his right hand off the steering wheel and intertwined our hands together. "I understand, and I'm always here for you Eve." he smiled. I smiled back up at him. "I keep having these weird dreams about you." I said looking out the window. "What do you mean *weird?*" Parker asked, trying to keep his eyes on the road and look at me at the same time. I sighed. "It's like, I'm watching you sleep at three in the morning, and the window is open, and the moon is shining... it sounds peaceful, but it actually is kind of creepy and eerie." I muttered. He laughed.

"Aw, you're a creeper!" he laughed and pinched my cheek. "Stop it! where are we going?" I asked playfully as I hit him on the chest. Parker smiled in amusement before he shortly pulled into the parking lot of a familiar Italian restaurant. He turned the engine off, and got out of the car. I got out of the car and Parker reached for my left hand and we started walking inside.

On the way to walking inside the restaurant, I felt something hard hit my back. I turned my head to see a powder white, blonde haired little girl standing about fifty feet away from us by the dumpster. I would have thought she was a regular girl, except for the fact that she had burning red eyes that were burning a hole into me. Parker was now a few paces ahead of me, and now entering the restaurant. I thought of another little lie I could tell him so I could go and handle *my* business. Parker held the door for me and I ran up to him while pretending to look for something. "Hey, I forgot my phone, get a table and I will find you." I said kissing his cheek. Before he could respond, I was outside the restaurant, pretending to walk to Parker's car.

"You know, I really don't appreciate you ugly, annoying evil roaches coming here to Earth, trying to attack me. I think I should start carrying some raid with me." I said walking towards the little girl. The little girl ran towards me, and tried to leap frog onto me, but

I blocked her with my favorite move, a chick kick to the head.

I definitely don't condone hitting kids, but she was asking for it. I figured that Scarlett probably thought that she would have a better chance at getting me killed here on earth because it would catch me off guard, which would be smart if I wasn't overly focused. The blonde haired girl and I exchanged blows to the face and upper body. I was surprised that this little girl was really getting some good hits off of me. However, it all came down to me putting her in a neck lock. A neck lock that Bobby had taught me, and I had begun to use quite a lot.

I sat on her back, and pulled her arms towards me. I placed my left leg under her chin to push her head towards me, and used my right leg for balance. I wasn't planning on killing the little girl, I don't think I have the heart to do that, but I did want her to feel pain. Enough pain to tell me who she was. "Tell me who the heck you are before I hurt you so bad, that when you start screaming, everyone in *Fermia* will be able to here you from down here!" I growled and tightened my hold on the little girl, who then started screaming. "Okay, alright... I'm Roxanna!" the girl cried out. I rolled my eyes. "Okay, and who sent you here?" I asked her still holding her. I already knew the answer, but I wanted her to tell me herself. "Why would I tell you that?" the girl panted. I bent her body even more. "Because you don't want me to break your body in half that's why!" I yelled at her. She cried out, but I didn't give in. "I was sent by Scarlett, she wanted me to kill you obviously." she whispered. I snorted.

"Well I've got a message for you to give to Scarlett, tell her to stop being a coward, and to bring it to me herself! Stop sending others to do her dirty work, especially since they can't get the job done." I said through gritted teeth, before letting Roxanna go. I stood up and patted my clothes clean, and started walking back to the restaurant. I turned back around and looked at the little girl who was on the ground rubbing her sore body. "Oh, and if you ever throw a rock at my back again, I will rip your head off, got it?!" I said more in a statement than a question. Roxanna glared at me.

"This isn't over Eve, it's not over until Scarlett says its over!" she said. I cocked my head to the right. "Well it's over for you, and it will soon be over for Scarlett too. Neither of you are even in my league, as a matter of fact, you are so far down the totem pole that you shouldn't even be talking to me my dear." I smirked, and started walking again. I heard the little girl growl. "Watch your every corner." she said. I chuckled. "Thanks for your useless advice." I said as I finally walked inside the restaurant. I only let her go because I really wanted her to deliver my message to Scarlett. Usually, I never let my opponent leave freely.

I found Parker sitting at a table all the way to the left. "Well, was it a hunt looking for your phone?" he smiled. "Ha-ha, yeah a treasure hunt." I said taking my coat off, and sitting down. "So, how long you have been dreaming about me... in my bed?" Parker asked. I laughed at his question and his intention to bring it to a sexual level. "Don't be such a guy; the dream had nothing to do with sex." He raised his eyebrows. "I didn't imply that, you did on your own." he smirked. I narrowed my eyes at him. "Yeah, okay, you're a guy; I know how all of you think." I said. But anyway, as for the dream, I've had it twice. But I can never get to the end of the dream, I always get woken up." I said sounding frustrated.

I was frustrated in trying to figure out what the dream meant. Before, my dreams would usually mean nothing, but now, most of my dreams are premonitions, which meant, I had to figure it out before it became reality. I couldn't *not* worry about it. Parker gasped. "Aw, so you were dreaming about me in your little nap today in the car, that's cute." He cooed, reaching his hand over to hold mine.

I looked at our hands. I wasn't sure how I felt anymore. To me, touching someone's hand can tell you a lot. If you like someone and you touch their hand, you feel a surge of something like electric...something that makes you get goose bumps, and I wasn't feeling that with Parker anymore, I was feeling something else. I was feeling hollow.

"I'm glad we are spending more time together, after your birthday, I didn't know what to think about us anymore. I felt I was going to lose you, and I can't lose you." He said sadly. I sighed. I hated lying and hurting his feelings, but these things had to happen because of my new life. I used to be so innocent, and now I'm lying, fighting, angrier than ever, and worse than anything, I'm actually a killer. I'm doing things I never imagined I would.

"Sorry about that, there's just been a lot of new changes in my life since I turned eighteen. I never mean to do anything to upset you." I whispered. I desperately wanted to change the subject; I didn't want to talk about the changes I had made, or the pain I caused Parker since I turned eighteen. I couldn't explain anything in great details to Parker.

"So, I'm happy we have five months until graduation." I smiled. Parker frowned. "I'm not...because things might change between you and I." he confessed. I was tired of the seriousness, but decided to go with his flow. "Why would you think that?" I asked. Parker looked down at our hands. "Well, you're going to away for college after we graduate right?" her asked. "I'm not sure... maybe... I don't know what I'm gonna end up doing with my life." I told Parker. I acted like I was confused, but I really wasn't. Obviously I had some idea of what was going to happen with my life, I was planning on moving to Permia for good after school ended. Life would be simpler for me if I lived there full time, I could be myself, and I wouldn't have to run back and forth from Earth to Permia, and in reverse. What I didn't know is, if Parker would be part of my life.

"Did you figure out what you are going to do?" I curiously asked him. Parker put his hands behind his head, and rested his head on them. "Take a year off, and see the world, and if nothing extraordinary happens in that year, I guess go to college." He answered. "Sounds like a good plan." I smirked.

Within a half an hour, we finished lunch and I drove Parker back to school so he could pick up his car. "Well, I had fun." I said putting the car in park. Parker got out the car, and rushed over to my side. He opened the door, unbuckled my seatbelt and pulled me out. He engulfed me in a tight hug. "You can't leave without giving me a real goodbye, and I had fun too." He said hugging me. I wrapped my arms around his waist and hugged him back. My senses taking in his Dior cologne.

"I'm happy your mine." he said just before he kissed me on the cheek. "I gotta go." I whispered, while pulling away from him. "See you later." he said while lightly kissing me on the lips. I got no major feeling from the kiss Parker had given me. This sudden hollowness towards him really made my heart hurt. It's like a dagger to the heart. I wanted to love him, I wanted him to be mine, but it's hard to believe in something you want if you have no emotion to push you to get it. It's like you wanting a chocolate bar, but you can't smell chocolate. You can eat it and taste it, but without all of your senses working, it's just not satisfying.

    I waved goodbye to Parker and watched him leave out of the school parking lot. I got in my car, drove to the right, and parked my car across the street at Ms. Burns's house. As soon as I made sure no one was watching me, I orbed myself to the front door of the Caylan mansion.

XXX

Scarlett's Box

With my sensitive hearing, I could hear everyone talking, so I headed into the kitchen where Marius was. I watched him pace around the kitchen with a book in his hands, muttering. "Hi Marius!" I greeted. He smiled at me. I hesitated before telling him my thoughts. "It's been too quiet when dealing with Scarlett head on and I bet something is gonna happen soon. I can feel it. I'm not sure when it's going to happen, but we all need to be ready. I got attacked today by a little girl." I said. Marius looked up at me. I could see worry in his eyes. "Don't worry, she was nothing that I couldn't handle, I just wanted to let you know." I said.

"Well, I'm glad you're okay, obviously you handled that well. I will have everyone to assist you with extra training. We need you sharp and prepared for anything." Marius said. I nodded my head in agreement. "I have to kick it up a bit on training with Bobby and Eli, hopefully their not busy." I said before heading to my room. I really wanted to sleep, but I knew I had a job to do. So for two hours I decided to practice hard. I needed to be in the best shape I could be for when that time came. The time for Scarlett and I to go toe to toe.

By the time I finished practicing, I felt like I had got hit by a bus. I was so sore that the hot bath I got into after practice, didn't even help my muscles relax. Alone in my room, I realized that this was the moment I had been waiting for all day, the time for me to get some sleep. I nodded off peacefully, but shortly began dreaming. Dreaming the same dream I'd been dreaming about. The one about Parker.

Parker was asleep, and the moon was shining through the open window. The clock on his dresser said six minutes after three a.m., and I got that eerie feeling once again. Parker was sleeping peacefully, and I watched him sleep. Shortly, a silver red sparkle appeared in his room and none other than Scarlett appeared. Even though this was a dream I still couldn't believe my eyes. I watched Scarlett look through Parker's clothes, photos and other items in his room.

A red smoke appeared almost next to Scarlett, and a large bald headed warlock appeared. "What took you so long?" she whispered to the warlock. "I'm here aren't I?!" he asked sounding annoyed. The warlock had a small black box in his hand that Scarlett ripped from him. Scarlett traced the pattern design on the box with her pointer finger before opening it. In her hands she took out a large red, brown spider. The warlock took the box away from Scarlett, and then along with me, watched Scarlett. Scarlett smiled, and then began humming gently. She continued to hum before she laid the spider down on Parker's stomach and started to speak.

> Fill his heart with fire and rage
> For the one I despise and hate
> One painful bite to the chest
> Brings their love a tragic death

I jumped up when I realized that those words weren't just any *words* being spoken by Scarlett. That was a cursed spell, a wicked spell produced by Scarlett. "No!!" I screamed and tried to remove the spider away from Parker, but I couldn't. This was a dream. I watched the spider crawl up to Parker's chest and Parker yelped and woke up. He reached up and turned the light on, but by that time the light actually came on and he looked around, Scarlett, the warlock and the spider were already gone. I watched Parker stand up, and confusingly looking around the room, and then I woke up.

I sat in my bed screaming the word "No!" I took deep breathes and tried not to freak out about what I had just saw in my dream. I tried to convince myself it was just a dream. It was all just a dream. "Eve! Are you alright?" Chaska asked as her and some angels walked into my room. "We could sense that something's wrong with you, what's wrong?" Eli asked. "Not to mention hearing her scream like a freak!" Destiny added. I breathed deep before speaking.

"I just had a dream or a vision whatever you want to call it, about Parker being bit by a spider. He was asleep in his bed, and Scarlett and a warlock appeared out of nowhere. The warlock gave her a box, and she cast a spell about the spider biting Parker, and filling his heart with rage for the one she hates. I can't believe she let a spider bite him! I swear to my father I will rip Scarlett's head off if they actually take one step near Parker's home, I swear I will create an even worse hell then hades!" I rambled and yelled.

"Calm yourself Eve; you don't know if that is *actually* going to happen, it could have been just a really bad dream." Chaska said. I tried to calm myself down before I spoke. "I want Josh to be the guardian of Parker now; he is released from me to go help the innocent that cannot face Scarlett alone." I said to everyone in the room. "I understand." Josh said. "Thank you." I said to him. I felt a little more relaxed that Josh would be guarding Parker, but I still wanted to orb to him. But what would he think if he saw me suddenly appear in his room, in-human like?!

"You really need to calm yourself Eve, look at you!" Marius said as he watched me begin to shake out of fear and anger. I got up and went to the long mirror that was attached to my closet. I looked at myself. I looked ready for battle. I was wearing a cream silk pajama shorts and tank top set, my eyes were bright purple, my skin had a glow and in my gut, I could feel the hunger and eagerness to hurt someone or something, while a hot sensation began to come from my hands. I no longer looked like an angelic Archangel... I looked more like a wizard princess, ready for war. "Well I can't be an angel all the time." I muttered to myself.

I calmed myself down and sat cross legged on the floor. "You all can leave, I will be fine." I said. I listened to all the angels leave, but turned around to see Bobby still standing in my room standing by my bed.

"How do relationships work here? Are you and Destiny a couple?" I asked looking up at Bobby, trying to change the mood. "I like her yeah, but we are only friends." he answered. "As for relationships in Permia, they are allowed. This is the final dimension it is allowed in, any place above, companionship, or marriage...doesn't exist. We need to know what companionship and what love feels like, so it is allowed." he continued. "So why aren't you and Destiny together, it's allowed, you've got nothing to lose." I said. Bobby didn't say anything. I looked at him and smirked. "Are you scared?" I asked Bobby. Bobby's eyes widened and he shook his head no. "I am not scared." he said. "Then ask her out! Use me as an example; you don't know if something horrible will happen to her one day. If you like her, tell her while you've still got time." I said.

Bobby sighed. "Fine I will." he said. I looked forward, but I could feel Bobby's eyes still on me. "Eve, I know you don't want to hear it, but I'm going to tell you anyway. In case you haven't noticed, you and Parker won't work out, not for much longer anyway. He's human, and each day, you're getting more and more in touch with who you really are. In the matter of seconds, when you became angry, you became a completely different girl. I think, everything happens for a reason, and I think you should break up with him...before something bad happens. Before your dream actually becomes a premonition." He said. "If you break up with him, Scarlett will probably leave him alone. You can save him, and keep him out of danger. She will only hurt the people that mean something to you, and you're supposed to protect the innocent, not get them killed." Bobby continued. "You being with him *can* get him killed." I just stared at Bobby, I couldn't think of what to say. He huffed in my silence and walked to my terrace. I watched him spread his large wings and fly away. Where he was going, I didn't know or care, what started to fill my head was Parker.

I already question if he would be part of my future. I already knew that I would have to explain myself to Parker *or* break up with him, but I didn't think I would have to worry about that right at this very moment. Yeah, I do care for Parker in some sort of way, and I knew it would break his heart if I hurt him, but he has to be protected no matter what. "Ugh, I need to do damage." I muttered to myself. I changed my clothes in to simple black shorts and a t shirt and went to Marius's room. "I need to go out, and do damage control. I need to get myself ready." I said. Marius nodded his head and together we walked out and into the Permian night.

XXXI

Short Practice

I flipped the vampire on his back and gave him a left hook. He reached for my neck and pushed me off of him." Eve get him!" Marius shouted. I got up and I ran back at him, he grabbed my right arm, twisting it and actually starting to hurt me. I did a split and did an overhead arm drag, making him fly into the air and land behind me on the ground. The restless vampire quickly got up, but was met with a savate kick and then a stake to the heart.

"Well, those last moves were definitely impressive, but it should have taken you a shorter amount of time to kill just that one vampire alone." I looked at Marius with raised eyebrows. "Mari." I said calling him the nickname I had made for him. "I just kicked some vampire butt, give me some credit. And besides, this was a fun practice and for you to critic me and my skills. It's not a real battle or anything." I said, while we walked out of the woods.

"Yeah, I suppose your right. But just so you know, you have to be much quicker and sleek. But overall, you were amazing. Just as powerful as your parents." Marius said giving me a side hug. I smiled and looked ahead at the beautiful white mansion that sat in front of us. "Get some sleep you've got school in a few short hours." Marius said. He was starting to really become like a father figure to me, and Winter and Elsa were perfect substitute mothers, even though no one can replace my mom or dad, it's wonderful to have them all around.

"Why do I have to go to school, it's not like I'm going to use any of the tools for a normal human job." I said in a whiney voice. "Because it gives you knowledge." Marius said with a smile. He then spread his huge wings and flew over the house and most likely landed by his bedroom window. I exhaled all my bottled frustration, and orbed to my room.

XXXII

The Breakup

For the last week, I trained extra hard. I gained a ton of muscle, much more quickly than the average human. I also gained tons of confidence. I was becoming a totally new girl. As time went on, I became more aware and tended to rely on my powers. I sat in bed as the sun came up, but shortly decided to get ready for school.

As I got ready, I thought about what I was going to say to Parker. Today was the day that I had to break his heart. I wasn't in a happy or angelic mood; honestly I wanted to cry on the inside. I grabbed my purse, and orbed to Ms. Burn's house, got in my car and drove across the street to school.

When I got to school, everyone was waiting outside as usual. I took a few minutes to compose myself before getting out. "Hey you!" Loren greeted me. "Hi!" I waved to her and to everyone else. "Hey." Parker said as he pulled me into him. I pulled away and looked down at my feet. I wasn't prepared for what I was about to do, but I knew it had to be done. "Can we talk for a second?" I asked him, still looking down at my feet. "Yeah sure." he answered. I started walking around the parking lot, away from other people so that it was just Parker and I. It was about a minute of just us two breathing before he spoke.

"Eve, what's up? We don't have much time before the bell rings, what you need to talk about?" he asked me. I decided to just spit it out. I decided to just be straight forward, and go from there. "We... we need to break up." I said bluntly. Parker's face and mouth dropped. "Why?" he asked with narrowed eyes. I exhaled deeply. "We just do." I replied. Parker shook his head in disbelief. "That's your excuse? Well that's not good enough Eve! Am I not good enough? Why are you leaving me? At least give me a good enough explanation!" he semi yelled. I bit my lip to keep myself from crying. It killed me to hurt his feelings.

"My life is too complicated, and in my life now, I'm afraid you and I won't work." I confessed. Parker pulled me into his arms and hugged me. "Please don't leave me." he whispered. I sniffled before replying. "I have to." I said pulling away from him. I looked up at him, and saw that tears were starting to form in his eyes. I couldn't face him anymore, so I walked away. I knew what I had done was the right thing, Parker would move on eventually and I knew I would be more relaxed if I knew he wasn't a target for Scarlett.

I started walking back to my car when I bumped into Josh; he took one look at my face and hugged me. "You ended it, didn't you?" he asked. I nodded my head yes. "It will all work out for the best." Josh said. I didn't realize I had been holding my breath until I let out all the air that had been building up inside of me. "I'm just gonna go home, and go to sleep, take my car and park it in front of Ms. Burns house please? It's the house complex across the street; her house is all white with a purple flag hanging from the mailbox." I said. "Of course, relax, and everything will be fine." Josh assured me. I half smiled up at him and then walked towards the gym. Nobody was over in that area of the school yet, so I orbed home and went to sleep.

XXXIII

A Familiar Stranger

When I woke up, it was twelve thirty a.m. I had a full four hours of sleep, and I felt refreshed and yet numb. I got up, straightened my hair, added a little bit of makeup and orbed outside to the front of the mansion. I didn't know where I was going, but I felt the need to walk. I didn't care about Scarlett or any danger; I had no fear in my body. I just had to move.

I orbed downtown, and sat on a bench that was next to *"Tommy's Sweet's"* Ice Cream shop. I was hidden in the by trees. And I felt like this is where I should be, I seemed invisible, something I hadn't been since my birthday. I sat there until the sky turned from violet to a plum purple. I was trying to figure everything out. Like: "how did Scarlett know about Parker?" And "why not anyone else as a target, why target Parker? why not my adoptive family?" I figured I would never get the answers to those questions unless I found Scarlett and beat the answers out of her, but finding her wasn't easy.

I continued to walk downtown until I came across the pub that Destiny and I stumbled upon the first time we came downtown. I walked inside, and looked around at the Permian's that were drinking beer, and other fizzy drinks. Some were dancing, and playing games like foosball and pool. I sat at the bar, for a few minutes, before I got that feeling again. The infamous feeling that someone was watching me. I got up to leave, and started on the dark path of the town.

I still had that feeling, and in that moment, I knew that someone was behind me. I slowered my pace, and pretended that I had no clue that *I knew* I was being followed. Then making sure to catch the follower off guard, I orbed in front of him or her and backed him or her up against the stone wall of Immortal University. "Why are you following me?" I asked before I had a good look at the guy who had been following me. After asking the question, I got a full look at him. He had almost shoulder length black hair that was pulled into a ponytail and matching facial hair. He had deep brown eyes, and a perfect smile. He had a mysterious aura, and I was a little intrigued. He was the guy from my dreams.

"I was just curious..." he said while pushing me away, so he could remove himself from the wall. His voice was deep, powerful, commanding and enchanting. I folded my arms. "Okay, so what about me has you curious? You don't even know me." I asked the mysterious guy. He smiled and leaned into me. "I never said I was curious about you." he whispered, and then started walking back the way we just came, on the dark path. I shivered.

I watched him walk away, and then I orbed back home. For the next few hours I wondered about the mysterious guy I had met. I wondered who he was, why he was he being all creepy and watching me, and more importantly, how long had he been watching me. More answers that I couldn't figure out for myself.

I was happy that for a few hours I didn't think about Parker. I also didn't think about Scarlett. I was at a weird peace and intrigued with everything around me for the moment. I orbed into my room and looked into the mirror. I was glowing, and I smiled at my reflection. I wondered why I was glowing, or how was I even smiling after the day I had. "I'm such a weirdo" I muttered to myself, before lying in my bed and reflecting on the hectic day.

XXXIV

The Underground

Later that night, I decided to go check out *The Underground*. I looked in the mirror and adjusted my black rebel crop top, and pulled up my black skinny jeans. I put on my black combat boots and leather jacket before orbing to the entrance of the underground tunnel.

"Hey, it's about time I catch you back over here." a girl's voice said. I turned to come face to face with a pink and purpled haired girl I recognized as Cami Jane. "Hi." I smiled at her. "So, I take it you're a wizard." She asked while slowly walking to me. "You don't know who I am?" I asked her confused and curious. She snorted. "Am I supposed to know who you are?" She asked. "Guess not." I said while shrugging my shoulders. "So how can you tell that I'm a wizard?" I asked her. "I seen you orb in." she replied. I nodded my head. We stood there for a few seconds in an awkward silence. "so, you gonna come in or what?' She asked. "Yeah, I'm coming in." I said. "Let's go then, I'll show you where to go." She smiled.

I watched her walk down two small staircases, and I shortly followed. Once down the steps we made one sharp left turn and then a quick right and we were walking down a seriously dark tunnel. Thankfully with my perfect eyesight, I could see everything. It was like night vision, without that ugly green color as a highlighter. "So what breed are you?" I asked breaking the silence. I could see her smile and point to her ears, "an elf." *I said to myself.* She smiled."

Cool." I smirked. We walked a little more down the tunnel before I began to hear noise.

As we continued to walk, the louder the noise got. We came across a steal door, which Cami slid open and we walked through. I now figured out that the noise I was hearing before was music, and laughter. We walked up a small flight of stairs before we came to our destination. I was surprised to realize that we were in an actual club. There was a dj, tons of people dancing, laser lights and fog. I could feel the bass in the floor and my heart started pounding as I got excited. Back on Earth, I always wanted to club, but never actually went since I'm too young. The club was dark and edgy but had a definite exciting and thrilling feel to it. Cami smiled at my reaction. "Enjoy yourself babe!" She said patting me on the waist.

I watched Cami walk over to the dj booth before I went to the bar and ordered a sprite and took in all the fun that surrounded me. I glanced to my left and saw the hot mysterious guy watching me again. I raised my eyebrows at him and he took it upon himself to walk over to me.

"Now, what is a pure angel like you doing in *The Underground?*" He asked. "How do you know I'm an angel?" I asked him. "Don't worry about that; just know that I know, I know exactly who you are." He smiled a closed lip smile. "So why are you here? And why do you keep watching me? What are you a lonely creeper stalker?" I asked curious. "Watching you? What you think you're just *that* special enough for me to watch?" He asked with a sarcastic chuckle. "I don't know, you tell me Mr. Stalker." I replied. His dark eyes twinkled and I could tell that he was enjoying this little playful conversation we were having.

"You know what, I like you. You're not what I expected." He said. I stayed quiet and thought about the comment he just made. *I'm not what he expected? Who the heck is this guy?* I mentally asked myself. "Just be careful, not everyone in here is friendly Eve." He said. I widened my eyes at him. "Are you friendly?" I asked. The stranger tilted his head to the left. "I cannot confirm or deny that, guess you're going to have to decide that on your own." he said. "What makes you think I care to find out anything about you?" I asked him with a straight face. "I don't know, maybe you care, perhaps you don't." he said. I looked at him with annoyed eyes and he gave me a tiny little smirk and walked away from me. Annoyed and a little confused about this mysterious, stalker, stranger guy, I decided to leave. I could use an hour of sleep to gain some clarity. Too much thinking has fogged my brain.

I made my way to the exit and I watched a guy walk with a girl headed down a dark tunnel in the opposite direction from the exit of the tunnel or the underground. Instead of following them, I decided that it was none of my business, they are probably making out like most kids do at our age. I firmly believed that until I heard the girl scream.

I groaned and ran towards the direction of the dark tunnel that the couple went in, totally annoyed that my act of duty called. I carefully walked down the tunnel I saw the pair walk to, oddly not seeing the previous couple, and only hearing water and the loud music from the club. I walked deeper into the pitch black dark tunnel when I finally heard a noise behind me. I turned around and immediately felt myself flying in the air and then landing on the floor after receiving a kick to the gut by the guy.

I dusted myself off before standing up. "You know, you could have picked a place where there's a bit of light to do this... oh never mind I guess you did it for my benefit, staring at ugly opponents do hurt the eyes." I said with a bit of sarcasm. Mr. Let's play in the dark monster got angry at my comment and ran at me. I swiftly lifted my leg and chick kicked him in the head, before giving him a full set of 6 right and left hooks. I pulled my dagger out of my boot and slowly circled around the guy on the floor. "What did you do with the girl?" I asked. The guy played the "I'm hurt and can't speak role", which only made me mad so I kicked him.

"Speak! What did you do with her?" I yelled and put the dagger to his neck. "I right here." she chuckled and backhand slapped me making me hit the tunnel wall and drop my dagger. The guy quickly got up and kicked me in revenge for kicking him. I held my stomach and I groaned as I stood up. "Oh a set up how lovely." I said. As I smacked the girl and picked up my dagger. I ran to choke the guy, putting my all into choking him, holding him against the wall, lifting his feet off the ground. I lifted up my dagger and was seconds away from using it on him until I felt myself being choked from behind.

The guy took my dagger and slowly walked towards me, the girl gripping me tight from behind. *Okay Eve, time to get serious.* I thought to myself. I had been playing with these two idiots, knowing that if I wanted to, I could have killed them a long time ago. Right when I was about to break myself free another figure appeared, it was a man's figure and he tackled the monster holding my dagger.

I grabbed the girls arm, flipped her over and picked up my dagger from the ground and stabbed her with it. In front of my eyes she turned to fire and then ashes and dust. I looked up to see the two men fighting. "Who the heck is this guy that tried to save me like a hero?" I asked myself. I watched them brawl and realized it was the stalker guy that *saved* me. I watched him knock down the monster guy and I turned to walk away, figuring that he can take care of himself and I was now really tired anyway. "Hey!" I heard him call after me and then he yelped. I turned and saw him being in an arm hold.

I ran over and punched the monster guy who then let go of Mr. Stalker. He stumbled back before I saw him draw a red element ball from his left hand. He aimed it at me but the stalker guy knocked me to the ground blocking me from getting killed. We rolled on the ground until I ended up on top of him.

I looked deep into his dark down eyes and he looked into mine. I felt a weird feeling in my stomach, but couldn't dwell on it as I heard footsteps running towards us and I drew my right hand back and threw my own element ball at the monster. I hit my target and listened to him scream out before turning into ashes. "Another one bites the dust." I mumbled. The stalker guy pushed me off of him and walked away. "Well, thanks." I whispered as I watched him get further and further down the tunnel.

XXXV

Increased Attacks

The next day, I woke up and did my usual routine before I headed off to school. I parked in my normal spot for school, and I wasn't surprised to see that David's car was parked beside mine instead of Parker's. I walked to my locker, and got prepared for class.

"Well, I'm not sure what's going on, but Parker is saying you cheated on him, so he dumped you, and everyone is talking about it." Loren said, as she took her place by my locker. I looked up at her. "Um, can I get a hello first before we dive right into the rumors?" I asked sarcastically. I turned away from her and grabbed my math book out of my locker. "You know what, I don't care what Parker tells you or anyone at this school, just know that I ended it okay. Obviously if he dumped me, I would be bawling with tissues from not expecting it, but instead, I'm standing right in front of you with a smile on my face." I smiled. Loren looked at me.

"Okay, cool." she said in before the bell rang. "Why'd you break up?" She asked. I couldn't think of a good lie, so I thought of the most used one. "I met someone else." I said. Loren's face broke out into pure happiness and I could tell it was only because she wanted the four one on who the new guy was. I was happy that the final bell rang so I didn't have to answer any of her questions.

The entire school day was awkward because of Parker. I saw him a few times in school, but of course he wouldn't say anything to me. I would notice he would look at me from out of the corner of his eyes but I didn't care. I did what I did for his safety, and I couldn't help but smile that a little bit of pressure was lifted off of my shoulders. I was thankful that I had Josh; he was the only one that didn't ask me what happened? Or is it true you cheated? Some girls even asked me to confirm that I had broken up with Parker, and when I did... they had huge grins plastered on their faces, because he was up for grabs now.

"Eve, can I see you for a minute please." My substitute English teacher Ms. Leach said. I nodded my head and walked into her classroom. She shut the door and closed the door window with a shudder. "What's up?" I asked as I sat on a desk. She turned to face me, and I noticed her face began to change into something hideous. Her eyes became black and her teeth went from crisp pearly Chiclet's to piranha sharp. "Here we go." I groaned.

"You know, I'm not shocked that you turned into the ugly looking thing that you are, it's just shocking that you would actually try to go for me in school, you've got balls. I hope not literally." I said as I jumped off the desk and tackled her to the ground. We rolled around and her knife sharp nail scratched my belly. Getting completely upset at the long diagonal scratch going from my rib to my belly button, I rolled us over so that I was on top of Ms. Leach. I banged her head against the floor, before quickly getting up. I grabbed her by her hair and planted her face into the ground with a Snap mare driver. I took my dagger out of my boot and slammed it into her heart. And just like the rest, Ms. Leach bursted into flames before turning into black ash and then dust.

I gasped at the pain of the cut on my stomach. I sat down and put my hands on my cut and willed it to heal. I willed for my cut to be painless. I felt my skin snap back together, basically gluing the opened wound together again. It was painless and a warm feeling washed over the area. Within a few seconds I removed my hands and the cut was gone. I was thankful for the pain to be over, but was upset that my white shirt was ruined. I slipped on my peat coat and used the sleeves of my coat to open the door. I immediately went to the bathroom and washed my hands before meeting Josh outside.

Josh and I watched Parker stand outside talking to a handful of slutty girls. "It's wrong for him to be like this, and spreading rumors, especially when you did it for his own good." Josh said sitting next to me on my car. I smiled at Josh. "He's human, he doesn't understand." I replied. Josh rolled his eyes. "Yeah, but there is still no reason for him to be a jerk or to spread lies." Josh said. I fidgeted with my fingers, mad that there was dry blood stained in my nails. "Is that blood?" Josh asked. "Yes, before coming to you I found out my substitute teacher was actually a demon. We had a lovely conversation in the English room." I said.

"Where's the blood from?" Josh asked. "She had really sharp nails; she cut through me like butter." I replied. "But I healed myself, I'm good." I assured him. Josh was just about to reply before we heard another person speak. "Josh, Eve... how are you two?" Ms. Burns asked, coming to stand by my car. "Good." Josh said. I nodded my head in agreement with him.

"Are you okay? I heard you had another run in with another Demon?" she asked. I sighed. "Yeah, I handled it well though." I assured her. She smiled. "Well, I just want you to remember to be careful, wouldn't want anything bad to happen to you or any loved ones." she smiled. "See you two later." she said just before waving bye and walking away. I wondered what she meant about anything *bad* happening to anyone else. Did she know about the dream I had about Parker? *I know Archangels, and angels can read minds, and listen in on conversations, but can wizards?* I asked myself. "That's a good question." Josh replied. I laughed. I totally forgot that Josh was sitting right beside me. I also forgot to block my thoughts.

I parked the car at Ms. Burns house as usual and orbed home. That's when I realized how much I like it in Permia more than on Earth. How much more comfortable I am in Permia. Instead of going inside the mansion, I walked to Pia's stream. I walked through the green grass, and pushed by tree trunks and bushes before I could actually hear the stream. I had a calm feeling flowing throughout my body until I had caught an image of a shadow that was on the right of me.

I bent down, faced the opposite direction and placed my purse, coat and books on the ground. I placed a hand over them, and transferred them safely to my room. Before getting up, I pulled out the dagger that is always located in my boot. I knew that as soon as I got up, I would be attacked by some demon creature behind me. So I slowly picked up the dagger, and slowly got up from the ground. Wanting to surprise whoever was behind me, I quickly turned around and pushed the dagger into the creature's stomach. I looked at what I stabbed and I pulled away from the hideous red faced demon that was now turning into flames, only to bump into something hard.

I turned around and stared at a second red faced demon who grabbed me by the neck. My neck was being crushed by a red hand, and I couldn't fight him off. I gasped to breathe, and closed my eyes. I thought this was my time to go; I would die by being choked to death. That was my thought, until I suddenly was able to breathe again. I fell to the ground, coughed and clutched my neck; as I watched the stalker guy that had been following me; snap the neck of the second red faced demon.

After we both watched the Demon turn to dust, he turned to me, and looked at me. He started to walk away, and I stood up. "Will you at least tell me your name, so I can say a proper thank you?" I asked the stalker guy. I was instantly attracted to him, freaked out by his stalker creepiness but still attracted. Something about him, made me drawn to him. I was overly intrigued. He turned around and faced me; his lips were in a thin pink line before he spoke. "Tess." he replied. I started walking a little closer to him. A swarm of butterflies fluttered in my belly at the sudden closeness between Tess and I.

"Well, thank you Tess." I said. He blinked his eyes once, but continued to stay silent, and stare at me. I couldn't look at him directly in his eyes, I didn't want him to know that I was weirdly developing a little girl crush on him, an unknown stalker stranger. I looked down and I bit my lip to focus on the pain instead of the butterflies. Not knowing what to say, I picked my dagger from off the ground and then orbed away from him Tess.

XXXVI

Asleep in Class

My clothes were a bit dirty from the fight, so I quickly changed clothes, nothing serious just a cream baby doll top, skinny blue jeans and black boots. I walked out my door and walked down the sun filled hallway. I touched and admired the beautiful paintings posted on the cream walls, and then walked down the spiral stairs and into the living area.

Just as I sat down, the door shut and a wet Eli walked in. "Hey, what are you doing wet?" I smiled at him. A towel suddenly appeared in his hands, and he wiped his face before he spoke. "I fell asleep in Earth History class, and let's just say, my professor has water as her element." Eli said. "Sounds wet." Chaska laughed.

"Hey, um... what do you learn in a class like that? Like what's the point in taking classes if we angels know the histories of the world and everything?" I asked Eli and Chaska. "Not everyone knows everything, lots of Permian's haven't even been to Earth." she said.

"Earth class consists of topics like Earth history, Earth geography. It's for us to get better understanding of Earth." Eli said. I nodded my head in understanding. "Marnie, your aunt, she thought it was important for Permian's to learn about the earth, because the human world is so different from Permia. She had sent some Permian's over to earth to learn. When they came back, they became teachers; they teach us what they learned about Earth. You could be a teacher here, teach Permian's about Earth." Chaska said. "I think my hands are already full with being future queen." I smiled at her, and then orbed away.

XXXVII

Just Like Any Girl

Parker had been missing from school for a few days and it made an angry and nervous feeling erupt in the pit of my stomach. At the mansion, I kept guards all around the entrances, and kept myself occupied with reading. Destiny and Bobby seemed happier, and they were looking like a real cute couple, but in the back of my mind, I didn't care. The only thing I could think about was the *"punched out of my body"* feeling I had in my stomach. It felt like something bad was going to happen, and when I felt this way, bad things usually did happen.

I put down my current reading book *"The Art of War"* and disappeared off to Immortal U. Out of curiosity I wanted to gain more information about my two different species. Before my coming to Permia, to me, angels lived in Heaven and they were part of God's "crew". I thought everyone had a guardian angel, and I knew that people liked to make statues and paintings of them. That was all of my knowledge of angels. I didn't know the different types of Angels, and what their true purpose was.

As for Wizards, aside from the wizard of Oz, Harry potter, Wizards of Waverly place, and somewhat of an idea of who Merlin was, that alone explains the knowledge that swarmed inside my head of what wizards were.

I figured being a queen, I would need to know about every

creature I would have to deal with. What were their power, strengths and weaknesses are. But I didn't want to just hear about it from someone else, I wanted my own information so in the end, I could form my own opinion about everything.

I was used to seeing the college at night, it looked scary looking around that time of day and in the daytime my thoughts about it didn't change a bit. It's creepy and dark...historic. But it also has an ancient beauty quality to it.

I started walking in a little hallway when I began to feel I was being watched...again. My *being watched* instincts were marvelous thanks to Tess. I looked behind me and saw no one. When I turned my body back around, and was ready to walk inside the building, was when I came face to face with Tess. I jumped back, and watched him smirk at me.

"Really?" I asked while raising my eyebrows at him. Tess didn't say anything, and I decided that, that was my queue to walk away from him. Even though I got butterflies from the sight of Tess, I had too much on my plate, and I didn't have time to worry about a guy who was only playing mind games with me. "Why do you keep following me?" I asked turning to face him. He put his hands in his pockets and slowly with *swagger,* he began to walk to me.

"Well... maybe I think your kind of cute." he smiled. Now even though I am a kick but Wizard warrior, I am still just a girl, and I started blushing, just like any girl would do after they heard a comment like that from a cute boy. I put my head down, and tried to hide my blushing so he wouldn't see the effect he had on me. "So what are you doing here?" Tess asked. I looked back up at him "reading." I answered.

Tess raised his eyebrows. "Reading...about what?" he asked. I folded my arms. "Mysterious creatures like yourself." I replied. He chuckled. "Sounds boring tell you what, why don't we hang out tonight?" he asked. My mouth dropped. Was he really asking me out? Did Tess just ask me out? Yeah, I was feeling more than ecstatic, but I decided to play it cool. "Why would I go out with you, you're a stranger?" I asked almost sarcastically. Tess came closer and slowly walked behind me smirking.

"Stranger. Am I now?" He asked. I stayed quiet. "well, we don't have to be strangers; we could be friends." he whispered in my left ear. I looked down at my feet, "oh we can? And how would that work? It's not like I can actually call you whenever I want someone to hang out with. You usually just stalk me and appear out of nowhere." I said. I couldn't even lie to myself, I totally wanted to connect with Tess more, and I was secretly hoping he would give me his number, but knowing how unpredictable Tess *seems*, I knew he wouldn't give me his number so easily.

"Hmm, it's not like we never see each other, and I'm not talking or randomly appearing, I would say it seems like we've just been bumping into each other quite a bit lately." He said. I shook my head at his comment. "I wonder how that happens." I said with sarcasm. "But it would be nice to be able to contact the guy that's asking me out." I said in an almost whisper.

I looked at Tess in his brown eyes, and then my eyes began taking in his simple black t-shirt, and dark blue jeans. He also had a silver chain with a seven pointed star on it. His pale right arm had a black and white tattoo of a bow, and I shivered a little at the sight of it. Something about this guy was bad, and I don't mean horrible bad, I mean sexy, cool, bad boy *bad.* "See something you like?" he asked smirking at me. I looked up and stared into his eyes. "Not at all." I smiled. He laughed at my smart comment. "Meet me here at eight." he smirked, and then walked down the hallway, and turned the corner. "What if I don't?" I asked as he was walking. Tess turned back to look at me. "You will." He replied before turning around and walking away again.

As soon as Tess was out of my sight, I orbed off home and raided my closet for an outfit for the night and I decided that I would study later!

In my closet were all light pastel colored pieces of clothing, it was *Arch wear.* I rummaged through my dressers, searching through the clothes I brought from Earth, but I couldn't find anything I believed was suitable for not only my night with Tess, but for my new life here in Permia period. If my life was changing, my wardrobe deserved a change to. I looked at the old clothes and asked myself how I even went about wearing some items of the clothing. Clearly my taste was changing. I groaned and set off for downtown. I seriously needed to get some shopping done.

I ended up buying two pairs of sneakers for training, two pairs of leather boots, a couple pairs of liquid black leggings, some leggings with cool patterns and some plain. I also bought some corsets to start my new wardrobe with. After shopping, I actually tired myself out and I wanted to go to sleep, all the energy that I had, had worn off. I did have a long day; I don't even know how I was functioning anymore. I felt like I had drank three cans of *Monster* earlier and now was the wearing off period. I laid on my bed, closed my eyes and drifted off into the darkness.

XXXVIII

The Date

By the time I woke up, it was seven p.m. Needless to say I rushed out of bed, jumped in and out of the shower and did my hair and makeup fairly quickly. Deciding to let my hair curl natural and apply a Smokey eye look and clear lip gloss.

I looked at the time and huffed when I realized I had an half an hour left. I decided to wear a pair of the plain liquid leggings I brought from downtown, a fitted and kind of fancy burgundy half sleeve shirt to match, and I completed the outfit with a pair of black booties that had a large wooden heel, stud earrings and my leather jacket. My look was definitely not angelic, but it wasn't exactly wizardish either. It was more classy, sexy and sophisticated than anything. I gave myself a last minute body check, and realized that I finally look my age. I finally look like a young woman and not a girl anymore. Good, I wanted to impress Tess, not show up looking like a twelve year old. Then I orbed off to meet Tess.

Once appearing in the hallway that Tess and I had been in earlier, I was happy to see that he was already there, posted in front of the brick wall. I took in his black jeans, black t-shirt under his red and gray plaid shirt. His hair was flowing down to his shoulders and he was checking the time on his black wrist watch. I was beginning to get used to his dark, grungy sense of style, as well as like it.

"Your late." he smirked at me. I walked closer towards him. "Hey, you're lucky I came, especially when the person I'm meeting is someone like *you.*" I said sarcastically. Tess looked at me with a confused expression. "Someone like *me?*" he asked. He started walking down the path that lead to downtown and I followed. "Yeah, a creeper stranger like you." I replied. Tess stopped walking and looked at me. "Me...a creeper stranger? I don't think so." he smiled as he pointed to himself.

I took a few big steps so that I was now standing beside him, instead of behind. I was happy that I wore heels, my five feet two inches frame would make me look like a child compared to his at least six foot frame. "Even my stomach started turning before I came to meet you... must of been a warning." I said while looking up into the deep purple sky. "Sure it was." Tess muttered under his breath. I laughed at his comeback.

We walked downtown and enjoyed the lights and sounds as well as the light conversation we were having. Obviously Tess and I's relationship would be flirty, playful and filled with mystery. He only let me halfway in when it came to telling me about himself, which was frustrating but intrigued me anyway. I learned that he is twenty years old and his birthday is in October. His last name is Draven. Tess say's only people he considers family knows his real first name. Tess is a nickname. Tess also has no brothers or sisters or family. Just friends that he considers family. He has his own place an apartment in the downtown area. He works at the Green Ridge Pub, which is why he was watching me when Destiny and I were over in that area. He didn't know he was going to see me, or so he says. "You wanna go to *The Underground?*"Tess asked me. I nodded my head yes.

Shortly, we appeared at the tunnel and began walking down the stairs. On the outside I played it cool, but on the inside I was freaking out. For some reason, it felt a little scary being alone with him in the dark. "hmm, I don't know if I should be here with you... how do I know you're not evil or something." I whispered to Tess. Whispering because it didn't seem fit for me to talk loudly in the empty, could be romantic but actually is freaky dark tunnel. "You don't." he said simply. I stopped walking and Tess turned back to look at me. He walked towards me, and I started to feel those butterflies again.

"Do you always do what the *good* guys tell you to do?" he asked. I didn't answer. True fully, before my birthday, I always did what the *good* guys told me to do. I never broke any laws, I always followed the rules. I never got into any fights or major arguments. And I was quick to make snap judgments and stay away from people that *looked* like rebels or sluts. Yeah, I had my moments of thrilling fun like sneaking out to parties, sneaking out late at night to go out with friends, and even running across a train track as a dare. That's as far as my *badness* went. In the words of Loren, I was an actual *good girl*.

Tess smirked at the fact that I left his question unanswered. He slowly circled around me until we were face to face. "Do you trust me?" he asked. The first thought that popped into my head was *No! Eve! Run away!* But deep down, I felt sure about Tess. The attraction I had for him was greater than the fear. The mystery that is him, captured the curiosity in me, and held a firm grip on it. Also for the fact that the warrior in me wouldn't let me be too afraid of him and I couldn't look like a scary cat in front of him, I decided to go with my gut. "Yes." I replied.

Tess then got behind me, wrapped his left arm around my waist and we continued walking. I liked the way his long arm snaked around my waist. I liked how we fit together, him being tall and me being petite and tiny. We walked a little more down the tunnel and we came across the same steal door that I remember coming across with Cami. Tess slid open the door and we walked through, and finally entered The Underground.

XXXIX

A Normal Girl

Tess and I danced for a while. I was surprised that he was actually a good dancer, given his bad boy image. In the moment of him twirling me around, I noticed my hands burned a little when Tess touched my bare skin. After receiving the tingly, burning sensation a few more times when Tess and I touched skin to skin, I knew there was way more to Tess than I *really* knew. And I was afraid that what I didn't know would be bad. I didn't want to know if it was something bad, I wouldn't let myself believe it if it was something bad. I ignored my hands, and silently healed them, replenishing the tingle with a warm soothing comforting feel.

To be out partying, felt a little wrong. But it was fun, hot, dark and loud, the exact opposite of home. My gut was telling me to relax and have some fun, and that's exactly what Tess and I both did. We were having innocent and yet thrilling fun. "Those are some friends." Tess said pointing to a group of young people. We walked over and he introduced me to them.

They were edgy and funky, and I immediately knew they weren't angels. However, I was drawn to them. They looked like a small group of misfits that actually fitted together. I somehow felt like I belonged in their funky little *tribe*. It's like they were my family and I didn't even know them yet. "This is Cat, Cat this is Eve." Tess introduced. Cat said hi just before giving me a friendly hug. She was beautiful; she had an olive skin tone with orange hair. She was wearing a retro 80's crop top with a girl posing in shorts on the shirt. She was also wearing black leggings and blue pumps. She was the definition of funky. He then introduced me to Luke, who wore a blue jean button up shirt, with dark blue skinny jeans and a snapback. Next was Noah, who was super tall. He had a brush cut, jean shorts and a plain navy blue t-shirt. They were all very nice, and had their own sense of style that I liked.

"How come I've never seen you around here before? Tess has never brought a girl here before." Cat said. I looked at Tess and smirked. "Hey, hey, guys... don't blurt out all the info, don't you know we are in the presence of royalty here. This is Eve, *thee* Eve?" Tess smiled. Cat's cheeks started turning pink. *Oh God.* I mentally said to myself, while cringing. I didn't want to be known to the world as some stuck up queen. Or someone they had to bow down to. Yes I'm a princess, but I'm still just a normal girl. When I'm out with friends, I want to escape that royal, warrior princess life, even if it's just for a few minutes.

I frowned at Tess before turning to his friends. "Please don't, don't act different around me than you would normally act when I'm not around. I promise I act nothing like a royal." I said in an innocent voice. "Oh no, we aren't going to put up a front, it's just that…your down to earth, and you're really pretty. I wouldn't expect to see a royal in here." Luke said. "Well I'm here, not your ordinary princess I guess. Just a normal girl." I said. "Alright then, how about we hit the dance floor?!" Luke suggested. I grabbed his hand, and lead him to the dance floor.

Things got really heated on the dance floor and I found myself actually enjoying myself with Tess and his friends. I felt like I was being a normal teen again. I didn't have any royal duties or revenge to seek. The only thing I had to worry about was having fun. Which is what I was doing until I looked at my watch.

"Holy crap, it's one thirty a.m." I said to out loud. I had to be up at six a.m. to get ready for school, and I needed my four hours of sleep to function. I pulled away from Tess and looked up at him. "I've got to get back; I have to be up in a few hours for school." I told Tess. He nodded his head that he understood, and we went to tell the others that we were leaving.

"It was so good to meet you Eve!" Luke said engulfing me in a tight embrace. "You too, I had fun. We all should hang out again sometime." I suggested. Everyone replied back with a mix of yeah's and sounds good.

Tess put his hand on my lower back, and started pushing me towards the door. As we left I heard a chorus of see you later's and bye's from his friends and even Cami. Tess slid the steal door to the left and we entered the dark tunnel again. I noticed Tess was quiet, and had a frown on his face. This boy seriously confused me sometimes.

"What's wrong?" I asked. Tess kept walking, and it took him a few seconds to actually respond. "Why was Luke hugging you like that, do you like him?" he asked. "What? No I don't, and a hug is a hug. He was hugging me like what?" I asked honestly confused. Tess sighed. "I don't know... close, and really tight." he replied. I stopped walking and smirked a little. "Wait a second...are you jealous?" I asked Tess. He didn't look at me; he didn't have the guts to face me. "No, no I'm not jealous." he said. I laughed at his weak response. "Oh my gosh! You're jealous of the hug Luke and I shared. Hilarious!" I said laughing. Tess got a little mad that I was laughing, and started walking faster.

I decided to change the subject for his benefit. But on the inside, I was happy that I made him jealous. "I'm glad your friends all acted normal around me, unlike the angels and council who were very formal and serious when we first met. Your friends, they were very mellow about meeting me." I told Tess. Tess chuckled. "We all know a little about you. Your mother is part of Permian History, so of course she's in the textbooks we have at Immortal, and in the library." He said. "A little about you is in there as well. It says how you were born, but shipped to Earth to be saved. How our world has hopes that you would return to take your spot as a queen one day." He continued.

I looked at him semi calm and semi in shock. Semi calm because I knew my mom was royalty, and if back on earth in the USA, we had to learn about whatever current president we had, then of course in Permia they would have to learn about the people that had control of this place. However I was Semi in shock that a little piece of me was actually in a *text book*. Never in a million years did I think I would be the topic of a history assignment. "That's all we know about you from the books. No one knows what has become of you, unless they meet you or know your back here." He said.

"Unless they see you out and about, or watch the news or something, I doubt that anyone even knows your back. I'm pretty sure, anyone that you meet is overly happy and shocked on the inside, and they just don't want to frighten you by acting crazy. No one knew what you looked like, or expected you to come home and actually stay. Not after eighteen years, our world is obviously *complicated*." Tess chuckled.

"I didn't expect me to stay either... but I felt that this is where I belong. I never really belonged anywhere back home on Earth." I confessed, as we climbed the stairs and started the pathway. "Well, I'm glad you decided to stay." Tess smiled. I smiled up at him.

As we came to a stop in front of Immortal University my lips turned into a smile as Tess and I faced each other. "How did you know it was me when we first met...I never told you my name, and yet... you already knew?" I asked Tess. "Well for one, you resemble your mom, Emirah." He said. I stared at him in almost disbelief. It was hard hearing that I looked like my mother, because from the pictures I've seen, I knew the comment was true. I just wished I could have been with her longer, or better yet... have her here with me today.

"Two.... there is no one like you around here. There's something about you, that's innocent, and yet exciting. You're just... special. And I've kind of been waiting to see if you show up and you did." He said. "And I did. But I am nothing special." I said. Tess looked at me wide eyed.

There was an almost daring silence that took over us as we stood in front of the school. "So, I had fun. Thank you for asking me out." I told Tess. He smiled. "Glad you enjoyed yourself." I began to walk away, when he pulled me into him by my elbow. "I'd really like to kiss you." He murmured against my lips. This was the moment that every girl dreams of with a hot guy, the first kiss. Will it be tender? Will it be rough? Will it be quick or sloppy? I couldn't wait to find out, I *had* to find out.

    I walked back up to him and stood on my tippy toes and leaned into him. Tess pulled me tighter and leaned down. Our lips met in a short but sweet and heated kiss. It only lasted five seconds and I wished it lasted longer, but I decided that it was best to keep it light and simple tonight, after all we just met. "You really are special Eve." He said. I backed away from Tess, touching my lips at the heated sensation. I smiled at him and waved goodbye and then orbed to home. It may seem rude, but this was just how Tess and I were, and I guess I'm not good with goodbyes, even if it's not permanent.

XL

Distracted and Confused

Living in Permia was getting to me a little bit. I wondered if I would still be able to be kind of *normal* meaning, can I go out and have fun, or will it get worse than what it is now? Lately I have been getting attacked on both worlds, and I wondered if this is what it would always be like now. I wished I could talk to someone about it. I didn't want to talk about it with anyone who would sugar coat this situation to me. Sugar is sweet, and my life at the moment, was anything but that. I wanted someone to be real with me, and say *yeah Eve, it's gonna be hard, but you were chosen to do it...so do it.* I needed tough love, and I wasn't getting that. I was expected to suck it up and just not have any problems with my new life. How I wish it were really that simple. I've become somebody an entire world and a half depended on. That isn't an easy title to hold .I didn't feel like an angel, I didn't feel like a wizard...at this point I more so felt confused.

For the rest of the week on Earth I pretty much kept to myself. Only getting into conversations with Josh, and somewhat talking to Loren and the others. I didn't mean to distance myself away from them; it's just that I had nothing to talk about with them anymore.

Back in Permia, I spent a little time with Tess, and most of my time trying to train, and study about Permia and my family. But I was so distracted by Tess and the kiss we shared days ago. Even Destiny noticed how unfocused I was.

"What's up with you? You're like in your own world?" Destiny said as we sat in the kitchen. I had my math worksheet in front of me, and the only thing that was written on it was my name. I sighed and blushed before I spoke to Destiny. "I met a guy." I said. Destiny dropped the meat she was about to put on her sandwich and rushed over to sit next to me. "Who? Is he from here or earth? Is he's from here?" she asked. "He's from here." I said. Destiny squealed. "Is he an angel?" She asked. That's when I thought about it, I didn't know what Tess was and at this point, I guess I didn't care what he was. "I think he is he would be living here if he were an angel right? And he doesn't live here." I said more than asked. "Okay point, than what is he?" Destiny asked. "Um, I'm not sure what he is." I confessed. Destiny's eyes bulged out her head.

"Dude, he could be evil, he could be a monster or something!" She said. "I doubt it, he's really nice to me, and the kiss we had was unbelievable." I said. "Wait, you two kissed?" She asked. "Yes." I smiled. A look of jealousy and envy became plastered on Destiny's face. I huffed." Dest, tell me bad things about him. I need to stop being so distracted and forget about him so I can focus on what's important." I said.

Destiny got up and went back to making her sandwich. "He's evil; he is distracting you on purpose so that he can kill you. He's disgusting and vile." She happily said. I snapped around to look at her. "Okay, stop." I said not wanting to hear any more of what she had to say. I liked Tess and that was that, and I couldn't deal with hearing false negative comments made about him. I just have to push myself to forget about him for a little while. I put my pen to my math sheet and began working.

XLI

The Truth

As the days went by Tess and I started hanging out a lot together. For some reason we understood each other. We just clicked. Out of nowhere, he sort of became my best friend, and I found myself wanting to be around him, or wondering where he was when we weren't together. Not in a crazy "where are you?" way. It was more of an "I'm lonely, where's my friend" kind of way. It was almost natural to have him around. But I wondered if I could talk to him on a deeper level, deeper than we have already gone.

We started hanging out so much that I noticed my own sense of style was starting to reflect his. My wardrobe consisted more of plaids and dark edgy pieces of clothing. I began to take more time styling my hair either letting it fall into curls or pushing it into a high ponytail. My makeup started becoming a little heavier; a purple Smokey eye was starting to become my signature look. I as a whole was more edgy. I was beginning to look more of a Wizard princess rather than an Archangel, but I decided to let my heart be covered in gold and white lace instead of my shirts and dresses.

I was walking alone downtown, lost in my thoughts as an arm snaked across my waist. I jumped and stood at a stance out of instinct from being attacked so much. I looked up at Tess who was smiling down at me. "You do that way too much." I said to him. "Do what?" he asked. "Watch me, and then sneak up...appearing out of thin air." I said. He grinned and let out a little laugh. We walked together in silence, but sometimes I would catch him looking at me, and sometimes he would catch me staring at him too. Tess was mysterious and he could make me curious about him, laugh at him or even afraid of him, all at once. It was almost scary how someone can make you feel all those emotions all at once. One thing I didn't mind though was that he always made me forget about Parker, who had moved onto multiple girls at school. "Hold on," I said, and Tess held my waist a little tighter. I orbed us up to the top of Immortal U.

We sat on the ledge looking out at the world. I remembered dreaming of this moment. "What's wrong?" Tess asked as I scooted over a little closer to him. I sighed. "Nothing huge really, it just... I feel so frustrated, I hate that I feel like I can't have a night off for fun, I always have to be on *future queen duty*. I'm sad because I miss my real parents. I'm angry because of what happened to them. I'm tired from training. And I'm confused, confused because even though it's stressful I love being in Permia, it's better than being on earth. But it's just so much to take in, and I'm afraid of what's to come." I confessed to Tess.

"I wish I could say it will get better, but honestly Eve... as long as Scarlett is around, I'm not sure if it will." he said. Tess said what I wanted someone to tell me, the hard truth. Tess put his arm around me and I shivered. He took his arm off of me and looked at me. "You cold? here." he said talking off his jacket. "Oh no, it's okay." I started to say, but Tess put his leather jacket over my shoulders anyway. "Thanks." I said.

There was a comfortable silence before I began to speak again. "Guys usually only give their jackets to girls they like...when they are feeling chivalrous." I said, looking at him through my eyelashes. Tess smiled. "What makes you think I like you?" he asked. "You don't?" I asked standing up. Tess stood up and we both stared at each other. We both leaned in until I jerked back. With my perfect hearing, I could have sworn I heard a noise not too far away. "Did you just hear something?" Tess asked looking around. I was too wrapped up in him to be certain but I for sure thought I heard a sound. Even though I wasn't a hundred percent sure, I would rather be safe than sorry. I'd rather be prepared for an attack instead of being attacked from behind. I walked a few feet away from Tess when it happened again. I was being attacked...again.

Three pale, bald sharp toothed creatures surrounded me. Demons. Two of them grabbed my arms and pinned them behind me. Tess ran up to the four of us, and grabbed one of the demons that were holding me. I head butted the demon that was holding my left arm behind my back, and round house kicked the one standing in front of me. "EW you guys are ugly! You make me sick!" I said as I knocked one to the ground and started on the other. I quickly glanced at Tess who was still going to work on the first one.

I took out my silver dagger and stabbed one of the demons in the heart, not even watch him die. I watched Tess take out a blade from his jacket that was lying on the ground, and slice the demon in the front of his neck. The demon screamed, and fell to the floor, soon after turning into fire ash then dust. The last one, had grabbed me from behind, but Tess grabbed him and slammed him into the floor. Right then, I saw my opportunity to kill the ugly Demon and I did, stabbing it in the heart with my dagger. "Glad you were here to help." I said to Tess in between breathes. "My pleasure." he said. I grabbed his hand and once again I could feel the heat rising on my hand from it. But I ignored it and quickly orbed to the busy downtown area of Permia.

I smiled at Tess as I let go of his hand and we walked side by side. "Really, I don't know what I would have done if I was alone, and had been caught off guard like that. I've been kind of out of it lately." I confessed. Tess wrapped his arm around my waist, and I turned so that we were facing each other. I leaned into him, and he leaned into me, and our lips finally connected and started moving in sync. After five seconds my lips felt like they were slowly burning on a low flame. I pressed myself into him harder and wrapped my arms around his neck. He ran his hands on my cheeks, and I let out a muffled groan mixed with a scream while we kissed.

The heat was becoming too much, it was getting hotter and hotter by the second. I pulled away and touched my burning right cheek, and looked at Tess. Tess had a shocked facial expression, "I'm sorry...I shouldn't have done that." he said in a low tone while looking at anything but me. "Demons and Angels don't mix." he said looking straight into my eyes. And before my eyes, a silver glitter appeared in front of me, and I watched Tess orb away for the first time. He left me speechless and angrier than ever.

XLII

A Heart to Heart

I orbed back to the mansion and crumbled on the floor in the middle of the hallway. I couldn't believe that I, the future queen of Permia had kissed my enemy, a demon. He charmed me, made me like him, he seemed nice, he was attracted to me, and I was attracted to him. But he's a *demon*. I couldn't fall for a demon! I let a few tears roll down my cheek, upset at my stupidity.

So wrapped up in my own muted thoughts, I didn't even notice Winter standing above me. "What's wrong? What's happened?" she bent down and asked me. "Ugh, it's a long story." I replied whipping my tears away. "We've got plenty of time, and I want to hear all about it." she replied. I stood up and walked into the sitting room and Winter followed. "Where do I begin?" I asked myself. I took a deep breath before I spoke.

"So, a very short while ago I met a guy here named Tess. He's really nice, attractive and he we've hung out a few times. He made me feel a bit normal and like I belonged. I even got girly butterflies and feelings towards him. So earlier tonight, I kind of got attacked and he was there, and helped me kill the nasty, ugly vampire, demon things, and I thanked him and we kissed." I said in a rush. Winter looked at me like I was insane. "Okay...so what's the problem?" she asked. This is the part that I dreaded, that I really, really didn't want to tell her.

"Well when we kissed, it kind of tingled at first and then we got more into it, and then it really started to burn. He touched my cheek and it burned. I kind of freaked out and pulled away. He said he was sorry, and then looked up at me and said demons and angels don't mix, and then orbed away. I never saw him orb before tonight. He just always appeared from out of nowhere." I said quickly, hoping she didn't comprehend what I was saying. But from the semi shocked expression on her face, I could tell that she heard me. "And now, I'm even more scared crapless about running this place! It's too much responsibility, and I can't even control myself when it comes to a charming demon." I admitted. "I thought he was a wizard or something you know; I didn't think he would be an actual demon." I continued. Winter sighed.

"First, I can imagine why you would be scared and nervous about being queen, you just found out about yourself and your parents as well. You just found out about your life being anything *but* ordinary. You have enemies that you didn't even know about, and you have to balance your normal life and a secret life. It's a lot to take in...But we aren't given more than we can handle." she said. I remained quiet. "Somewhere deep down, I know you feel like this is where you belong. You didn't understand your identity and purpose on earth. I could see it in your eyes when we first met in October. Now, you look more aligned." She continued. "Yes, it's hard to adjust to the fact that your purpose isn't about you. Everything in life, no matter what realm we are in, is hard. And in the end, it's always worth it."Winter continued.

"Now, as for this Tess guy." she huffed. "You need to stay away from him. Keep what has happened, between the three of us only. Angels and demons *don't* mix, that's the exact definition of good vs. evil. That's like mixing devil's food cake with angel food cake and eating it!" she said. I let out a tiny and low chuckle at her comment. "I know it will be hard, but just like any young couple that goes through a breakup, it's painful, but it doesn't last long. You can and *will* get over him in time. Focus on what you should be focusing on." Winter said. I sat and continued to listen. "You must also be careful Eve, you may be one of the most powerful beings here, and even though it wouldn't be easy because your practically immortal, but you can still be killed, and anybody will do anything to get that *one* opportunity to kill you." Winter said.

I looked up at her in surprise. "How can I be killed? Am I not immortal enough?" I asked her. I didn't even think to ask about this before, totally not knowing how to truly protect myself yet. "You can only be killed with *The White Fire Dagger*, the most powerful dagger in all realms. The dagger is cursed and bound to kill anyone that is wounded by it. No one has ever been strong enough to survive it, or be quick enough to heal their self before the toxins spread through the victim's body and killing them, victims including your mother." she said.

"So, you can heal yourself before getting killed by the toxins in the dagger?" I asked her, ignoring the fact that she just mentioned my mother in our conversation. I didn't want to talk about my mother anymore, it would only make me cry some more. She nodded her head yes. "Yes, but no one has *ever* done it before, when you get punctured by that dagger, everyone is too shocked to react, and so they panic and lose the time. But if you are quick enough, it is doable. The pain is excruciating though." she said. I stayed quiet.

"I have a question, and you don't have to answer if you don't want to." She said. I only looked at her for her to continue. "How did you handle being down there on Earth? How was the first eighteen years of your life?" Winter asked. I sighed before answering. "I was told that I was brought to the hospital as a missing baby. Shortly after that, my adoptive mom Mena, found me and took me home. I've been with her ever since. It's definitely been hell, maybe not the actual hell, but certainly a version of it." I admitted.

"It's no fun to be called names, criticized or judged. Mental abuse it's a form of physical pain, it damages your heart and mind. But somewhere inside was a faith that I've always had. A faith that I knew one day I would be out of that house, and away from that awful family for good. I just didn't think it would happen like this or even this soon though." I chuckled and slightly sniffled.

"I'm sorry you had to go through all that you did Eve, but now you are home, where you belong." Winter smiled. She scooted over and hugged me tightly. I thought about her words. *You are home, where you belong.* I exhaled and relaxed as I realized that she was right. I relished in agreeing to the fact that I was now *home* where I belonged. "Well, it is two a.m., you should get to sleep, if you ever need anything...I am always here Eve." she smiled. I gave a small smile back to her. "Thank you so much Winter, I needed this talk." I replied. "My pleasure, happy dreams." she said before quietly walking away. Shortly after, I orbed away and went up to my room as well.

I stared out at planet earth. I started thinking how much my life has changed. This all started in October, when Winter told me my fate. Did I ever think I would turn out to be an Archangel Wizard Princess? Not at all! I started thinking about how I just abandoned my adoptive family, and how they probably didn't even realize I was gone. *I'm grateful that this change happened.* I thought to myself.

I have a bed now; I'm no longer in a basement. I'm royal now. "A modern self-saving Cinderella with powers or something," I muttered to myself. Even with all the chaos, I knew I had to be grateful. I thought about all that Winter had said until I began to fall asleep. I was hoping my dreams would give me answers about what to do. But as soon as I started dreaming, jet black darkness took over me, and I would end up in a dreamless sleep.

XLIII

Unfriendly Friend

I woke up and counted down the days until I didn't have to wake up and orb off to earth for school anymore. "Only until June." I whispered to myself as I checked myself in the long mirror that hung in my closet. The red V-neck and blue jeans matched well with my ponytail and minimal makeup. I honestly didn't care for how I looked on earth anymore. I was starting to feel that I didn't have to impress anyone there anymore. But for the sake of my future title as queen, I practiced having that aura and upkeep in my appearance. No more sweat pants outside the house for me. I groaned to myself and orbed to school.

"Hello my future queen, how are you?" Josh asked, walking beside me on the outside connecting bridge of our school. "Please don't remind me." I laughed. "I'm good, and you?" I asked the guardian. "Well you know angels hardly ever feel less than great." he said. I rolled my eyes. "Lucky you, it sucks to be a mix breed I'm always stressed out now a days. Thank God I have the Archangel/wizard sleeping habits; if I had to get normal amounts of sleep, I'm afraid I would have had multiple strokes by now." I said half sarcastically.

The first bell rang and I scoffed at the sound. "And that's the bell, time for three super boring classes." I said to Josh. He laughed. "Who are you telling, where's the challenge, when you know all the answers for all your class work before your teacher even explains the subject of learning or directions?" Josh replied. "Being able to read minds, and being supernaturally smart, the fact that we know practically everything...is just amazing." I said to him. "Couldn't agree more, see you later." Josh said as he headed into his classroom. I meant what I said about being supernaturally smart being amazing, I managed to keep straight A's in all of my classes without even trying. But being supernaturally smart, doesn't excuse us from being late to class, and getting detention. And because I didn't want to be late for class, I started speed walking, and bumped smack into of all people, Parker.

He looked a little different to me, and I couldn't put my finger on what it was that was different about him. Even though a weird feeling ached in my body while in his presence, I was happy to see that he was okay; he hasn't been in school for over a week. "Sorry about that." I said picking up my books and pen from off the floor. "It's fine... no harm done." he replied while reaching down for his blue folder and an ice pack.

"Hey Parker...even though we are not together anymore... it would be nice to be friends." I said to him. He titled his head to the right. "It would be nice...but no, we can't be. See, my parents taught me to never talk to strangers, and since I think of you as a stranger now, it wouldn't be right." He replied smugly. "Why would you consider me as a stranger?" I asked clearly confused. "Because you're not the girl I met in October." Parker said.

"No kidding!" I muttered under my breath. If it weren't for my life changes, Parker's comment would have felt like being cut open with a knife, but now with the life I live, I've heard worst comments. I watched him grip the ice pack in his left hand and my heart started beating a little quicker. *Play it cool Eve, don't act worried.* I thought to myself. "What happen to you?" I asked casually pointing to the ice pack. "Some kind of bug bite." Parker said. *Oh great, what the heck is going to happen to him? Is he going to turn into friken Spiderman now? Let's pray that Scarlett hasn't done any damage to him.* I mentally spoke to myself.

"It would be best if I didn't talk to you anymore." Parker finished. I rolled my eyes at him. "You know what, I was only trying to be nice...but I can see that now that was a mistake." I said while walking away from him, and heading in the direction of my class. I knew Parker really well to know that he's *not* really a snob, and that he's probably behaving this way towards me to save himself some heartache. I couldn't take it so personal.

By the time my last class came around, I was starting to feel like something was wrong. I telepathically told Josh to keep his senses sharp, and be ready for anything. I felt like something was going to happen, but I wasn't sure of what or how soon. I alerted Marius and the others as well, telling them to keep their guards up and keep the mansion secured tightly. My stomach had felt like someone had punched it out of me, overall my insides were twisting and the feeling was obviously not okay with me. "Hopefully I am overreacting. I've got to be overreacting." I mumbled to myself.

After the bell rang and I put my books away, I walked to the parking lot, and my stomach almost fell out of my butt. Standing by Parker's car, a sight took me by surprise, and I didn't know exactly how to react "Scarlett?" I asked in shock.

XLIV

Mind Games

Scarlett pulled out of her embrace with Parker, and looked at me. When she realized that it was me, a wicked grin took over her face. "Of all the days I see you again, it would be here! What are you doing here and with Parker?!" I asked angrily. I felt a hand appear on my shoulder and looked up to see that it was Josh.

"Oh, have you met my friend Parker? Actually he's kind of like my best friend." she smiled evilly. "Don't let her get to you, control your anger, we are surrounded by humans." Josh said in my head. I breathed in and out, and tried to relax myself, as I watched Scarlett walk towards me. "See, you've been hurting and killing all of my friends. And more importantly painful, you took away my best friend so I have to get you back." Scarlett said whispering to me. "What do you mean?" I asked confusingly. Scarlett put her hand to her heart and fake gasped. "Oh, I see you haven't caught up with your Permian history, seems like Tess has some explaining to do, don't be so hard on him though, he's been replaced." she smiled and folded her arms.

On the inside I wanted to cry as well as throw a fireball in her face, but I refused to let Scarlett see me like that, and I couldn't let human kids see me in action. "You can have Tess, as long as I have Permia in the end, and your ass ends up rotting in a pit of fire, *which* you will be. I don't care who you *take* from me." I smiled at her. Scarlett frowned, and tried to slap me, but I blocked her by grabbing her hand and pushing her to the ground.

I laughed at her, and started walking away and headed to my car with Josh following behind. "I'm coming for you Eve; you better stay on your toes!" I heard Scarlett yell. I turned to her and laughed. "So much talking, and little action, how is the ground treating you baby cousin?" I asked her. Parker's eyes widened as if he just found out that Scarlett and I were related. And I walked away and got in my car.

Josh got in on the passenger side and we sat in a scary silence as I drove to Ms. Burns' parking lot. "I am such a horrible person, how did I let this happen?" I asked breaking the silence. I ordered more guards to watch over Parker, I needed to keep a close eye on him. Scarlett's plans to torture me went up another level by her getting Parker to stand by her side. Scarlett caught me off guard. The whole time I thought if anything, she would kill Parker, not let him live and seduce him. The anger flowed through my body and I only thought of revenge. My vengeance on her will come soon. But soon didn't feel soon enough.

XLV

Warrior Princess

The sky was a pale purple, the color of lavender. The winds increased, and the Permian trees grumbled. "Eve, why are you so upset? You have to solve whatever problem you're having, the winds you're creating are horrid!" Marius said to me telepathically. I muted my mind, blocked him out and watched the arrow I had just release hit the target directly. I couldn't tell anyone besides Josh about Parker. I had to deal with that specific problem by myself. I hadn't seen Tess for an entire week and some days. As much as it pained me...it angered me even more.

It pained me because, he was a great friend, I easily trusted him, and let him into my bizarre life, and he had hurt me and then left like a coward. It angered me because I let myself let him get closer to me. And it angered me that Tess had failed to mention who or *what* he really was. And it definitely angered me to know that he actually knew Scarlett, and they had possibly been in a relationship together.

I laid down on my belly on the ground in the backyard, tired from training hard. Goose bumps started to form on my arms and I quickly sat up, and looked around. I spotted nothing, well that is until a silver shimmer shined in the front of me, and Tess appeared. He stood about fifty feet away, staring at me. I saw confusion and maybe even sorrow in his eyes, but I didn't care. He was a demon, and I had to do what was right. Tess slowly started walking towards me, and I stood up. I grabbed an arrow, and attached it to my bow, and aimed for Tess.

Tess dived out of the way and began running as I launched a series of arrows at him. Growing tired of the bow and arrow, I grabbed my father's staff. I watched Tess run behind a tree, and I aimed for it, burning a hole into the tree and knocking it to the ground.

This motion repeated itself three more times before Tess climbed a tree top. I breathed in and out slowly taking time on my aim, before aiming the staff for Tess and striking him. I watched him fall from the tree top and I put my staff in my less dominant left hand. With one motion of my hand, I forced him over to me and dropped him to the ground. I pulled out my favorite dagger and walked in front of him. "How dare you come here? How dare you actually have the guts to show your face to me?" I asked Tess with gritted teeth. Tess didn't answer; he was too busy trying to catch his breath.

"You're a demon! *And* you actually know Scarlett...why didn't you attack me? Why didn't you kill me? You had so many chances!" I yelled. Tess stood up and I tightened my grip on my staff. "I wanted to kill you, at first I did. Scarlett filled everyone's heads with vile lies about you. But then I met you, and saw how innocent you are. How pure, curious and strong you are. I fell in love with you the first day I laid eyes on you, and I fell harder the moment we met." Tess said. I narrowed my eyes.

I couldn't love Tess; I couldn't have feelings for him. People of his kind aren't supposed to be with *my* kind. But why do I feel like I'm just telling myself lies. I'm denying my true feelings for Tess. "I can't love you. Everything we had, every moment we shared wasn't real it was all a lie. I feel nothing but hollowness towards you." I said with almost no emotion. Internally I felt defeated. I felt weak, and I honestly I just wanted to cry a river. Scarlett was winning. Tess is a demon, and Parker is standing beside Scarlett. How could I control an entire dimension when everything I do is wrong. Every positive thing

I try to do, turns into a negative. My crowning date was approaching quickly; it was in a week and two days to be exact. The angels held me at a certain standard and it was all just too much pressure, too much weight on my shoulders. At this point, I didn't want to do it anymore. I didn't want to fight.

I looked up at Tess. "Kill me now." I said dropping my staff to the ground, and giving him space and opportunity to do his worst to me. Tess looked at me in shock. "Go ahead." I said looking into his brown eyes. Tess shook his head no. "I can't." He said lowly. Tess walked over to me cautiously. I did nothing but close my eyes and avoided the tears from actually falling from my face. With my eyes still closed, I could feel Tess inch closer and closer to me, and soon he held me in a tight embrace, rocking me back and forth." Everything will be okay." He said as he kissed the top of my head. "Everything will be okay." He repeated.

I wanted to fight him off but I couldn't, I don't think I had the will power in me to do it. I felt so weak that if Scarlett had come to kill me at this very moment, she would have done it fairly easy. I also had to figure out if I could really forgive Tess for not telling me what he really was. I know that if he would have told me first before getting to each other, I probably would have killed him.

Also, with me feeling more than weak in this moment, I needed him. I needed him to keep me sane and strong. Even if being with him or loving him is wrong, it was one less thing that was pressuring me. Tess was always more like the anecdote for my pressure, he became my best friend and whenever I was with him, I felt at ease, and my weakness solidified and I became stronger.

After pulling out of the hug, Tess looked at all my weapons on the ground. "What are you doing?" he asked. "What does it look like? ...I'm training." I said to him. I tiredly sat cross legged on my blanket. "I can help you train. I could tell you haven't really practiced on your wizard powers as much as you've practiced your Arch traits." He said. I looked up at him tiredly. "The way you were using your staff. A pro would have hit me on the first strike." He smirked. I snorted at his comment. "I don't know...maybe you being around me, while Scarlett is alive...maybe it's not such a good idea." I suggested. Tess sighed. "Don't worry about me; I'm not afraid of Scarlett. And besides, Scarlett will be expecting a lacking in your wizard instincts, and we can't have that can we?" He asked. I shook my head no. "Now, let's practice." He said as he grabbed my staff. To gain some knowledge and leverage over Scarlett, I decided to bottle up and dismiss my issues with Tess and save them for a later day. I grabbed my staff and joined him in the middle of the field.

XLVI

Focused for Scarlett

With my crowning date in two days, every entire being in the Caylan mansion could feel that something was coming. To be ready, I knew I needed to practice my wizard powers. I needed to strengthen my powers as a whole, even though I am comfortable with using and controlling my archangel powers. I needed to be ready, and I promised myself I would be ready.

I ended up missing out on school for an entire week to train with the wizards. I practiced with Ms. Burns, Luke and Cat. From them, I learned to control my powers, and create a bond with my staff. I learned that I had to trust my powers, and that it had to trust me. I started running eight miles a day, and would do some martial arts, or upper body strength positions to go along with my staff play with Tess. Cami even taught me spells and how to keep calm by practicing yoga.

Each day I practiced, my body would kill me but I looked more like a warrior. More lean, and more poised. I became more focused than ever, I became fierce, and everything I did was absolute. I decided to only focus on Scarlett for now. She was my main target, and after dealing with her, I could focus on what was really happening with Parker, school and ruling Permia. Also for now, others would join me in protecting the innocent, I couldn't focus on the innocent and focus on Scarlett and the incoming damage that I

Hidden

felt was to come, at the same time.

XLVII

First Valentine

I was resting on a chair on my terrace, putting a fishtail braid in my hair with my eyes closed, when I felt something touching my face. I didn't move because I didn't know exactly what it was at first, until I noticed that it was very, very warm and caressing my cheek, it was a hand. I kept my eyes closed, and after a few seconds, I grabbed the *hand* that was touching me, and suddenly opened my eyes.
"What are you doing?" I asked Tess. Whose heart, I could hear, was beating rapidly. "It's safe to say that you just scared the hell out of me!" he laughed. I smiled at him and let go of his hand, while healing the heat that his touch gave me in the process. "What are you doing here?" I asked him. "Just wanted to see you, and it is Valentine's day." he replied." Do you like them?" He asked as he handed me a vase of blue, purple and turquoise orchids. "I love them; they are beautiful, thank you so much." I smiled and leaned up to peck his lips.
"Orchids are my favorite you know." I smirked at him. "Yeah I noticed, whenever we went for a walk and we passed the garden by Immortal, you would always look at the Orchids." He smiled. "Oh the stalker watcher you are *Contress Draven!*" I smirked. Tess cringed when I called him by his first name. "Your evil!" he joked. I snorted.
I sat the Orchids on the floor next to me and watched Tess sit down on the chair beside me. I couldn't think about spending a great Valentine's Day evening with Tess until I finally got something off my

chest. Something that I had been putting off, but I couldn't handle it internally anymore.

"How did you meet Scarlett? Were you two a couple?" I asked him in a more angry tone than I expected. "Where did that come from?" he asked me with folded arms. He wasn't angry, just confused by the sudden subject. I huffed and walked into my bedroom and put the orchids on my dresser. Yes, I am a bit of a drama queen. "I saw her again, she made a visit to me at school and she told me..." I started. I *was* going to tell Tess the entire story but then I decided to leave Parker out of it.

"She told me you two were best friends, and not to be so hard on you when you explained yourself to me, because you've been replaced." I said. "We never dated, we were only friends." Tess said. I shook my head in disbelief. "Don't lie to me Tess." I replied. "I am not lying to you Eve!" he said through gritted teeth. The one thing that Tess hated more than being called by his full name was when he was being called a liar. But can you blame me for calling him one?

I turned away from him, not wanting to look at him. Tess grabbed my arms, and pushed me against the wall. After turning my head to the right, not looking at him, he put his finger under my chin and pushed it up so I had to look at him. "We were only friends, and I didn't want to tell you because I was afraid of how you will react. I didn't want to have to deal with how you are reacting right now, and it's about something, so little as friendship." Tess said.

I pushed Tess away, and rubbed my burning chin. "She's my cousin and arch enemy Tess! If anything you should have told me sooner!" I yelled at him. "I knew if I would have told you, you would have thought I was with her, on her side, and not give me the time of day. I wanted to be with you, so I decided that I couldn't take that risk!" he yelled. I wanted to easily forgive Tess, but my anger was building and I was ready to burst. There are *too* many secrets being kept between us. I pushed Tess with so much force that he flew into the wall, and landed in a thud.

I grabbed my iPod and sat on my chaise. Scrolling until I came across one of my favorite songs *All mixed up* by *"The Red House Painters"* Tess got up and snatched my iPod away from me. I looked at him with wide eyes and was ready to say something but he beat me to it by speaking. "I'm sorry for not telling you about me being *who* I am, and about Scarlett...just stop acting like you don't care about me and stop being stubborn and listen to me!" Tess commanded. "I am not being stubborn, I am being a smart future queen, and if I have to cut you off I will, you can leave Tess!" I shouted as I walked over to my mirror. Yeah, this was yet another horrible Valentine's Day. Valentine's Day was never my favorite, maybe because I'm always single on that day.

Tess walked over and snaked his pale arm around my waist. I closely took in of our reflections in the mirror. His pale skin contrasting and yet meshing nicely with my golden brown tone. "I'm sorry Eve, what more do you want? And I'm not leaving, because I like you too much to leave. But I am sorry." he said. I turned to look at Tess and I gulped down the lump I had in my throat, and I could feel my heart beating out of my chest. I felt a fire in the pit of my stomach, and I knew internally I had forgiven Tess. Isn't that what angels and humans are supposed to do? Learn to forgive?

Tess kissed me softly and our lips sizzled. However I couldn't control myself and didn't care to stop. I pressed into him wrapping my arms around his neck. After a few minutes, I realized what we were doing and what was hopefully about to happen. I Pushed Tess off of me and he landed on my chaise. I then got on top of him and put my mouth on his. I even pushed my hips closer into his.

From the back of his throat, Tess let out a few groans. "You feel so damn good." He whispered to me. I looked at Tess with my heating purple eyes. His eyes were glowing an electric blue, and the only thing I could see in them, were desire and lust. I knew what *I* wanted, I wanted him, and I could tell that he wanted me, and I knew what we *both* wanted. But, it felt like making out with him was bad; it felt like something I shouldn't have been doing. I felt a little guilty on the inside, but how can you believe something is bad when it externally feels right, and even feels right to your heart.

Being with Tess felt right, and that outweighed the bad feeling. I pressed my lips against Tess's lips. Tess pulled my cream colored silk tank top off and his hands roamed my shirtless body. I felt my skin burning, it was burning like fire. I opened my once shut eyes, and looked at Tess and gasped. His hands and face was turning red from touching me. He pulled away from the kiss, and put his thumb to my cheek, which immediately started to heat up. "We need to stop. It's too hot." He whispered. I nodded my head in agreement.

Tess and I stared into each other's eyes, mine fluorescent purple and his electric blue, knowing we should stop because of the painful heat and yet we re-attached our lips together, not wanting to stop because of the wonderful heat. I decided the uncomfortable burning sensation needed to hinder, therefore I willed a healing to *both* of our bodies. My body became warm, the burning sensation hindered by the healing.

A cool, refreshing feeling took over my body; I looked down at Tess, and leaned down to him. "Better?" I asked in a whisper. He smirked at me. "Much, thank you." he said, just before pressing his lips to mine. I closed my eyes, and enjoyed the warm pleasure once again. I tugged the bottom of his shirt, and he received the hint and removed it from his body. I took in every inch of his beautiful pale torso.

I stood up and took Tess's hand and led him to my bed where the rest of our clothing was removed. Even though every time we touched skin to skin it burned, I felt something for Tess that I never felt for anyone else before, not even Parker.

My heart exploded for Tess. Our connection was intensely passionate, magical, mysterious, and thrilling. We both enjoyed the comfortable but indescribable feelings we both received from one another. He made me feel like I was ready to be queen; everything with him was somewhat easy. Easier than just dealing with the Angels. Tess got me; he understood the good and the semi bad in me, the good and bad that I didn't even understand myself.

I rested my head on Tess's chest. My first time was beautiful, and an experience of it's own that I do not regret. Our heated but healing bodies intertwined, and as both of our eyes began to flutter, we fell asleep in each other's embrace. Tess and I both were at peace.

XLVIII

Pained Lover

After that wonderful night with Tess, I hoped to wake up in pure bliss; however, I didn't wake up feeling at peace anymore. I woke up to a scream, a male screaming. I quickly sat up in my bed to see that Tess was laying on the floor screaming in pain as Marius's staff forcefully ejected it's power into Tess's body. "Stop!" I yelled as I raised my hand to Marius, knocking him and his staff to the floor. "What do you think you are doing?!" I yelled at Marius, as I covered myself in a sheet, and ran to Tess's aid. "I thought he was going to attack you Eve, I saw him standing over your bed, and I thought he was going to harm you! He's a Demon!" Marius yelled.

    I looked at the burns on Tess's body as he was shaking, screaming and curled into a ball. "Get out!" I told Marius in a whisper. He stood there without saying a word, and I turned to glare at him. "Get out!" I yelled full of anger. Without question, or hesitation, Marius disappeared from my room.

    I wanted to cry while watching Tess in pain, but I couldn't let him see me cry. I didn't want him to worry about me, when *he* was the one that needed worrying. I put my hands on Tess's ribcage and pressed hard. A warm tingle sensation and a white glow began to pour from my hands and on to his body. Tess screamed in pain. "Relax babe, try to relax." I whispered. Whenever I healed Tess, it was always the both of us being healed in the process. The only other solitary person I ever healed was myself. I didn't know if trying to heal a demon alone would work, but I had to try. I kept my hands on Tess for three minutes before finally removing them.

I then sat back on my bed and watched him. I couldn't do anything but watch and wait now. He had stopped screaming, but he was still trembling on the floor. Once he had stopped screaming in pain, is when I realized that my own body was covered in burn marks. The Archangel genes I had been blessed with from my mother had simmered the sting, and the true side effects I would normally have had if Tess touched me, if I were simply an Angel. I silently thanked my Mother for being a Caylan; I silently thanked her for being an Archangel, and blessing me with the ability to heal myself and others.

XLIX

Tess's Truth

Minutes had passed, hours had passed, the moon and sun even passed, and Tess was now sleeping somewhat peacefully on the floor, in the same position he had been in. I went out on the terrace and looked at the moon.

"Hi." Tess said, coming from behind me, and wrapping his arms around my waist, just minutes after I had gotten up. "You scared me." I said just before gently hugging him. "Easy little one, I'm still burning hot." he said. I looked at his red toned abs, and I looked up at him, "Seriously or are you being cocky?" I asked. Tess looked into my eyes. "Serious." he said with a little chuckle. I then backed away from Tess. "How come that happened to you, why'd it take so long for you to heal?" I asked him, once again a little embarrassed from my inexperience in Permia health. Maybe I could take a class on that in Immortal U.

If Marius had done that to me, if he would have zapped me, it would have felt like a little shock... but it literally burned Tess, I don't understand why what happened. I thought to myself. "Well, we are different species, what may hurt me, might not hurt you and vice versa. Marius is an elder and I am who I am, which means he can cause some damage to me. Dark elves aren't that powerful." Tess said. "And besides I woke up burning a little bit from us lying with each other, guessing you stopped healing us when we fell asleep." Tess said.

I turned my back to Tess and looked at the sky. "What?" He asked. "Just thinking how, I feel bad that we can't be intimate with each other without burning... and also the fact that it's been six weeks since we first officially met and I feel like I know you, but I don't know you. Are you a dark elf? Or a demon? Tess who are you?" I asked.

Tess took my hand in his and I immediately healed us both before we had a chance to burn. "A rouge Dark elf, that's fallen for a kick ass Archangel Wizard princess." Tess admitted. I looked at him. "Why rouge, what happen? I thought you were a demon..." I asked more then said. I wanted to know everything about Tess, the *Dark elf* that I lost my virginity to, the *dark elf* that I was basically intoxicated by.

"My mother was a light elf; she was pure, good, beautiful. I think that's what draws me to you, your light and purity. My mother, she fell in love with my father who was a dark elf. I was only three when the war for Permia started so I don't remember everything, but what I've been told was that, my mother and father both died in the war." Tess said with his head down. I stayed silent; I didn't really know what to say at first.

"Maybe we're not so different from each other after all." I said after a while as I cupped Tess's cheek. Tess deeply exhaled. "I was placed with my father's friends who were dark elves, since I have no family left. I was taught to fight and protect myself, I was taught to steal, and how to survive on my own. Dark elves don't abide by the same rules light elves do." Tess said. "I wanted to go to live with the light elves, but they don't accept you if there's an ounce of dark elf in your blood. So I ran away, I was tired of the life that I was living." He said.

"I was wondering in the shadow forest one day, and I ran into Scarlett. Dark elves are not allowed to be with any other species but our own even for companionship, so Scarlett cast a spell and turned me into a hybrid. Making me a half dark elf and demon, that way she could be with me. But I never saw her in that way. I found her as a comfort, it's lonely when you're surrounded by no one but yourself on a daily bases." He said. I wanted to scream at him, but choose to keep listening.

"We lived in her mother's cottage in those woods until they began to hunt for her after she killed the rest of your family members. They, the council torched her cottage; thankfully I wasn't in the cottage at the time. Neither was Scarlett, and we ran away from the shadow forest, we ended up coming here, closer to the town." He said.

When Tess realized I was going to keep quiet, he continued talking. "With Scarlett, I felt like I was still at home, with the dark elves. Surrounded by evil, lies and deceit. Eventually I left her, set my own rules, and made a living for myself." Tess continued. "So, you left because you wanted to be good?" I asked him. Tess smiled a little. "Just like you have to find the balance of good and evil in you, so do I. Scarlett said there would never be any good in me, but my mother was a light elf, so good has to be in here somewhere." He said touching his chest.

"There is good in you, I've see it, I've felt it... you just have to stay around the good, to remain good." I stated. "It's not that simple, I'm a rouge elf demon hybrid, people don't take chances on a guy like me, it's a miracle I have the job and friends that I do. If they only found out I was a demon…" Tess started but I cut him off. "You're only half demon, so stop calling yourself a demon, and only that. I took a chance on you! More than an hours' worth of a chance on you…. and it was worth it, and you will always have me." I admitted.

It felt good to admit my feelings towards Tess. He pulled me close and gave me a hug. I immediately blessed him with a healing so I wouldn't hurt his naked upper body. "I'll always bet on you, my Elf." I chuckled. "Thank you." he said seriously while we were embraced. On the inside just a little, it did bother me that Tess was half demon. But if I can keep him on the good side, I will. I'd do anything to keep him good.

"Here this is for you; it was the rest your Valentine's Day gift, but things kind of led to other things. I was going to give it to you when we woke up, which is why I was standing over you." he said while pulling something from his pocket. "Sorry about that, I feel so bad that happened. It was majorly wrong for him to do that." I replied. "He didn't know, he thought he was protecting you. By the way, you even look beautiful when you wake up." He smirked. "I really don't." I blushed.

Tess gave me a ring. It had a dark purple heart with a gold crown around it. I didn't want it on my ring finger, so I put it on my thumb. I looked up at him and smiled. "Thank you, it's beautiful." I gasped while giving him a quick hug. "You're welcome." he smiled.

I stayed silent and looked down at the ground. "What else is on your mind?" he asked. I sighed. "My ex-boyfriend, Parker... Scarlett's done something to him. I feel like I can't do this, like I am a bad person for this job. Me helping people is a joke." I confessed to Tess. "You're not a bad person, this is a hard job." he replied. "I'm supposed to protect the innocent, and I let her get parker." I said sadly.

Tess carefully placed his hands on the fabric of my shirt on my shoulders, careful not to touch my skin. "You can do anything you want, if you want to, you have the will power to do so. Power, an unbelievable amount of power is inside of you, you just need to bring it out of you." Tess said, comforting me. "You're a future queen; life isn't going to be simple for you. But you don't have to do it alone; you don't have to do *any* of this alone. Let me help you." he said. I looked into his eyes and saw honesty and truth, and I had to believe and trust in him.

Even though Tess is who he is, and I am who I am, I knew that he had a secure spot in my heart. I had more in common with him than anyone else. We both are hybrids of breeds pure and considerably evil. We both lost our parents in the same war. We both were loners, and are somewhat used to being lonely. We were that way until we both found someone who replaces the loneliness with love, laughter, sarcasm, mystery and understanding. I looked up at him and leaned in, and he leaned down. We met in another slow, soft and warm kiss. "Thank you for this, and thank you for being you." I said, wrapping my arms around Tess and giving him a hug. "Anytime." Tess replied kissing the top of my head.

Tess stayed with me that night. We both were in my bed, but we kept to ourselves, I didn't know if he was totally healed or not, and I didn't want to hurt him. Tess slept peacefully, but I was wide awake. I had a few uneasy thoughts inside my head.

I had been neglecting school so I could train hard, and if I kept neglecting it, I wouldn't be able to graduate and permanently move to Permia after graduation. I decided that I have to let go of some things. Right then I decided to hold off from training. Now I was growing a little tired of waiting for Scarlett, and I felt that I had practiced enough anyway, so I was ready for her.

Also, regardless of the amazing chemistry between Tess and I, it scared me to think that Scarlett would go after him. How badly he got injured from Marius, made me scared. If he reacted that badly to him, he would die from one zap from Scarlett. Reluctantly, I knew I had to also hold off from Tess for the moment. I realized my true feelings for him, I realized I love him and I would do anything for him, and that includes protecting him with every fiber in my being. Even though I love him, I can't risk him like I risked Parker. Parker, he was a whole other issue. I had decided on a plan, then it was time for me to close my eyes, and that's exactly what I did. I shut my eyes, and dreamed of darkness.

L

The Law

Tess was gone when I woke up. I knew he had to go to work, and I thought I would surprise him by showing up to *The Ridge*. As I got dressed, I noticed that I was getting used to the "Arch Wizard Princess" look I had developed, it was now effortless. My high ponytail, grey tank top, purple jumpsuit and black boots looked nice on me. I was a new me, a confident me. A beautiful me, that now I actually felt and believed in.

I orbed downstairs to where my Angel family were spread out in the family room, I breathed loudly to get their attention. "Eve! You need to explain yourself; you are not acting like a future Archangel queen!" Elsa screamed. I looked at her with dull eyes. "You can't be with a demon Eve, you're an Arch, and it can't be done." Chaska tried to explain. I rolled my eyes. Did they honestly think that I didn't know that what Tess and I were doing was bad? Did they think that I didn't wonder about how this will affect Permia? They were all going on as if I just dismissed what Tess and I truly were. Like I just dismissed the burn we both felt whenever we touched each other's skin.

"You guys need to listen to yourselves... I am not just an Archangel! I am the daughter of a Wizard Warrior... I cannot be angelic every second of the day, that's not who I Am." I yelled. I then turned to Chaska. "And as for it can't be done...I am an Archangel

Wizard Warrior Princess! Can't be done? Years ago I'm sure everyone told my mother that she and my father couldn't be done, that I couldn't be done. But I am here." I huffed. "Basic rules and such things, don't apply to me. I make the rules okay, I am the judge, the sheriff, and I'm the one with the badge of significant leadership, I make the rules here! I am the law!" I stated. I mentally calmed myself down.

"I will always be an Archangel, and I will do what's right for our people, and even all of you. But I will also do what's right of me. The Archangel *and* Wizard side of me. As long as I am protecting, saving and guiding, I don't see any harm." I said. "But that boy is a demon. Demons cannot be good. They also can't be half good, and half bad. Demons are just as soulless as vampires. You are not evil, Zion wasn't evil." Marius stated. "You can't see...."Elsa started. I raised my hand up to stop her from talking. "That boy, Tess... is good. His parents died in the same war as mine. He met Scarlett and she turned him into a demon, naturally he's an elf, light and dark. And he's my responsibility." I said. "As for me, my father my not have been exactly evil, but he didn't live purely in Archangel Ways, he was a wizard. He cut corners and did whatever he wanted, and chose to stand beside my *mother,* pure good." I looked all of my Arch family in the eye.

"I'm practically half of each, half good and half bad but I represent good. So why can't other's do the same?" I asked. "We have to stop judging people so quickly family." I said before I walked away. "An Angel and a Demon, that's a tragic love story, waiting to be written about." I heard Marius mutter before I orbed to the tavern.

LI

I Love You

I sat on one of the stools and watched Tess work behind the bar. "Hey." he smiled when he saw me sitting there. "Hi, when you get a break, I need to talk to you." I told him. Tess stopped pouring a drink. "You okay?" He asked. I hesitated before answering. "Not really." I replied. "Okay, meet me outside in three." he said just before opening two bottles of birch beer.

I waited outside and mentally rehearsed my speech for Tess, just before he came out and bear hugged me from behind. "You have to stop doing that!" I laughed. "What's up?" he chuckled. I took his hand and led him to the path that led to Immortal U. Standing in the dark; I looked up at Tess and then looked at my feet. "This thing we have together has to be toned down a little for now. I need to really focus on school, and Scarlett. It scares me to think that she can and possibly will come after you. I'm not saying we need to break up for good, just tone things down before everything gets too reckless and crazy." I announced.

Tess's smile fell. "Seriously?" he asked. I hesitated before answering, I was a little afraid of what he would say, how he would react. "Yes, I don't want to start something so serious with you, and then something bad happens I can't hurt you like that. I don't know what I'd do if something horrible happens to you. And it seems like my life is just getting more, and more complicated." I bit my lip, to protect myself from almost choking up. Tess put his put his finger under my chin and lifted my head up so that I could look at him. He took my cheeks in the palm of his hands, and kissed me deeply.

Automatically I closed my eyes and instantly I had felt a hot, tingly sensation. On my lips and cheeks. I also felt somewhat weak, and lightheaded. No other guy could kiss me, and make me feel the way Tess did. I wrapped my arms around Tess's neck; he then suddenly lifted me up and I wrapped my legs around his waist. "That was unexpected." I whispered before kissing him again. "I wasn't prepared to say this at all, but it seems like this is a good time to tell you." He said, out of breath and just before he put my feet back down to the ground. "I love you Eve." Tess admitted. I swear when I heard him say those four words, I wanted to fly to the sky, on a magic carpet or float on a cloud. This was the first time anyone has ever said "I love you" to *me*, and I actually felt something back. It was scary, yet exciting, and just lovely. But the fear I had in my body was fiercely strong.

"I really love you, so don't push me away, everything you're going through, we can go through together, you don't have to handle all of this alone." Tess continued. "After everything we've been through, especially the last week or so, you can't do this. You can't just let me go." He said. I looked down at my feet, and tried to think of happy thoughts so that I wouldn't tear up. "I love you too Tess." I said, now looking straight into his eyes. I backed away from him and then orbed to the front steps of the Mansion.

I didn't know what to say, I didn't know how I was feeling. These were new emotions that I've never felt before. I panicked, and had to disappear from his sight. He was making me change my mind, change my plan, and I knew I needed to stay focused, but... I also *needed* Tess.

I looked to the sky for a few seconds before heading inside. I was hoping my mother would have seen what had just happened. I hoped she would randomly show up, and give me advice. "Hey!" I heard being yelled from behind me. I turned around and Tess came into view.

"Really?!" I said to Tess in more of a statement rather than a question. "Why would you walk away like that, after eight weeks Eve?" Tess asked, he was getting angry. "That's how you want us to end? You care for me Eve, you know you do, and you know I care for you, so stop being so scared, and stop thinking negative... and just be with Me." he said rushing up to me and caressing my cheek. I breathed deep and was just about to give into Tess before I heard my name being called.

"Eve!" Josh yelled after appearing right in front of Tess and I. "Is everything okay?" I asked concerned. Josh ran up to me. "No! Scarlett just had some of her men ambush me! I was watching Parker's house, when it happened; I'm guessing she was watching me the *entire* time." Josh said trying to catch his breath. "Where's parker?" I asked scared. "With Scarlett." Josh confirmed.

Suddenly Josh and I both fell to the ground. My ears were burning from hearing loud torturous screaming and cries for help inside of my head. Usually communicating from our minds is easy, a little alarming at first, but you get used to it, but this... this was causing an unbearable pain to my brain, and ears. The person screaming was clearly in pain.

"What's wrong?" Tess asked helping me up. "Someone's mentally screaming for help, and screaming so loud that it almost blew my ear drums." I said. Tess ran into the house and called for Bobby and the others, who within one minute all flew down or ran out to Josh, Tess and I. I looked at my family, and realized Destiny was missing. Destiny had been the screaming voice I heard in my head. I was just about to speak when Tess yelled "Get down!" and tackled Marius, Chaska and Bobby, knocking them to the ground and saving them from a huge fireball.

I ran over and helped Tess up. "Looks like the *demon* saved your lives." I said to the three on the ground. Tess helped each one up and I could hear reluctant thank yous from the angels and elder. "Clearly, Scarlett has called for the start of war. It's time people, get ready." I said looking at each individual in the eyes. "She would choose to attack you right before you're crowning." Tess growled. Marius had ran into the house to summon the other angels, elders and council members.

Shortly after he returned a massive colony of angels appeared from out of the sky followed by vampires, centaurs, wolves and even elves, along with other noble creatures that were coming to land in front of the mansion.

"Tess, I need you to go get Cat, Noah and everyone else, seems like the battle is about to begin." I said. Tess got up and immediately orbed away. I knew that this was the moment Scarlett had been waiting for. This was the time that Permia could shift to evil, and Scarlett would possibly take over the Earth. Or, I would reign and restore Permia back to peace, restore balance to the world, and avenge my family's death.

I then mentally spoke to my family, and told them to get ready for war. Then I sent out a silent prayer asking for strength and a victory over Scarlett. Nothing would stop me from ending her.... Nothing.

"Where are you? Destiny!? Where are you?" Bobby mentally tried to communicate. We all heard Destiny faintly say that she was in North side of the woods. Just as I got my composure back, Tess and a large group of others showed up. Over the past few weeks, we had been working with tons of people on my training and preparing ourselves for this moment.

"What's going on here?" Cat asked. "Scarlett has finally set up an attack." Marius said. "She has Destiny in the North side of the woods." Bobby added. Cat cocked her head to the side. "How do you know that it's Scarlett?" she asked. "Because no one else has the guts to kidnap an angel. Let alone, start an actual attack on the mansion. A fire element ball was thrown at Marius, Bobby and Chaska. Tess saved them." I said. Everyone nodded in understanding with me, and Cat high fived Tess.

"I'm not sure what Scarlett has planned but I'm ready to be done with her, and I'm going to need everyone's help. There's no telling how many Demons or what she has in her Army." I said. "I'm down." Luke said. I smiled at him, and the others who smiled back. "What do you need?" Tess asked stepping in front of me. I sighed. I looked down at all one hundred and fifty to one hundred and sixty Permian's in front of me and the council and elders to the left of me.

"I need Elsa, Jay and Joy and ten others to guard and protect the

East of the woods. Josh are you okay to fight?" I asked. Josh nodded his head yes. "Yeah, where do you want me?" he asked. "You, Chaska and Winter, you guys and thirteen others guard and protect the West." I announced, adding more protectors as the open coasts in the woods got larger. "Eli, Cat and Luke, with fifteen others guard and protect the South." I ordered. I turned to look at Marius. "Marius, round up the elders and council and please protect our home. Don't let anyone enter where we rest our heads." I said.

"Tess, Bobby ten others and myself will cover the North side." I said. "Everyone else, go straight into the field." I added. I knew that this wasn't going to end well. If that vision I had about Tess, Bobby and I walking through the woods is accurate, then I know something bad is going to happen to me. But I have a job to do, and Scarlett has to be dealt with no matter what.

LII

Beginning of War

I orbed up to my room and grabbed my staff, and put two daggers inside my boots. I stood in my room for a moment, and closed my eyes. I silently prayed for everything to work out, and for there to be minimal destruction. I silently prayed for everything that was about to happen, to *not* be as bad as I knew it could be.

I felt arms wrap around my waist, and I automatically knew it was Tess. "Everything will be okay." he assured me. I turned to face him. "Will it?" I asked him. He cupped my cheek in his hand; once again I felt that hot tingle that was starting to become familiar. "It will, and I will be by your side the entire time." he said. I nodded my head, and took his hand. I led him to the terrace and we peered out to the glowing woods of Permia, unable to see the evil that filled the grounds, but currently able to feel it around us. Tess and I orbed down, and I sent everyone on their way.

That left me, leading Tess and Bobby and the others into the Northern side of the woods. "This is kind of creepy." Tess said removing some of the brushes that were in his way. "Stop being such a scary cat." I chuckled. Tess looked at me. "I'm not a scary cat, but this is just eerie and freaky!" he smirked.

"Hey, um can we just focus on finding Destiny, imagine how scared she is." Bobby said. It kind of broke my heart how much he cared for her, and had to hear her suffer. To know that she was currently in pain and as of right now, and he couldn't do much about it. "Yeah, your right. Sorry, stop talking!" I said as I pushed Tess. Tess turned to me and pushed me back. "You stop!" he said. "Okay, I'm going to the right." Bobby said heading off in the direction he said he was going. "Yeah, both of you and four others should go to the right, you other six should go to the left and I'm going to go forward, if I need you I will scream." I said. Tess pouted while other's nodded their heads in agreement. "Okay." Bobby said as he continued to walk away. I smiled at Tess. "Be careful. "He whispered as he quickly kissed me. I watched him run off and catch up to Bobby and the others.

Before proceeding to go forward. I kept walking in the glowing forest until a red and orange color caught my eye. I slowly walked towards it, only stopping when I was a few feet away from it. In front of me were dead trees and glass, all burned. I frowned at the dead part of the forest. I looked at the three men who were sitting at a campfire. *I remember this.* I thought to myself.

While they were talking and laughing, with my staff firmly in my hand, I began to walk towards them. "Hey, you guys started a party without me? You should be ashamed of yourselves!" I said sarcastically. "It's Eve!" one of the guys around the campfire shouted. Before I knew it, all three "men" were facing me, and that's when I realized, just as I did in my premonition, they weren't men, they were ugly disfigured goblins! They grunted, and made weird animal like sounds to me. But I stood at a strong stance and didn't take my eyes off of them. I was fearless. I wasn't afraid of anything.

"You three are the ugliest *things* I ever saw, I feel bad for your parents!" I smirked. One of the goblins charged at me and I threw a fire ball at him, immediately frying him to a crisp. The second and third came after me at the same time and I put my staff to use. I battled with them using a blend of Bobby and Tess's teachings. I was just getting started when the second goblin jumped on my back, knocking my staff out of my hand and knocking me to the ground.

The second goblin lifted me up, and held my hands behind my back, as the third goblin slowly approached us, but I wasn't intimidated. "Well that was nice and cheap! you jumping on my back, that was such a cheap shot." I said sounding out of breath. The third goblin walked in front of me, and took my neck into his hands. I thought he was going to choke me but he tilted my head to the left and bit me. I screamed loudly and he let me go but only to smack me hard. The bite on my neck and the sting sensation on my face almost made me shed a tear. But instead of crying, I got angry.

I kicked the goblin that was in front of me, and flipped the second one off from holding me. I grabbed my staff and smacked the second one across the face with it. I then chick kicked him, making him land into the campfire he had built. I was beginning to feel almost tired, but I knew I only had one more to kill. I was just about to charge after the last goblin, when Bobby and Tess showed up. They surrounded the goblin, and held his arms so that he was unable to move. I walked up to the goblin that bit and smacked me, and slapped him across the face with the staff. He fell to the ground, so I picked him up, and threw him into the large campfire.

I fell to the ground and took some deep breaths. "Where were you two? Did you find Destiny?" I asked. "Scarlett had this side filled with goblins and vampires!" Tess said angrily. I felt tired, and blinked my eyes a few times. "What's wrong?" Bobby asked. I looked at him. "Just fought three goblins for the first time, and one had the nerve to bite me, sorry if I'm a little tired guys." I said to them both. Tess and Bobby looked at each other worriedly before they grabbed my arms and together, we went walking through the forest.

"We have to be quiet walking through here; Scarlett could have anybody out here ready to attack us." Bobby said. I snorted. "I can't wait until I find her so I can beat the hell out of her, literally." I said. Bobby gasped. "Language!" he whispered. Tess laughed. "Sorry, Mr. Angelic One." I whispered.

We were just out of the forest, and I could see the mansion lights, when I heard whispers from another voice inside my head. They were whispering some other language that I never heard before. Something foreign and not understandable. I couldn't really describe it, but it made me feel bad, worried, I knew something bad was going to happen. "Eve, are you okay?" Bobby asked me. I didn't respond, I couldn't open my mouth. Numbness and blurriness filled my eyes, and then, my world went completely dark.

LIII

Meeting the parents

The world around me was changing, from light to dark, to images of my life, images of me before my change, and after. The images stopped, and I recognized the setting I was in. There were beautiful glowing trees and grass around me, the sky was light purple, and the lake had glowing blue water streaming from it. I could see the beautiful fish swimming, and playing with one another. I was dressed how I was before I saw darkness, a plum purple jumpsuit and my hair was tied in a high ponytail. I dipped my hand in the water, right when I heard a voice I didn't recognize.

"Eve, how did you let a demon bite you, let alone touch your beautiful face?" a woman asked. I looked around, wondering where the sound was coming from, but I couldn't find anyone. "My daughter, I asked you a question." the voice said. I stood up. "Mom? wait am I dead? Am I dead?" I asked obviously confused. "Yes this is your mother my beautiful daughter. You are not dead, just hurt. How could you let this happen to you?" she asked. I bit my lip. "Um are you talking about Tess or that ugly goblin thing touching my face?" I asked. "The goblin, Tess may be half demon, but it doesn't mean he is bad. He wasn't born a natural demon. Love can make the impossible, possible." She clarified.

"Tess really cares for you, but keep in mind that you are an Archangel Princess and your life with Tess will be complicated in other's eyes. As you know Angels, don't do unpure things." she continued. Even though she I couldn't see her, I nodded in understanding at her words.

It was shocking that I was talking to my mother. I've had to wait eighteen years to just hear her voice; I sat on the grass and let a few tears roll down my cheeks. I never thought that this would happen. This was once again proof to me that all of this supernatural, other realm bullcrap wasn't *bullcrap*.

"It's alright." she cooed. "Just talk to me." She said. I sniffled before I spoke. "Well, the goblin thing just happened, and as for Tess. We can't even kiss without feeling a burning sensation and even though I don't want to, I think I should end it, it's less complicated if we aren't together." I said. "First as for the goblin, you need to be healed, you are in a battle Eve, you cannot be already weakened *before* going against Scarlett, the world needs you." My mother said.

A splash of water from the lake splashed onto my face. I gasped from shock and even a little fear. My face was instantly cooled, and I felt relaxed, and more charged than ever. "Now, as for you and Tess, you are part Wizard, therefore you will be attracted to both light and dark, but just because it's dark or is supposed to be dark through a stereotype, doesn't mean it's actually evil. You have human emotions that only *you* can battle, the angels won't understand. You have to make them see." She said.

"You have instincts in you that they don't have, as well as have an infinity to feel and react positively when you feel a darkness approaching. We all know what we're *supposed* to do but that doesn't mean we always do it, and it doesn't mean it's always the right decision. If it feels right, then go for it, and if it doesn't stay away from it. We all have to battle against the good and evil in ourselves, and obviously, you are no exception, future queen or not." my mother said.

"You know we are *always* watching you, and we love you no matter what. But you cannot be in a deep sleep for much longer Eve, you belong in Permia, continuing our legacy, and protecting both the worlds innocent from any evil." A deep voice said. I looked up to the sky. "Dad?" I asked. I heard a deep laugh come from somewhere in the sky.

I sighed and smiled. "It's good to finally hear your voices." I sniffled. "You have grown to become a beautiful young woman Eve, and you have done and will always do us proud." My dad's deep voice said. "Why me, this is too much to handle!" I said in a whine. "We never receive more than we can handle, and you're an Archangel Wizard Warrior Princess you are so much more powerful than you know Eve, we need to show you something, look into the lake." my father said.

I looked into the water and saw my face, but my face was soon distorted and the image of Permia appeared in front of me. Only, it wasn't the same Permia that I was used to. This Permia was dirty, and covered in black and ash from being burned. The tree tops were brown and no longer glowing. The Caylan Mansion was now discolored.

Downtown had become a shopping center for Robbers, and Immortal University looked like it was under construction. The beautiful people I came to know and love in Permia had been shipped to Earth. Forgetting who they were, and forgetting about Permia, as they lost themselves and had taken on new identities.

Some evil being demons of Permia shipped themselves to Earth, and terrorized the humans on earth. There was no one to stop the madness; Scarlett was standing in the middle of all the chaos laughing, and throwing fire balls at buildings, cars and people. "And all of this will happen if I die?" I asked my parents. "Yes," my mother said sadly. "Leading Permia won't be easy, not at all, but you can handle it, and remember we are always watching you, we are always with you Eve. We both love you so much." my father said.

"I love you both too." I said closing my eyes tight to fight the tears that I knew would be coming quicker. When I opened my eyes, I shockingly looked around at my surroundings. I was lying in an infirmary bed.

"Eve!" Tess yelled as he rushed over to me. But I couldn't speak, and then once again, I was pulled back into darkness. But this time, it wasn't pleasant on the other side.

LIV

A Battle in the Mind

It was dark, and cold. But more importantly, Scarlett was standing a few feet in front of me. Her red eyes were boring into mine, and she was holding the white fire dagger in her hand. "Scarlett?! How the heck did this happen? Where are we?" I yelled asking her. "It's nice to see you too big cousin. Oh, and we just took a little trip inside your little head. What better way to kill you. At least your semi asleep." She smirked. "How did this happen?" I asked shocked. "We *are* all magical beings. It wasn't that hard." she smiled.

Right then at that moment, I wanted to claw the lips off of her face so she couldn't smile at me but I didn't, I had to control my anger, and not let her get to me. "Okay, so why are we here Scarlett? Are you scared to face me in the real world, don't worry baby cousin, if I were you I'd be afraid to face me too?" I chuckled at her. I could see that she got angry from my comment as she gritted her teeth and tightened her grip on the dagger.

"Well, of course I figured what the hell; why not kill you while you're weak. If I waited until you were stronger, that wouldn't be smart now would it?" She asked. I decided to forgo on telling her that I had been healed by my mother, and just let her find out for herself. It was better for me to let Scarlett think that I was tired and weak. She would believe that she had an advantage over me when in all actually she didn't.

"Ugh, you're as dumb as you are evil, if you really think I would let you kill me. Weak or not, in the end Permia is mine." I said to her while grinding my own teeth. Scarlett tilted her head to the left. "Hmm, well let's see when this enters your blood stream. You know the white fire dagger is the most powerful dagger. It's killed many Archangels before you, including your pathetic mother." Scarlett said. Now I was really pissed, how dare she even mention my mother's name! I could feel anger rise through me even more, and I knew with my new buildup of anger, I was capable of things I couldn't even imagine.

I rolled my eyes. "Okay, can you please stop talking so I can just kick your ass?!" I asked her. "Tsk tsk, foul language for an Archangel! And you shouldn't speak to me that way you know, especially when I have a lethal weapon in my hand, it just might end up in your heart." Scarlett smirked. I had had enough of hearing her talk so I started moving towards her.

I inched closer to Scarlett, when a ripple effect appeared in front of her, and out of the ripple appeared Parker. Parker adjusted his suit jacket and stood in front of her. "Parker!?" I screamed. I couldn't believe my eyes, seeing him appear here inside my head and next to Scarlett. "What did she do to you?" I whispered. I looked into his eyes and realized that they were now black. So black that they looked like he had deep abyss's for eyes. It actually scared me.

He was dressed in a tight black shirt with a black blazer and even with the blazer on, I could see his huge new arm muscles. He also wore dark blue jeans and black boots. This wasn't the Parker that I was used to. I was used to the football; chivalry isn't dead, beach loving Parker. I studied him for a minute before he grabbed me and held me in front of him, making me an easy target for Scarlett.

Scarlett took her time walking towards me with the dagger in her hand, and a smile plastered on her face. To the right of us, I noticed Tess orbed in. He ran over to Scarlett and knocked the knife out of her hand.

I untwisted myself from Parker's now unfocused grip and gave him a hard kick to the stomach. I looked at him stunned before running over to Tess. "How did you get in here?!" I asked giving him a hug. "Thank you for saving me." I whispered in his ear. "Well, back home you woke up in the infirmary, and then you passed back out. Then you were twitching, mumbling about Scarlett and the words "my head" you were sleeping very uneasily. I figured something had to be wrong, and I came in." Tess said.

I didn't want anyone inside my head anymore, and made a decision to leave. I turned my head and looked at Parker and Scarlett who were sitting on the ground watching Tess and I. "Scarlett! If you want me, fight me in Permia, not here." I said. I tugged on Tess's arm and he looked at me. "Let's go, I'm ready to get out of my head." I said looking up at him.

"Don't walk away from me; don't leave me for her Tess!" Scarlett yelled. Tess turned to look at her. "You're in love with the girl whose job is to kill us! To kill our kind! Don't you see the idiocy!?" She yelled. Tess didn't say anything to Scarlett; he just took me into his arms.

Just as Tess and I started to orb away, I heard footsteps of someone that was running towards us, and in the blink of an eye, Tess reversed our position of me in front of him, to him in front of me. Tess had let go of me, and fell to the floor. I looked down and saw the white fire dagger sticking out of Tess's upper shoulder blade. I pulled the dagger from his back and then bent down to him and held him in my arms and immediately started to heal him. As I looked up and noticed that Parker was staring at us laughing. "Everything is going to be okay." I told Tess. That was our comforting phrase to one another.

I wasn't actually sure if everything would be okay, though. Tess was breathing heavily and his eyes had gone from electric blue, to his natural brown. He looked sleepy. "Seems that's another point for me Eve." Scarlett said smiling. I ignored her. "I took both of your boyfriend's lives away from you. And very shortly, I will take yours. Meet me at the cliff overlooking the ocean if you still think you are fit to run Permia. If not, tuck your tail between your legs, and get the hell out of my world. Pathetic girls don't belong here." Scarlett sneered. I didn't care about anything Scarlett was saying, I only focused on Tess. "Don't close your eyes Tess." I said to him as I pushed some of his hair out of his face.

I looked up to Scarlett and Parker, and I couldn't take them laughing. I gently laid Tess down, and then I got up and ran over to them, and knocked them both to the floor. I took the dagger and stabbed it into Parker's heart. I then quickly walked back over to Tess, and put in back in my arms before I felt the sting.

The sharp sting came from the lower area of my back and out my stomach. "Don't you know better than to turn your back on a royal?!" Scarlett said just after she stabbed me with the dagger. The pain scared me so bad that I accidently orbed and popped up out of my sleep. I had returned to the hospital bed with Tess still in my lap and the dagger still injected into me. I felt like I was on the verge of death. I closed my eyes and yanked the dagger out of me before lying down on the bed.

LV

Romeo and Juliet

"What the heck happened?!" Bobby yelled. I was crying too hard to even reply back to Bobby. "Eve!" Bobby yelled almost sadly. He put his hands on my cheeks and directed my face towards him, so that I had to look at him. "What happened?" Bobby asked. I took a few deep breaths before answering. "Move Tess away from me and heal him. On his shoulder." I groaned and ordered.

Tess was cradled in my arms and Bobby gently moved him to the lower part of the infirmary bed that I was laying on. Bobby gasped when he saw a pool of blood pouring out of my stomach and onto the hospital bed sheets. "Eve!" He cried out. I held my right hand out to tell him to stop, as I put my left hand on my stomach and healed myself.

After five minutes of going in and out of consciousness and feeling hot and cold, I finally got the strength to speak. "Parker... Parker stabbed Tess with the dagger, then I stabbed Parker with it, and then Scarlett stabbed me with it." I rambled. "Okay, let me help you." Bobby said. "I'm fine... just keep helping Tess." I whispered. I wasn't at hundred percent but I could feel myself regaining my strength.

I pulled myself up and crawled over to Tess and I put my hand on Tess's wound and tried to continue to heal him, but I couldn't tell if it was working or not, but I wanted him as healed as he could possibly be. "See, you do care for me. You were just too scared before." he said between breaths, finally opening his eyes. Tess was becoming paler and I could tell that he was nodding in and out of conscious just as I was. "You would think about that in a time like this." I tried to smirk. But the pain and the tears in my eyes prevented me from doing so. "I don't know, this is kind of like Romeo and Juliet, just don't kill yourself." He tried to laugh but only started choking. "Hybrids take a little more time to die rather than pure breeds or humans. Different breeds handle injury's differently." Bobby told me. I didn't want to think of Tess dying, I couldn't imagine it. I let my tear's pour down from my face for a brief moment.

"Hey stop crying, you're not the one in pain here." Tess said. Bobby shook his head. "Actually she's been stabbed too." Bobby announced. Tess's eyes got silently a little bit bigger. "What?!" he asked, trying to sit up. "I'm fine... I'm more worried for you." I assured him. "You're so stubborn; you care too much for others rather than yourself." Tess whispered. "That's what makes a good queen." Bobby added.

"Is this working? Are you feeling a little better?!" I asked panicking. "Getting stabbed by that dagger usually leaves the victim in death. It's hard to cure any creature that has been wounded with it; it's a miracle that you both are as well as you are." Bobby said. I started crying again. I knew it was because I had, the strength of my mother fully charged in me that *I* would be okay from the stabbing. I really wasn't worried about me; I didn't want to lose Tess. I couldn't lose Tess. I hoped that the powers within me along with Bobby's attempt to heal Tess, healed him enough to let him live.

I sighed and wiped my tears away. "I have to go, I have to go find Scarlett and protect the world." I said. I slowly got up from the bed and looked down at my bloody shirt and cat suit. "Really Eve, let me see your wound. You can't go out there hurt." Bobby said walking towards me. "I'm fine." I tried to assure him. I unzipped my suit, and pulled my top up. What I saw stunned me.

A vertical semi thick scar about the length of four or five inches sat right above my belly button. It made me even angrier than I already was. I wanted to kill Scarlett. Even though I have gained a large amount of confidence, I can imagine how insecure I'm going to be about this.

"Well, you really are a royal, you healed yourself up. Not even your mother was able to do this." Bobby said. I nodded at him sadly before I pulled my shirt back down and put my shoes on. I then grabbed my daggers and staff. "I have to go." I said. "I will be here when you get back." Tess whispered. I didn't want to leave Tess, but I knew I had to. With Tess saying he would be here when I returned I found it not enough. I wanted Tess to promise me, promise me and guarantee me that he would be here when I got back. But I knew that I couldn't ask him to promise me that, I could only take his already spoken words for it.

I leaned over and gently kissed Tess, and got ready to orb away. "Be careful, she's been toying with you. I will be there as soon as I'm done here with Tess, you sure you're okay?" Bobby asked. I sighed. "Just take care of Tess, bring him home and take care of him there." I said before orbing away.

LVI

The Final Fight

This world, these magical beings and magical powers, my new life, doesn't seem fun anymore. I thought to myself as I orbed to my room, and changed out of my bloody clothes. I put on an all black cat suit, which seems to be my signature fighting wear.

It's like everything is just getting harder and harder. but I'm willing to push through it, for the sake of my parents and for the people who need and believe in me. *But how much harder is it going to get?* I wondered to myself. I grabbed my staff and orbed outside of the mansion. I then walked back to the north end of the forest, and headed towards the cliff. I silently thanked the God above and my parents that I could see well in the dark purple sky. I also prayed that my mother and father would be with me during this fight between Scarlett and I.

I finally reached the cliff that stood above the Permian Sea. Scarlett stood there staring at me with her green eyes which immediately turned red when she laid her eyes upon me. She was in attack mode, and my insides twisted in disgust for her. "I know it hurts to lose your regular, ordinary, pathetic human life *and* your human boyfriend, *and* then get your cousin's sloppy seconds killed, all in the matter of three months. You're so heartbroken, and you know you just want to give up. So give up Evie." Scarlett said. I knew she was trying to play mind games with me, but I wouldn't let her. I just wanted to destroy her and get back to Tess. I looked at Scarlett holding her silver staff firmly. I didn't say anything to her, I only charged at her.

I drew my staff, which she blocked with her own. We staff played for a while, it seemed like we were those programmed star wars characters. Whenever I would strike left, she would block, and whenever she would strike right, I would block her. I finally had enough of the stupid pattern and kicked Scarlett in her stomach. Scarlett flew into the air, hunched over and glared at me before getting up and giving me two sidekicks to the stomach and one to the face. Not taking her kicks too kindly, I back smacked her and she then did the same to me.

I hit Scarlett in the face hard and she then kicked my face in. I then lifted my staff and hit her across her face with it. Scarlett backed away and smiled. "Oh, it seems I underestimated you Eve." she said angrily as we both were standing at a stance with our guards up. "Good." I said smiling at her.

Scarlett threw an element ball at me, which looked to be like the element water. I took my staff into both my hands and aimed. I ended up hitting the element ball like it was a softball. It bounced off of my staff and flew back at Scarlett hitting her in the chest. I charged at Scarlett with my staff ready to strike her; however Scarlett blocked my staff by grabbing it and hitting me with it, sending me flying almost over the edge of the cliff.

I quickly crawled and got up, and got away from the cliff and tried to chick kicked Scarlett across her head but I ended up missing. Scarlett jumped over me and kicked me from behind, making me slide onto the ground. My hands gripped the edge of the cliff, saving me from falling over. She then ran at me at full speed took my entire body into her arms and ended up smashing my back on the hard ground. I coughed and groaned before rolling over and standing up.

Scarlett threw another element ball at me, which thankfully due from her stumbling, she missed and it landed in the sea. I threw an element ball at her, and she ducked, the fireball hit a far tree in back of her. I ran to Scarlett and head-butted her and gave her a knee to the gut. I drop kicked her and then did a backflip to get some distance from her before I grabbed her head in a headlock and slammed her head to the ground. I smiled at her as I watched her stumble to get up.

She tackled me to the ground, in which we both were rolling around like bowling pins. She ended up on top of me, and started choking me. I punched her away from me, then reached up and head-butted her one more time. I removed my left foot from under Scarlett, and kicked her so hard, that she flew halfway off the ledge. She was left barley holding on to the edge.

"Eve, help me, we are blood... you won't let me die, will you?" she asked in an innocent tone. I walked over to her, and Scarlett quickly grabbed my leg, knocking me down, and lifting herself back up and onto the cliff. She was using *me* as a ladder. I looked down behind me at Scarlett, and kicked her in her face. She lost her balance, and slid back down, dragging me with her.

Scarlett was holding onto my left foot. I screamed and held onto a rock that was attached to the cliff. I kicked Scarlett's hand off of me and only for a second, watched her fall before down the cliff before I pushed myself up to hold onto a rock and orbed safely back onto the cliff. Out of breath, but happy, I grabbed Scarlett's staff and threw it into the sea. Then I grabbed my own staff and orbed back to the mansion.

I telepathically called for Bobby, and laid down on the grass in front of the house. A few seconds later I heard steps being walked towards me. "Are you okay?" Bobby asked helping me sit up. I tiredly looked at him. "Sorry to sound rude, but do I look okay? Scarlett gave me all she had. She put up a great fight!" I said. Bobby's eyes widened. "She's dead?" he asked, sounding almost shocked. I nodded my head yes. "How's Tess?" I asked him, almost afraid to hear his answer.

Bobby nodded his head vertically. "He kept his word, he said he would be here when you got back, and he's still here, hurt but here." Bobby said. Happy tears started streaming from my eyes. "Joy, Eli, Jay, and three others, are all dead. Destiny is fine, she's a little traumatized, but she's okay." Bobby said. I shook my head in understanding, but I still had tears pouring down from my face, now tears of sorrow. "I can't believe I got six people killed." I said more to myself than to Bobby.

I started doubting myself. "How can I lead when I get people killed?" I asked myself. "Everyone dies and moves on to another life, you can handle this. You did well my daughter." I heard my mother's voice say from out of the clouds.

I looked up to the sky and smirked just a little, I was happy that I had got my revenge for her and the rest of my family's death. Bobby flew me to my terrace, and helped me into my room. "Thanks Bobby, for everything, I'm gonna get some rest." I said to him. Bobby caressed my cheek. "You deserve it. Sleep well Eve." he smiled, and then left my room.

LVII

After the Fight

I went into the bathroom and took a quick hot shower. I watched and felt all the dirt from the battle fall off of me and enter the drain. I got out, and quickly got dressed. I didn't even want to look at myself in the mirror. I knew I looked as horrible as I felt.

Even with all the guilt and tiredness I felt, I felt something that I never felt before, an actual pride in who I am and where I come from. On earth is the place where I am a nobody. That's the place where I didn't know who I was, and I really didn't fit in. But here in Permia, I revenged my mother's death, saved the world, and I am a future queen. I *am* somebody here.

I spotted Tess all cleaned up and asleep, in my bed. I pulled the duvet a little, and got under with him, happy that I had on pants and a sweater; I didn't have to worry about getting burned. I chuckled at the fact that he was wearing all white. I could only imagine his reaction when he realizes he had been dressed by the angels. "Did you get her?" Tess asked in a husky voice, with his eyes closed. I looked up at him, and then laid my head down on his chest. "Sure did." I replied. "I'm proud of you." he whispered. I smiled. "Yeah, I saved the Permia and the earth; I think proper sleep is well deserved." I smiled. "I agree." Tess smiled back. "Yeah, a hundred days of sleep sounds great." I said with a bit of sarcasm.

I closed my eyes, and began dreaming which in the beginning

actually seemed peaceful. I was laying in the field, looking at the light green and blue tree tops in Permia. The sun was shining brightly and blended nicely with the lavender sky. I suddenly sat up from the grass, and was zapped back to the cliff, where Scarlett and I had just battled.

I was overly upset that I had returned back to this place after such a short time. I didn't want to be reminded of the war I had just been in. I began to walk away, but a grunting noise stopped me in my tracks. I turned back to face the cliff, and I saw nothing. Figuring that it was just my imagination, I started to walk off again, when laughter filled my ears.

I slowly turned around, and I saw a hand reach the top of the cliff. The hand was followed by a face, Scarlett's face. My eyes widened at the sight in front of me as she reached up the cliff with a wicked grin plastered on her face.

The End

Purchase other Black Rose Writing titles at *www.blackrosewriting.com/books* and use promo code PRINT to receive a 20% discount.

BLACK ROSE writing™

CPSIA information can be obtained at www.ICGtesting.com
Printed in the USA
BVOW04s0848110215

387261BV00010B/373/P

9 781612 96419